A Threatening Fragility

Lela Markham

Published by Breakwater Harbor Books

A Word from Lela Markham

Thank you for reading my book. If you enjoyed it, please take a moment to leave me a review at your favorite retailer. Only with your help can writers like me reach more readers. I appreciate it!

Since I published *Life As We Knew It* in 2015, some lovely people have contacted me concerning the book, complimenting me on the themes of faith and libertarianism found in its pages. I appreciate your support. While not a work of Christian literature, I have tried to be true to my faith and the beliefs of the larger evangelical Christian body while also showing Christians who make mistakes and act badly from time to time. I will continue that effort.

Transformation Project is at root a polemic against our rigged system of elites telling all of us "lessers" what to do while failing miserably on so many levels in their attempt to centrally manage the society. I hope I present the arguments in an entertaining way.

In *Life As We Knew It*, I introduced a president who came to power through a rigged system and in *Objects in View*, I showed his appointees attempting to manipulate horrific events to their personal benefit. In *A Threatening Fragility* I delivered on my promise that things could only get worse. So where am I headed with *Thanatosis?* I'm not telling, but the definition of the word might be a clue. But don't worry. I promise it will be entertaining.

I've called this series a "cozy apocalyptic". It doesn't focus on major events and world-stage actors. The town of Emmaus can only react to what is decided in other locations. My heroes aren't out to save the world. They just want to save their town. Yet, I also believe that the mighty mustard plant grows from a tiny seed. It is the reaction of the people of Emmaus to events beyond their control that will determine the future they live in.

Ultimately, that is the same power that you and I have. We can't affect what goes on in Washington DC. If the last few elections haven't proven that to you, you haven't been paying attention. We keep swapping one crazy train for another within the Beltway and that should prove to us that something is badly damaged within our system. The election of President Donald Trump doesn't convince me that the system isn't rigged by the elites in the two major parties as they seek to keep us enthralled to their agenda. This is not a political argument, but a reasonable observation by a small-l libertarian. Despite that, I believe we can affect things right where we live, by educating ourselves and our children, by encouraging our neighbors to do the same. Our rescue will not come from whomever is in the White House or on Capitol Hill, but it might just come from us.

Lela Markham

Thanks!

This book is dedicated to my lifelong friend and mentor Richard "Dick" Vance Underwood who went to be with the Lord in the week before the completion of the draft of *Objects in View*. The character of Dick Vance is a good representation of my friend, who I miss, but I expect to find canoeing a heavenly river when I get there.

No book is the work of a single individual. The author gets all the glory, but standing behind every published writer is a host of support personnel. Thank you to my beta readers, Shelly M. Lamb (who will soon publish her first book) and Alia M. Bierwag (check out her book *The Travelers* on Amazon), my editor Lauri Sliney and my husband and son for giving me cover design advice and final proof-reading.

This book contains short snippets of several hymns that have given me comfort during dark times. Although copyright laws allow my very incidental use, I want to thank John Newton (*Amazing Grace*), Horatio Spafford (*It is Well with My Soul*), Robert Lowery (*Shall We Gather at the River*) and the anonymous sailors who wrote *My Boat is So Small* for composing amazing music and lyrics. *My Boat is So Small* is one of two songs I can sing in Inupiat and I was so glad to discover it's a popular tune among bluegrass musicians so that I could have an excuse to work it into this book.

Table of Contents

Table of Contents

"We are punctual, a stressed, marked characteristic. We need order around us, in the house, in the life, although we live by irresistible impulses, as if the order in the closets, in our papers, in our books, in our photographs, in our souvenirs, in our clothes could preserve us from chaos in our feelings, loves, in our work. Indifference to food, sobriety; but this, we admit, is the part of the war against a threatening fragility." Anais Nin "The Diary of Anais Nin, Vol 1: 1931-1934

A Threatening Fragility
Book 3

Transformation Project

Prologue

You never know when life will turn on a dime and leave you standing in the middle of the road wondering what ran over you. Nobody could prepare for life as we knew it to end.

Because Emmaus grew its own food, we were more prepared than the cities to handle the surprise, but we were still stunned, mourning our old lives and trying to figure out how to cope with our new ones. We scrambled to reorder our world, to make the best of a difficult situation, to find a new normal ... never recognizing we fought a fruitless war against a threatening fragility that would soon consume us all.

Even as we prepared our own disaster plan in the absence of government aid, it turned out government had plans for us that we never would have expected.

JT Delaney

Sunday

Four Days After
The End of Life as They Knew It

Community in Peril

Emmaus, Kansas

He'd have swatted away the bright light shining in his eyes if he could have felt his hands. Marnie spoke words he didn't understand and he thought he heard Rob reply to her in Chinese. He floated free of the ground and drifted into blackness.

A roan mare raced by him at rocket speed, mane flying like flags, a swirl of dust kicking out behind her as she fled from a storm of enormous proportions, black and purple clouds boiling from horizon to horizon.

Shane walked on the wall. He stepped down from the dresser to the plaster, astride the photo of a surfer shredding a full-curl wave. He could feel the surfboard against his toes.

His eyes closed. When he dragged them open again, Vi stood before him, a shushing finger to her lips. Her long gray-streaked black hair hung loose, flowing over her shoulders, down past her hips, obscuring her white cotton nightgown.

"Don't tell them," she whispered.

"Tell them what, Grandma," he wanted to ask but his lips were melting.

Exhaustion dragged his eyelids down. Next time he opened them, *she* danced before him in scarlet silks, a diaphanous veil covering her face and waist length hair. Her lower belly swelled with a baby. Bang, pop, bang and blood began to seep down her gown.

Shane snapped awake, sitting up, gripping the edge of the mattress as the room dosadoed round his head. Sunlight spilled across the pine floor reminiscent of a Wyeth painting. He stared at his shoes set neatly to the side of the closet door.

My bedroom? How'd I get here? He'd been playing guitar at Callahans. There'd been beer and bourbon and ... *How much did I drink?*

The room tilted at a 30-degree incline. Outside in the hall, he could hear Rob and Jacob talking in low urgent voices. He slid forward on the mattress, put his feet on the floor. He still wore his jeans, t-shirt and socks. *I didn't put myself to bed.* He hated wearing socks to bed. Even passed out drunk he'd have taken those off. Had there been a plane? He vaguely remembered a claustrophobia attack ... or, er .... Something rattled the house from the north.

He pulled himself to standing and wobbled across the slanting floor to the door, where Jacob was turning to follow Rob into the back bedroom.

"What the hell just blew up? Someone bombing us?"

"I can see smoke northeast other side of Mission Ridge." Shane followed Jacob, the floor leveling out as he went. Everything still felt a little off-kilter, but his head started to clear. He didn't have a headache and it didn't feel like he'd puked. He usually puked if he drank heavily, which provided a good reason not to. He just felt like he wasn't quite here, as if at any moment he might start walking on the walls again ... or maybe through them.

Through Jacob's north-facing window, they could see massive billows of smoke, black and oily.

"It looked more like a huge grass fire when I came to get you," Jacob explained.

"You feel up to coming with?" Rob asked Shane who grabbed a water bottle from Jacob's night stand and drained it.

"Where's my 9?" Shane wiped water off his chin. Rob gave him a weighing look, then shrugged.

"I'll get it. Meet you at the truck as soon as you can get there. Pa, see if you can scare up the fire department. Looks like Brady's Tanks."

Shane donned his shoes while Rob raced up Willow Creek Run. Everything still had that slightly otherworldly feeling, but he knew one thing fairly certainly. Rob had put him to bed because he had taken control of the 9 mm that now sat between them on the bench seat.

"Was I rude last night?"

Rob favored him with an odd expression. Far to the southwest, Shane heard the growling siren of a fire engine.

"You don't remember?"

"Weirdest damn dreams I've ever had." *I've never blacked out before.* "I was at Callahan's and then I was walking home. There was music at the church and then .... What the hell is that?"

Ahead, the sky over the corn fields boiled with murky black smoke. A malevolent fog swept down to the ground, shrouding the way ahead. Shane closed the vents while Rob slowed. Debris lay in the road, in the single street of the Tanks. Flames shot high and hot from what remained of the diner. Several other buildings were on fire, flames voraciously consuming their century-old wood. Shane stripped off his t-shirt and began wetting it with Rob's water bottle.

"It looks like the diner blew up. Les and Molly lived above it. Oh, god! That's bad! STOP!"

Rob slammed on the brakes, swearing, swerving to miss a mangled hunk of metal in the roadway. Behind the conflagration of human structures, backlit by the dawn, was a much more frightening sight. Rob grabbed the CB mic.

"Anyone with their ears on. All hands to Brady Tanks immediately. Bring buckets, hoses, blankets, anything that can transport water. The corn fields are on fire. Repeat, the corn fields are on fire."

Regret

Casa Blanca Hotel
New York City, Times Square

"Call me Lilly," she had said when they were in the sauna, wrapped in towels and feeling warm and comfortable. Kate could see the sweat on her pale shoulders and above the pink of her upper lip. "After living through something like this, we're friends. Maybe we can even find a way to go west together."

"Julian seems keen on the idea too. If my husband doesn't show up soon, I think that's an excellent idea. It should be safe enough with a man along."

"Julian, huh? Hmm, I suppose. The doorman would be better, but I don't think he'll leave his wife and kids."

"No, he wouldn't. You don't like Julian?"

"No, I like him well enough. I just don't think he'd scare anyone away from us. He's got that laid-back IT vibe going."

Kate had laughed, because it was true enough.

"I bought a gun this morning," Lillian had said so matter-of-factly that Katherine had almost not believed her.

"A gun?! What for?"

"Kate darling, the world is not a safe place. My husband has a dozen guns in California. This one's not a really good gun, just a 22, what they call a Saturday Night Special. It only came with five bullets and I don't trust how old they might be, but …."

"Who sold you a gun?"

Not that it mattered now as the dream sauna's warmth dissolved into the cool evening air of the street. It hadn't been raining last night, but in the dream the pavement shimmered.

Bang, bang, bang. "Stop, we'll shoot!" Lillian's little squeak seemed so inadequate for the taking of her life. And then there'd been the door to the hotel. Katharine pushed through it and blinked at the ceiling. Bang, bang, bang.

"Katharine, wake up!" Julian's voice filtered through the thick wood door. Katharine rolled off the bed. The window washed light gray with early morning dawn. She freed herself from the entangling sheets and stumbled to the sitting room. Another knock came on the door. Her chemise clung damply to her curves.

"I'm a mess. I'll meet you downstairs later," she told him. Though singularly unhungry, she recognized him as a nice man who deserved her to answer him. Besides, she might need him to get out of here.

"All right. I'll have them brew us a pot of coffee. Don't be too long. I'll have Gillam unlock the door if you keep this up."

She'd had too much wine last night and told him she thought Lillian was her fault. She'd given him good reason to worry about her. On the other hand, she didn't want him to think she was given to unreliability.

Katharine stripped her silks off and left a trail of them on the floor to step into the shower. The water beat warm on her greasy hair and slid in sheets down her back. She settled herself on the travertine marble floor of the shower and let the water flood over her. Everywhere she looked, she saw Lillian's blood on the pavement.

She's dead because I wanted a sauna. How stupid could I be? Stanley warned me. My own heart should have warned me. What has living in Kansas done to my instincts? I used to know better. Didn't I?"

Tears mixed with the water. Lillian hadn't been a friend. Katharine had not acted as a friend. And now it was too late. Sobs wracked her.

"Shhh," he said as he slipped into the shower behind her, hands gently caressing her back. "Everybody makes mistakes, milady. I'm coming. Don't be afraid."

His hands eased around to her stomach, pulling her back into him. She relaxed backwards and, with a jolt realized that she'd dozed off and dreamt Joseph's arms and comforting words.

She smacked off the shower and reached for a thirsty Turkish weave towel. Twenty minutes later, she descended the grand staircase into the lobby of the Casa Blanca Hotel, dressed casually in slacks and a simple blue silk blouse, wearing minimal makeup and with no evidence that she had been crying for the last eighteen hours. She was Katharine Sullivan, wife of an American scion, not Kate Lansing, daughter of a sanitation worker. Kate could fall apart and revel in being a drama queen. Katharine must hold her head high and project an impression of calm.

In the lounge, some of the hotel guests were watching the news. She paused because it didn't look like the perpetual-loop news cycle that had been playing for the last four days. The ticker said something about food stations and then showed footage of people lining up along a New York City street.

When Marshall Ellerby came on the air, someone turned up the volume.

"Although I never expected to be the acting president, I am rising to the challenge to provide care in these troubling times. While FEMA is tied up at various locations around the nation, Bunnell & Wilson is providing food for the New York City area starting today."

The camera cut back to the news room where a well-dressed female commentator faced an equally well-dressed male reporter.

"Ellerby appears to have risen to the challenge of his temporary position, Carl. There's obviously no precedent for the designated survivor becoming president, but who else is left?

"Well, Marilyn, analysis of the film prior to the DC attack indicates that Speaker of the House Francine Maricle and Secretary of Education Anna Byers were not present on the Mall. We're working to verify that both of these women in the line of succession are still alive. Speaker Maricle was supposedly on her way to her home state of Alaska for a family emergency. Secretary Byers was supposed to be at the speech. It is possible she was there and our video analysis simply missed her."

"So what's the line of succession among the three?"

"Maricle would definitely be first, followed by the Secretary of Education, followed by Marshall Ellerby."

"What a disappointment if he isn't president! He's doing such a good job."

"Agreed, Marilyn. Ellerby ... as the head of Homeland Security Marshall Ellerby amassed the sort of experience the country needs right now. Anna Byers, who became Secretary under former president, has been an educator and education advocate. President Dotson retained her because of her fine credentials, but those credentials are not related to national defense or dealing with terrorist attacks."

"What about Maricle?"

"She was an eye doctor in Alaska before she was appointed to the House upon the death of the lone representative of Alaska, who had served for more than four decades -- was in fact the longest sitting Republican Congressman ...."

Katharine wandered off toward the cafe. Who seriously thought an eye doctor from Alaska would make a good president?

Demon Dance

Emmaus, Kansas

Yesterday's heat had done its job too well. The corn had already been dry, ready for harvest, perfect carbo-fuel for a conflagration. Flames leapt up in the gold brown fronds, crackling like popcorn. Rob joined Shane at the bed of the truck, pulling out a shovel, finding a padded blanket in the job box.

"That isn't going to do us any good without water," Shane said as he wrapped the wet t-shirt around his lower face.

The fire found new fuel, lighting the morning sky brighter with every passing moment. Shane turned to scan the area. The water tanks stood on the far side of the burning town.

"You smell that?" Rob shouted over the roar of flames. Shane sniffed, nodding. "Diesel. This whole area could go up."

"And you just called everybody here. You need to direct them away. If I wrap myself in the blanket,

I should be able to make the tanks without losing any skin. Maybe we can douse this thing before the diesel ignites."

"You're nuts!"

"Yeah, but I'm right and you know it."

As if to emphasize the need for heroics, a propane bottle from one of the buildings exploded, flattening the building and sending debris in their direction. Shane used his shovel to toss the flaming debris out of the bed of the pickup.

"You need to back up across the main road. Go. Get out of here."

The fire truck pulled up then and Chief Frear, hearing Shane's plan, had the pumper first wet him and then lay down a path to the tanks as he sprinted through the fire with the blanket wrapped over his bare back. The acrid smoke stung his eyes and flames licked at his legs, quickly drying the water in his jeans. The water in his makeshift mask filtered the worst of the smoke. He reached the stairs to the first tank. The metal steamed from the heat of the fire. A cooling spray from the fire hose rained down on him, sizzling as it boiled off the metal railings. He raced up the first flight of stairs. The heat and smoke dropped away, so he paused at the landing to catch his breath and drop the blanket, still feeling the effects of last night.

Below him, flame ate at every building in Brady Tanks. The second pumper truck arrived up and a variety of trucks and cars parked on the far shoulders of the county roads, pulling shovels, blankets and buckets out. The corn field fire had already spread to a second field. Another propane tank in the town blew, sending people scattering. Shane climbed faster.

The tanks were auxiliary water in the event of a drought affecting the wells. From the high vantage point of the maintenance deck he saw hoses running off toward the irrigation arrays. This one tank had a relief valve, a giant nut before the hose that, Shane hoped, would let out enough water to douse the building fires, so the corn field fires would be manageable. When he'd been up here yesterday with Les, he'd noticed the maintenance deck held a job box that wasn't locked.

He found a wrench that was longer than his arm, clamped it on the nut at the base of the relief valve and started cranking, throwing his full weight back to pull it toward him. Slowly, slowly, it turned. The wrench began to vibrate, shaking harder with every pull until water smacked him in the chest so hard it slammed him against the railing, forcing him to turn away.

Water sprayed in all directions, pounding against his back harder than the fire hose, causing him to stumble. As he clung to the railing, smoky steam stung his eyes. He blinked away the tears. Staring out across the fields, he could see dozens of fires, miles away, billowing smoke up into the sky. Then he forgot all about that as he saw *her* walking through the flaming fields.

No, come back. Leave them alone. It's me you hate.

She turned and stared at him, her hatred boring into his soul. Her hajib had dropped from her face and her features held a terrible beauty. He dropped to his knees and crawled under the worst of the spray to reach the stairs.

I've got stuff to do. I am not indulging this crap today!

He grabbed the now sopping blanket from the landing, pulled his t-shirt mask up to cover his mouth and nose, and headed down to the ground to help his neighbors fight the fire.

Morning Milking

Alex Lufgren lifted his head from attaching a milking cup to a restive cow's distended udder. His nose twitched. That smelled like smoke. Farmers feared fire because of all the hay and manure that made such good fuel, but this time of year was especially concerning because dent corn burned like firewood. He walked out of the milking theater, eyes scanning the barn, seeing nothing amiss. Outside the big sliding door, just a trace of smoke hung in the air. Alex couldn't see anything on fire in the immediate area, but the smoke worried him. He trotted up the stairs to the hay loft and then climbed a ladder to the cupola, which afforded him a 360-degree view of the dawn-blushed prairie. Here to the west of town, he could make out the trestle bridge over Wolf Creek and the top of the water tower. The ridges to the north and west blocked his view in those directions.

He heard her coming, of course. His parents had never bothered to fix the creaks and groans of the stairs because they couldn't hear them, but he could … and liked it. Poppy had always wondered why she couldn't sneak up on him. She couldn't hear the creaks on the stairs either. Hearing was his superpower.

"What's burning?" Keri asked. He turned, surprised to see her here in the cupola. He'd expected his sister, not his wife. She was dressed for farm work, her honey blond hair pulled back in a single braid. They'd been to church last night, so would use today to get a jump on harvesting. He'd kind of forgotten that she would join him. A married man of only four months, and his wife a teacher from a non-farm family, he hadn't really thought she'd volunteer for farm labor.

"Looks like a fire the other side of the ridge."

"Do you hear that?"

Listening, his ears only caught farm noises, but then on the edge of his hearing, he could make out a siren.

"Where's that coming from?"

She shook her head, then pointed west.

"Smoke's coming from the northeast."

"I hear another siren from the east. And, I think there's smoke to the west too."

His stomach tightened with apprehension.

"What's going on?"

Alex' cell buzzed. He read the message aloud to her.

"Jeremiah him say Vance corn on fire. He recommend we start harvesting quick. Micah."

"This just keeps getting better and better." Keri shook her head.

"You sound like Shane."

"Well, he is my brother."

Never had brother and sister been so distinct from one another. Shane being dark of hair and skin and Keri being light, but more than that, their personalities had never been alike. Still, they had the same fount of wisdom in parents and grandparents.

"He's different."

"No kidding. According to Jazz, he shot two people yesterday." Alex had heard that from Clem the vet and then from his cousin Jeremiah he'd heard that Shane needed prayer, but with no details. "He had a good reason, but ... he walked up to the church last night like there wasn't a care in the world."

Alex squeezed her shoulder. While he hoped never to be in Shane's position, he thought he understood it a bit. In situations like this, maybe you couldn't afford to take a high moral ground if you wanted to live. After all, he'd agreed to harvest corporate fields that had ostensibly been abandoned because he deemed it better to harvest and hide the corn than have it taken to an undisclosed location where they had no assurance they could draw from later? By God's standards, stealing didn't differ from killing people who were in agony and going to die anyway. That latter might actually have been compassion. He had no answers to these questions, so, like most good Christian people faced with a conundrum, he changed the subject.

"We've got a lot of work to do. I got to get the cows hooked up for milking. Can you handle the goats so I can get to the fields?"

"I can. And Poppy should be headed out here soon enough."

"Nah, Noah's holding church, so she should go since she didn't go last night."

"Do you know what Mark and Alice have planned?"

"They're adults. Able to make their own choices. I'd better get back to those cows."

At the bottom of the stairs, he met Mark coming into the barn dressed for work. Mark and his family were migrant farm hands who had been in town only a few weeks, but since the bombs, they'd become close as family ... well, ordinary in-laws, the sort you hadn't known since kindergarten.

"Alice and Pete will be joining in a few minutes. You got a job for me?"

"I gotta get the cows hooked up for milking. There's a big fire northeast of town. We need to get going on the fields. Can you check the fluids on the harvester and top off the fuel?"

"Yes, sir." Pete materialized behind Mark. "Put the kid to work too."

"Pete, tell Poppy that I need the bunker silo cleaned out. She should show you where that is and then go to church. She can take the old truck. I don't think Joe will ticket her. He's far too busy with real issues right now. We'll need her back here right after service. She's to go to the back 40 and cut sod."

"What for?" Pete asked.

"She knows."

Pete frowned, but then said "Yes, sir" and disappeared from sight.

One ... two ... then three of the cows let out mournful sounds. Whatever his issues might be, they knew it was well past time to milk the cows.

Slouching into Town

Josh Callahan woke up with a suddenness, blinking into the dawn. His internal clock said it was later than he'd planned to awaken, but the sky outside looked gray. In the darkness of the truck, the others breathed quietly. He sat up, pushing back from the steering wheel, smelling smoke. The gray sky shifted to expose a patch of blue. He opened the door and coughed.

"What the hell is that?" Kowalcsky asked, straightening in the passenger seat.

"Corn field fire," Josh identified. He slid to the ground to look around. Smoke drifted across the road. He climbed back into the truck. "Hold your piss. We need to get out of here." He banged on the window between the two sections. After what seemed way too long, it slid open.

"What's up?" Monahan asked. "What's burning?"

"It's a corn field fire. We need to get out of here before it attracts a lot of attention. Is everybody in?"

They were, so Josh fired up the van and drove westward. They passed a few cars headed toward the field. He settled his cap more firmly so as to shade his face, but waved companionably. As soon as he could, he turned off on one of the gravel roads. Though slower going, this roundabout route meant they encountered less traffic that might ask why a commercial vehicle fled the scene of a corn fire after a three-day downpour. A close inquiry would find escaped convicts and this little run for freedom would be over.

"It's been a fairly wet summer," Josh explained as he paused to let a convoy of vehicles speed past. "The corn shouldn't be burning."

"If you say so." Kowalcsky seemed more interested in trying to get a radio station than the mystery of multiple fires. That was, until they passed the third one in 20 miles

"That's got to be arson, right?"

"Yeah, probably." Josh slowed down to let a slug of speeding traffic go by on the paved road before he drove across it into another gravel section. "Corn can burn if it gets dry, but it hasn't been that dry."

"Could it have anything to do with radiation?"

"Hell if I know. I only know about corn fields because I was a volunteer fireman back in high school."

"Are they fun to fight?"

"I never fought one. Most farmers are pretty careful not to let their money burn, you know?"

"Oh, I hadn't thought of that. So, why would people burn them down now?"

"Maybe someone was mad at the farmers ... or they could be corporate fields. Now that the police are busy with a crisis, could be people thought they could get away with it."

Kowalcsky gave him an odd look. As they neared Emmaus, smoke hung heavily in the air. Josh swung wide to the north, trying to avoid the traffic and the fires themselves. He knew the back ways from his days running moonshine with Shane Delaney, who had been very talented at avoiding the police. Kowalcsky noted the helicopters going overhead and then a big water tanker, asking questions Josh couldn't answer. Finally, they were on County Road N, and Josh turned into the compound's long driveway.

Kowalcsky got out with Dan when they got to the locked gate. Dan apparently remembered the code because the gate slid open after he inputted it for the first time. They all bailed out with Kowalcsky and Dan detailing people to carry crates of food into the central structure.

The windows of the above ground section had been boarded up, but the code here worked too, so they entered the dim interior. Patterson took a flashlight into the depths of the complex and soon the lights came on.

"Are we on the grid or off?" Dan asked when Patterson came back.

"Off the grid. I thought we didn't want to alert your brother we're here."

"Just wondering. Could we be on the grid?"

"Yeah, technically. You want it to be, boss, say it."

"No. This is good for now."

"I'll check the battery bank. Not sure if it's been maintained in all this time. Ditto the windmill and solar panels. They look good and we have lights, but I have no idea if they can power the whole complex after five years." Patterson wandered off.

The dim room smelled of dust and Josh's skin crawled at the chance of encountering a spider web in the darkness.

"I'm going to find some tools and get rid of that plywood."

"No." Dan's voice cracked. "For now, we want to look like there's nobody here. After the truck is unloaded, take it around to the back of the building. I know we would all like to see the sun after all these years, but we want to stay out of prison, so we have to be smart in what we do."

"Yes, sir."

Josh went outside to lean against the truck and think about Wendy Schoenfeld and Sarah Wyatt. He wondered if they were still in town. His fantasies of the last five years flitted through his mind ... what he would do with them, separately and together ... after all that time in prison, rubbing bellies with a pretty girl seemed like a dream. The other guys stripped all the crates and boxes out of the truck, then Josh took it around back. He took his sweet time returning to the building. Despite the thickening smoke and the roar of equipment not far away, standing outside in the air and sun without a guard on the wall felt like heaven.

Battling the Dragon

Andrew Bennett cursed the slowness of his harvester. He could see the flames shooting high above the fields as he worked his way down the road to reach the field. He had it going as fast as he could -- about 20 mph -- but the fire moved faster.

He'd just started coffee in the kitchen, pleased at the restored electricity, when he'd smelled the smoke and gone outside to see the sky east of his farm boiling with ash. He'd barely reached his truck before the first fuel tank blew. A quick drive-by had convinced him that they needed a fire break and he'd turned back toward home for his harvester.

How much corn did we lose while I was deciding what to do?

The #1 water tank blew a gasket and wetted the remains of the town, knocking down the closest fire, but the conflagration already raced toward Dick Vance's farm. The grass fires of old had created their own wind that fanned the flames even more. If corn field fires were similar, buckets and pumper trucks couldn't stop it as long as it had access to fuel. Andrew had to cut it off first.

He swept down Vance's driveway, seeing Dick had had the same idea. He and his sons worked furiously to redirect their circle irrigation. Dick paused long enough to wave Andrew through. Now the harvester slowed to a crawl as it sucked up stalks and spit them out into the collector trailer he hadn't had time to disconnect. That meant this corn would be saved.

The shears made crunching noises like cows chewing as Andrew cut a wide swath through the field. Smoke twisted up into the sky, the roaring off to his right reminding him that he might be losing a huge investment if he didn't beat the fire. On the far edge of Vance's field, a group of young men wielding old-style harvesting tools began flailing away, chucking corn into a truck as fast as they cut it. Vance and his sons dragged hoses behind the harvester, disappearing into the corn stalks to fight the monster. Flames shot up above the corn to his right. He couldn't afford to be frightened in this all-out battle against the conflagration. He aimed for that group of furious workers and red-lined the harvester.

All Is Not Quiet on the Western Front

Seattle, Washington

The sound of distant gunfire woke him. He rolled off the bed toward the interior of the house and squatted there in the dark, listening. The gunfire didn't repeat. The neighborhood around the house lay perfectly quiet. He couldn't even hear traffic out on the interstate. He crept to the patio doors and peeked through the curtains. Nothing moved. After checking the latch and slid bolt, he padded out to the living room. Duke, the black Lab whose house this was, was staring at the southwest corner of the house, ears twitching. When Geo petted his head, he whined softly.

It wasn't a dream if the dog heard it too. .

The street out front of the house was as quiet as the side yard had been. Geo let himself out the door, standing in the dewy Seattle pre-dawn in his underwear. He waited a good five minutes before going back into the house and locking the door.

Duke wagged his tail and went to curl up on his bed. It was 5 am. Staying up occurred to him, but he didn't want to make noise that would awaken Wes, so he went back to the bedroom.

He'd found a tablet no doubt belonging to Joyce, the now-deceased homeowner, last night, so he opened it now and scrolled through the files and links she had. The Seattle Times was mainly running rewritten press releases, claiming the martial law restrictions would be gradually lifted this week and fairies would be handing out free unicorns at noon on Monday.

Geo sighed. He wondered how long the people of Seattle would put up with this sort of nonsense. Nobody had elected Knight Industries to control the city. On the other hand, a voice that sounded a good deal like his father's, nobody elected the US military to do it either.

Out of curiosity, he logged into Facebook and was surprised to find that it was still there. It made sense that Menlo Park, being so close to San Francisco, which hadn't been nuked, would still be there, but he would have thought the government would put it on lockdown. Certainly, it hadn't been available when the military had been in charge. So what did that say about Bunnell & Wilson's commitment to the US Constitution?

Geo shivered. He heard Wes roll over in bed. He scanned through the Facebook posts. Most were foreign posters. Not a lot of Americans ... but a handful from the Seattle region. Assuming Joyce had her password saved on this machine, he could log out to look at his own FB and then come back. He might get some mileage out of pretending to be Joyce.

That's evil. His sister Jazz would have said that, right to his face. And she would be right. It was evil to let people believe their friend was alive when she wasn't. On the other hand, it might also be a really good way to find out what was going on in the world.

He leaned back against the pillows, contemplating Joyce's avatar. He chewed his lower lip, thumb hovering over her photo. He sighed, logged off her profile and logged onto his own, going to see if Jazz or Michael had posted anything since the bombs, but neither had. Neither had his parents. His brother Jim had posted two days ago. He was serving overseas. It occurred to Geo that if someone was looking for him, entering into conversation with his brother might make him easier to find. IP addresses could be traced, after all. But he didn't want his family worrying about him. Geo updated his status as safe and then logged off.

Horses

Emmaus, Kansas

In her dreams, her parents' house in Seattle sat prettily in a gentle shower. Yellow flowers bobbed against green grass. She remembered the sound of roller skates on old-style pavement. Her mother stood on the porch, looking young and alive. Mom turned to look across the street, her eyes widening, flinging a hand up in front of her face as flames engulfed the porch. Thick smoke filled Nevada's lungs.

"Mom," Kim sounded anxious as she shook her. Nevada opened her eyes, staring at her daughter in the gray light of morning. "Something's wrong."

The smell of smoke had followed her into waking.

"What is that?"

"It's like a forest fire, but there's no forests, really, so I don't know."

Nevada stuck her head out the open bedroom window. Smoke drifted in the warm air, wafting in from the east, collecting between the house and the barn. In the barn, the horses were whinnying and she could see movement beyond the open doors.

"We should do something about that, right?" Kim asked.

"Yeah. Get your clothes on. We'll be able to see around the area from Mr. Delaney's deck after we get them settled.

It took no time to don jeans and hiking boots, tucking in the shirt she slept in. Kim joined her as she headed across the yard to the open barn doors. She could see why the horses were panicking. Leaving the doors at both ends open to encourage a breeze had created a tunnel that concentrated the smoke. As they walked, the wind rattled the doors and caused the horses to rear.

The roan mare the Delaneys called Rocket kicked at the gate of her stall, causing the other horses to stomp and blow. On the far side of the paddock a row of trees and a creek separated the property from the road. A convoy of vehicles sped by. Nevada stared at the field of corn across the road, sniffing the smoky air.

"What is it, Mom?"

"I think corn can burn." Kim's eyes widened. "We're fine. The creek should keep us safe. But horses don't know that. Let's get the end doors closed. Maybe they'll calm down if they can't smell it so well."

The first set of doors at the house end closed quickly, but the wind grabbed one of the second set and they struggled to pull it closed. Just as it closed, the latch on Rocket's stall shattered and the mare galloped toward them. Nevada slapped the bolt home as Kim flung up her arms and waved the horse away. As Rocket turned, nostrils flaring, her haunch raked Kim's side. Crying out in pain, Kim tumbled into the door. Nevada ran forward to grab the horse's bridle. Kim caught the reins with her right hand. Rocket pulled and threatened to rear, but they hung on the leather, using their weight to keep her controlled. They forced the balking mare into the free stall, closed and latched the gate and then Nevada wrapped a rope around the latch and tied it off to assure there'd be no more escapes.

When she turned back to compliment Kim on a job well done, she saw that the girl had sat down in the straw, cradling her arm against her chest, her forehead damp with sweat.

"You're hurt?"

"I think maybe it's broken."

"Let's see."

Nevada wasn't trained in first aid, but she could see the lump forming a couple of inches above the wrist.

"Well, looks like we need to go to the med clinic."

Lazy Americans

Someone had organized a bucket brigade from a truck tank to wet blankets wielded by whomever volunteered. When the first pumper truck ran dry, the second one took its place, but several farmers showed up with water tanks and spread out along the roads to try and slow and control the wildfire with low-flow hoses and wet blankets. Rob had lost track of Shane in the confusion, but there was no reason to be any more worried about him than any of the other couple of hundred people who were now spread out along the fire line, wielding buckets, shovels and wet blankets.

A majestic wall of towering flame expanded outward, the fiery monster seeking new fuel like some demon beyond their control. The gentle breeze had risen to a dashing wind, feeding the torrent of flames that leaped along in resistless splendor.

But resist it they did, with every bit of strength and every tool they possessed. Vern Carlson, who didn't even own a farm, drove his dump truck across one field, flattening the stalks so that others with pitchforks could scoop them up into the bed, while women raked away the root balls and more stubborn stalks, leaving a wide area of mostly cleared ground that would slow the fire's advance. Bennett was using his harvester to try to save the Vance place, where someone had turned on the irrigation system to try to dampen the flames.

Rob despaired for a bit when the water stopped spraying from the overhead tank, but it didn't matter. Not much remained in Brady Tanks to burn. The fields were the concern now ... the fields and the houses and barns beyond.

More people began arriving to relieve those who had arrived earlier. These were townspeople being neighborly, risking physical harm to save their friends' farms. Chief Frear detailed them to strategic points and called Rob to him.

"According to Jacob, we've got it seventy percent contained." Frear handed him a bottled water, which Rob chugged.

Rob had been too busy to realize that his father had been flying, using the duster as a spotting plane. He hadn't even thought about the need for an aerial view.

"There's nobody answering at the Forest Service. A pilot from that commuter that landed volunteered to see if he could get a water dumper in the air. He and Joe found a plane, so he's about ready to take off."

"What will that do for us?" Rob poured the last of the water over his head. "Seems like a water pistol trying to put out a forest fire."

"I've seen the Forest Service just end a fire by hitting the leading edge just right. Joe says this guy has experience, but it's been a few years."

"I guess it's better than nothing. Have you seen Shane?"

"Yeah, several times." Nate grinned. "When I trained him as a volunteer firefighter all those years ago, he was crazy and a danger to himself. He's still crazy and a danger to himself, but he knows what to do without being told."

"So, I shouldn't worry about him?"

"I wouldn't go that far, but it's probably not going to do you any good. He'll still do what he's doing."

Just then, Rob spotted Shane dragging someone free of a line of people wielding shovels along this edge of the fire. He yelled for assistance while the man clutched his chest. Two of Nate's crew closed in on him with a stretcher and took over. Shane stumbled to his feet, wiped sweat off his forehead and pulled up his improvised mask to return to the fray.

Rob and Nate met the firemen at the ambulance. Mike LaRoche, the high school principal and superintendent of schools, was barely conscious, fogging up the oxygen mask as they loaded the stretcher.

"Looks like a coronary," paramedic Chad Balloch said. "Straight to the clinic, don't stop for reds."

"That could be anyone of us," Nate remarked to Rob as they walked back toward the fire line. "Lazy Americans working hard in the dog-day heat, totally unprepared for a crisis like this."

Rob nodded, decided to ignore his own heart in this, sighed and went back to work.

Gathering in Silence

Poppy Lufgren noticed half the congregation was missing when she pulled up in the parking lot. People were fighting the prairie fire. Alex had forbidden her to go. Sometimes he could be so bossy.

The red oak trees that lined the parking lot and framed the front of the church had turned copper with an occasional hint of scarlet, testament that the dog days were coming to an end.

Poppy checked her hair in the mirror and grabbed her Bible. She'd planned to dress nicely for service to impress Pete, but Mark said he had to work and Alex said she had to go to church. She normally loved going to church, but lately ... the world seemed a lot less rosy right now.

Mrs. Thomas waved at her as Poppy entered the lobby. She knew a few signs because she'd lived in Emmaus so long and cared enough to learn a few. Poppy signed "fine" to her and "how are you?" She turned and bounced down the stairs to the fellowship hall where the Deaf congregation met.

Poppy sometimes went upstairs with Alex and Keri since they could interpret for her, but it was easier to come down here and have Uncle Noah preach.

Uncle Noah, big and tawny like most Lufgrens, had been about 10 years younger than her parents, so he was still fit and healthy and had kids a bit younger than Poppy. His youngest daughter was Hearing like Alex, giving hope they were maybe breeding the deaf gene out. Noah's wife lost her hearing to an illness at age four, so had been born into a Hearing family. Poppy counted herself lucky not to have been born deaf to Hearing parents. She'd learned language from her parents from the beginning, learned all the nuances of being deaf in a supportive Deaf community. Alex could hear perfectly fine, but he was Deaf because his parents had been Deaf. Those born outside the community couldn't possibly understand. Barbara was a great aunt and she could sign like a native, but she hadn't grown up with the same values.

"You, how you?" she signed upon seeing Poppy. She stood with Joelle, cousin Micah's wife, who had been raised in a hard-of-hearing family. Poppy felt much more comfortable with her than Barbara, though both women had met their Lufgren husbands at KSD, the residential school for the deaf in Olathe. Poppy wondered briefly if Olathe still existed, being only a half-hour from Kansas City. She had hoped to spend her last two high school years there to prepare for college. Barbara continued signing.

"Me good me. Alex he harvest he."

Several of the boys raced by, mouths open in unheard clamor. If they got too loud, someone would come downstairs to gently remind them that others could hear what they could not.

"Fire north there. BIG. Jeremiah say fields his safe, but BAD."

"Smoke west too."

"You're pulling my hair!"

"Truth. World gone crazy."

Someone flickered the lights to get everyone's attention. They sat down on folding chairs and Noah stood up behind the lectern.

"World gone crazy," he signed. "Sermon title. World we live today." He weighed the two scenarios from hand to hand. "Man bad to man. Many people die. We-all angry … easy … yes, natural. Jesus Him say 'love who hate you.' Hard. Many people die. Angry. Scared. Helpless. God say 'love'. This world we live now this."

He preached for another 10 minutes and then they prayed. Deaf didn't bow their heads and close their eyes like Hearing. You only did that when you were alone. They signed their prayers to God. In this small group of a dozen people, those listening pantomimed lifting those prayers heavenward. And then Noah announced they were having a short service today because he needed to go harvest his fields before they burned up. Poppy sat in the truck watching people come out of the church. Joe the deputy wasn't around, not that she could see anyway. Assured she'd not get in trouble for driving without a license at only 15, she started the truck and drove back toward home.

Watering Station

Jazz Tully parked Jacob Delaney's old green pickup across the road from the fire line and climbed up into the bed to hold a sign she had hastily scrawled WATER on. Soon, she had people gathered, taking bottles of water from the flat cases in the bed.

From across the road, she watched the ragged line of men and women who were fighting the fire. The flames were shooting far above their heads. The smoke shifted momentarily, revealing the blue roof of the Vance's farm house and the big red barn beside it. Gooseflesh raised on her bare arms despite the heat.

She'd also brought several plastic jerry cans of water, which people seemed grateful for.

Colleen Bennett, Andrew's wife, wetted her hair, which she'd piled up into braids on top of her head. The water trickled down her face in black sooty streaks.

"Thank you for doing this. People get so caught up in fighting the fire, but we need water and food to fight the fire."

"That's what Mr. Delaney said. How's it going?"

"I don't know. The edge I'm working on has been beat back by several feet. Reminds me of how I met Andrew."

"I don't understand."

"We were on fire fighting crews out in Idaho."

"I'd love to hear about it sometime."

"Yeah. We should get together ... " she sighed "... after we take care of this."

She finished her water bottle, tossed it in the trash bag Jazz had provided and grabbed another bottle to take with her.

"Hey, Ms. Vance," Jos greeted as he grabbed a water bottle. He was in her US History class. "Have you heard if we're making progress?"

"I haven't."

"I figured since you're driving Mr. Delaney's truck while he's flying the fire, maybe he'd had told you."

"Nothing so far."

He nodded, grabbed a second bottle, and headed back toward the fire.

A part of her wanted to go join the firefighters on the line, but she didn't know what she'd be doing and people kept coming for water. Eventually Captain Frear came for water and he told her the fire was contained, but they were awaiting an aerial drop to knock it down still further.

One of the Bennett girls, who she didn't know very well because they were home-schooled, pulled up with a stock tank of water on a flatbed trailer. Jacob's truck bed was nearly empty. Jazz handed out her last few remaining bottles of water, gifted Miss Bennett with her sign, and then drove back to the feed store and her apartment on the second floor. The streets were practically deserted, except for a couple of crews of teenagers, dressed in hazmat suits, who were cleaning up radioactive roadkill. There was only so much one could do and she suspected she'd done that, but getting rid of the health hazard was as important as fighting the fire, so she asked the kids who had organized them, then got into her car to drive over the Emmaus Road Baptist Church to done a hazmat suit. A contingent of women were getting ready to go sweep an area of yards and old orchards on the eastern end of town.

Staying busy in trying times was important, her mother would say. She just prayed she would hear her mother say it once more. With her parents in Florida when the bombs went off, she didn't want to think about the possibility that she might not hear her say anything ever again. It was far easier to scoop up dead squirrels and worry about your lifetime exposure to radioactivity.

Resistance Has Consequences

By noon, the aerial drop had knocked the fire down enough that the bucket brigade and shovel crews could put the rest of it out. They'd saved the structures outside of Brady Tanks and lost several acres of corn ... several days' worth of food for the town. Shane leaned against the side of Rob's truck, his tan deepening in the hot sun. Frear walked up to him.

"Where's your dad?"

"I don't know." Shane blinked, bleary, blood-shot eyes scanning the milling line of blanket-and-shovel-wielding folks halfway across the field.

"Too much fun at Callahan's last night?"

"That and I didn't eat anything before this fandango." He scrubbed a filthy hand across his sweat-soaked hair. "What's that?"

Frear held up the fragment of electronics in his hand.

"I think it's a detonator."

Shane straightened, leaned in. He'd been a curious kid and Nate felt heartened that he hadn't outgrown that. That mind would be a terrible thing to waste.

"How do you know?"

"I took an arson course. It would explain why the diner's big tank blew so soon in the fire."

"When we got here I could smell diesel and gasoline. I thought maybe it was just from the cars, but that combo is used as an accelerant." Shane got a foggy faraway look on his face.

"What?"

"When I was up on the water tower, I didn't have time to think about it, but there were other fires. Come on. I'll show you."

Shane dragged up the stairs but he'd never been one to complain. He might have been slow just so Nate wouldn't get out of breath. From the maintenance deck of the water tower, they could see at least a dozen smoking fields, some of them in nearby counties. Two of them had helicopters with buckets working over them.

"I guess that's where the Forest Service went," Shane suggested.

By the time they reached the ground again, Jacob had arrived with Dennis Hoffman, the copilot from the commuter plane who had been forced to land at Emmaus Airfield the night the troubles had begun.

"That was good work with the plane," Shane complimented.

"I flew one summer for the Forest Service in Alaska. I'm just glad there was no terrain to deal with."

"Yeah, the deck in Kansas is pretty much a deck, though you do have the Heights here to be concerned about."

"You sound like a pilot."

"Yeah. This man here taught me everything I know."

Jacob guffawed.

"Boy's too modest. I got him started. He went way further than I ever thought. Don't run off, Nate. We need to talk to you and Rob ... and probably you too, Shane." Rob had seen them and was walking across the scorched ground toward them. Soot blackened his face, dripping into his beard in demonic streaks. Dick Vance and Andrew Bennett also drifted their way. Dick's beard had been singed. Andrew's shirt had several burn holes.

"We saw dozens of other fires out there," Jacob told the group as soon as Rob joined them. "There were a couple of helicopters with buckets fighting them, but it looked like most were ground assisted – farmers and townsfolks."

"I did a second run west of here, doused the worst field near Mara Wells after Jacob talked to me," Dennis explained. "I was out of fuel, so I couldn't do more."

"How'd you even get the plane?"

"Joe knew about the Forest Service station, so we gambled there was a plane there and there was.

But it didn't look like anyone had been there since before the bombs."

"So, who's operating the bucket helos?" Rob asked. Dennis shrugged, but Shane cleared his throat. He wiped sudden sweat from his forehead. Under his tan, he seemed gray.

"In Miristan, there was a crew that used to do something similar with the poppy fields. The ground crew would first arrive, make demands. If the demands weren't met, the crew would fire the fields. Then a pilot would put out the fire. The demands were usually met after that."

"A crew?" Rob asked sharply.

"Dad, believe it or not, I don't know how to scoop water with one of those things. I can't say I wouldn't have learned if they'd ordered me to, but it wasn't me. My point is --." He swallowed convulsively, blinking. "--has anyone made any demands on the town that we refused?"

"Yup," Dick said. He and Andrew exchanged glances.

"A USDA agent came to the cooperative meeting last night." Andrew pushed back his wet hair with a filthy hand. "He didn't exactly make demands, but he was strong in his suggestions."

"Which were?" Rob asked.

"That we use their storage facilities up at Wendat Lake and allow them to control the corn for us."

Rob growled.

"Alex gave me his card last night at the church. I figured I'd call him on Monday, say we weren't interested."

"Resistance has consequences," Shane said.

"Like hell," Andrew retorted. "I'm fueling up my harvester as soon as I off-load Vance's field and I'm pulling my corn today. They can't burn it if the fields are empty."

"Same with me," Dick said. "Don't usually hold with working on Sunday, but that got shot to smithereens this morning anyway, so may as well get to work."

"Shane, we need to let the others know," Rob said. Shane's face darkened.

"Do you need some food, son?" Frear asked softly.

"Click Michaels got your radio up and running," Dennis said. "We pulled it up on our way over here. If you radio him, he'll put it out on the air."

"I wasn't suggesting you drive around in a circuit again," Rob told Shane. "Pa, you take care of getting that on the radio. Shane, with me. "

"Before you go, Rob, I need to tell you -- I think someone blew Les' propane tanks to cover up the arson."

"Might not have been for that," Dick chimed in. "Don't expect you'd notice since this isn't technically inside Emmaus, but I own this land, what sat under the Tanks. Les owned the building, but I bought the land off of him about 10 years ago. I was pretty vocal in that meeting."

Andrew and Dick headed off toward Dick's place. Rob leaned in to look at the detonator and Shane sat down abruptly on the ground and put his head between his knees. Frear immediately dropped beside him.

"You okay?"

"Dizzy."

"You need to eat something. I'll help your dad get you into the truck."

After Rob drove away, Frear looked back to the fire scene. The tanks were all that remained. They'd found two bodies in the wreckage of the diner. Identity couldn't be established, but nobody really doubted that Les and Molly had perished in the fire. People headed back to their own farms and homes, getting ready for the harvest, nursing some burns, some folks having lost corn. They'd have to figure out who had done this so as to keep them from doing more harm in the future. Deputy Joe Kelly walked over. He looked neat and official in his uniform. He'd been helping with first aid and detailing people to where they were needed, so he looked hot, but clean.

"Passed Dick Vance back there and he said you think this was arson. I took a course in that back in the Academy. Can I help you?"

"Yeah. Firemen don't have police powers. Normally this would fall to the police chief."

"I'm not that, but I'm the only cop remaining." Joe's voice wavered.

"Yeah." Nathan wished he had time to be sad. "Let's walk the scene."

Extraordinary Circumstances

Dr. Callahan traced the fracture on the computer image with a purple-clad finger.

"Yeah, it's a nice simple fracture. We'll get you fixed up in no time."

"Will I need a cast?" Kim asked. She had an ice pack wrapping her wrist now.

"Yes, for a few weeks, until it stabilizes. Up to six. The good news is that the bones are still aligned. It's just a fracture. I won't need to set it."

Nevada squeezed Kim's shoulder.

"It'll be fine, sweetie. I broke my wrist when I was just about your age. I fell when I was roller skating. It's really not that big of a deal."

Kim nodded. She looked pale, but not in a lot of pain and the wrist hadn't swollen much on the drive over here. Nevada had packed it in frozen peas, which the nurse had complimented.

Lila, the nurse, began setting up to apply the plaster. Dr. Callahan lifted the ice pack away.

"Swelling is minimal. That's good. This won't take that long --"

A clatter of noise sounded in the hall. Dr. Callahan instructed Kim to put the ice pack on and then turned to check on it. A moment later, a fireman stuck his head in the door.

"Lila, Marnie needs you in the other room."

Lila assured Kim she'd return in a minute and then hurried out with the fireman. Minutes ticked by ... 15, 30. Nevada could hear commotion on the other side of the wall.

"What's taking so long?" Kim asked. "It's really aching."

"I think it must be an emergency."

Eventually Lila came back into the room. She looked drained, her full lips drawn.

"Sorry for that," she said. "It was a heart attack. Let's get that arm casted so you can get home."

"Is he okay?" Kim asked.

"The patient?" Kim nodded. Lila shook her head, sighing heavily before lifting away the ice pack. "Good. Swelling is still minimal. How's your pain?"

"It hurts, but not so bad so long as I don't try to move my fingers."

"Good. This is a nice simple fracture, nothing at all to worry about. Casting will take a while. Might as well get to it."

"Isn't the doctor supposed to do this?" Nevada asked.

"Dr. Callahan has official business she has to take care of. I've done dozens of casts though."

Lila set about coating Kim's arm in a protective crème, then carefully wrapped her forearm in a cotton padding and then the plaster bandages. She finished just when Dr. Callahan came back into the room. The doctor had washed her face, but she'd clearly been crying.

"Are you okay?" Nevada asked, speaking low so Kim wouldn't hear her.

"I will be. It's just … even as a family doctor, you can expect to lose patients, but I've lost quite a few this week."

"These are extraordinary circumstances. You're doing fine."

Dr. Callahan gave her a grateful smile and then went over to inspect Kim's cast.

"It'll take a little time to dry and then you can head home. The fire's just about out, by the way."

"That's good. Do they know how it started?" Nevada asked.

"Not that they've told me, but I'm sure they'll broadcast it on KERB."

"It's back?"

"Started this morning," Lila said. "I don't know who the guy is who is doing the announcements, but he's been doing a good job of keeping everyone updated."

"We'll tune in. It's been so strange, being so out of touch for the last few days. Is the Internet back?"

"Spotty," Dr. Callahan said. "All the news networks are playing the same government-issue press releases. My grandfather-in-law pulled up the Wichita stations on his seaman's last night and they're playing old music and government press releases."

"So, the guy doing KERB is ...?"

"Town announcements and whatever he can get off the Internet. He's playing a lot of music too."

"So, where's DJ Bob and the others?" Kim asked.

Dr. Callahan suddenly misted up and turned away. Kim winced guiltily and shook her head to indicate she didn't need the details. They weren't with us anymore. She didn't need to know more.

"I don't know what's wrong with me," Dr. Callahan croaked. "I'm not usually a crier."

"You've had a tough week," Lila diagnosed.

Nevada didn't know Marnie Callahan very well. Tall, slender, fit, with long dark auburn hair that she kept in a French braid while at work .... Were her blue scrubs a little tight around the middle? Her face seemed fuller and a bit flushed from the last time Nevada had seen her for her annual woman's physical. She'd gotten married this summer. Surely, a doctor knew how to prevent pregnancy, but ...

It's not my place to point this out. She's a doctor. I'm sure there's a pregnancy test available.

Dr. Callahan monitored Kim's pulse, blood pressure and temperature one last time before releasing her to home.

"Take it easy for the next few days. You can go to school, but you'll want to keep the hand elevated and no riding for at least a week. Come back for a follow-up appointment on Friday. My advice to you is that you stay away from Rocket until the cast comes off. Ride Taffy. She's a rocking chair ... and my horse, actually. But no horses at all until I give the go-ahead."

Kim assured her she'd do as instructed and Nevada realized that meant she would have to take care of five horses all by herself for at least a week.

"Don't worry, Mom," Kim said as Nevada started the car. "I'll tell you what to do. You won't have to do it all alone ... just the physical part."

"Well, thanks, kid. I appreciate that I'll have your moral support. I also appreciate that you waved off Rocket before she could run right over me to get through the door."

"You're welcome." Kim looked down at the white cast on her arm and sighed. "You're worth the price."

"Well, at least you can still dance," Nevada pointed out.

Kim giggled.

"Thanks, Mom."

Nevada tuned the radio to KERB and listened to a strange new voice tell them about the progress on the fire in the fields east of town.

Involuntary Solitude

Danny's stomach rumbled. He'd tried drinking water to keep it at bay, but it had been at least 12 hours since he'd eaten and could no longer ignore his hunger. With no other prisoners and no windows to track the passage of time, the cell's bars seemed to grow closer with every hour. The clock he couldn't see ticked louder. Had they forgotten about him entirely? He'd tried shouting sometime earlier, but his voice just echoed back to him from an empty building. First there had been the wail of a fire truck and, more recently, he thought he'd maybe heard vehicles outside, but nobody answered his shouts, so now he lay on the bed, staring at the concrete wall, trying not to cry.

When he heard the footsteps in the hall and the sound of the outer door being unlocked, he rolled off the cot to stare at the uniformed cop who entered with a bag in one hand.

"I'm sorry," the cop said. "I meant to bring you breakfast, but things got a little hectic this morning."

At least it wasn't the old man who had brought him food yesterday. He'd been there when ... well, when ... and his bright blue gaze had felt like lasers boring into his soul.

"There's laws. You can't not feed me."

The cop stared at him for a moment before holding the bag through the tray hole. Too hungry to resist, Danny grabbed the bag and ripped it open to reveal the contents. He'd never tasted a better roast beef sandwich, even with wheat bread.

The cop pulled up a chair and seemed to settle in. He had a clipboard and pen.

"I'm Deputy Kelly, by the way. What's your full name?"

"Why should I help you?"

"Well, there's a question there, sure. I suppose you could not tell me your name and I could find out some other way. Either way, you're going to answer for your crime."

Danny's appetite disappeared. He chewed resolutely and swallowed.

"I didn't mean to hurt that guy. He grabbed for the gun."

"Did he? That's not what Jacob says."

"Jacob .... Is that the old man? He couldn't see everything. There was a wall in the way."

"Couldn't he? Okay. So, your story is that it was self-defense?"

"Yeah. I mean, I shouldn't have shot him, but I was scared and he was aggro."

"So, when I enter your photo into the computer, what am I going to find? This your first time being an idiot or do you have priors?"

"It's not like that, man. My grandmother would kick my ass for getting into trouble."

"Sounds like a good granny. She raise you?"

"Yeah."

"Jacob said you're from Chicago. Is that where she lives?"

Danny nodded.

"Okay, no name. What brought you to Kansas?"

This cop had a sense of humor at least. He'd never had much experience with cops before. He hadn't expected them to make jokes.

"My uncle and I went to Denver coz he had a presentation at a school. We were coming back when they stopped us on the highway. We were playing cards when he suddenly freaks out and tells me I need to go. He hands me this gun and says run."

"Why?"

"I didn't know why until I looked back. The Army was burning the cars."

The cop's blue eyes seemed sad.

"Yeah, I heard about that. Why didn't he go with you?"

"He did. He tried. He was in his wheelchair, but when we got to the road's edge, he couldn't follow and then they saw him. He told me to run. What's my grandmother going to say?"

Deputy Kelly took a deep breath and let it out slowly.

"Your grandmother was in Chicago, Jacob said."

"Yeah."

"They nuked Chicago."

"She's okay."

Joe sighed.

"I hope so."

"She's fine!"

Danny could see the pity in the cop's eyes. He slammed his back against the wall, stared at the floor, head pounding with anger. "I don't want to talk to you."

"Yeah, okay. I'll be back with dinner. We'll see how much of this form we can get filled out then."

"Go to hell."

"Hmm. Feels like we're probably living there right now." He stood up and moved toward the door. "I'll see you later. Enjoy your solitude."

Jokester

Alex slowed the harvester and climbed out of the cab to talk to his cousin Micah.

"See you against corn can't almost."

Micah liked to tease, but Alex couldn't argue that his blond hair and tawny tan took on a chameleon quality around harvest time. Although a Lufgren, Micah took after his Italian mother with dark hair and brown eyes. Alex signed "ha-ha" in response.

"Jeremiah he say lose zero corn him, but want harvest today him," Micah signed. "Jonah say he collect his and help Zeb him." Alex nodded before replying in sign.

"Me work fast, but limit time machine." One side of Micah's farm road had been cleared. On the other side, the corn still nodded in the sun. "You need help you?"

"No. Easy."

"Super farmer strikes again?"

Micah chortled, laugh lines appearing around his eyes and mouth. He always found a reason to be cheerful.

"Me collect one field. Relax ten minutes, next field collect. Me rolling."

More likely, he'd worked in the dark, doing what was necessary. The heat dried the corn too fast, which led to fires.

"You place put all?"

"Silo behind wood lot, storm barn, bunker silo. Thumbs up."

"Me go. Call if you need help you."

Alex climbed back into the harvester. Micah's farm road was the quickest way to Shane's two fields. Getting his own corn in concerned him, but he could work his fields at night. He knew them well enough. He didn't know Shane's fields at all because they were corporate fields existing in the no-man's land between Jericho Ridge and Mara Wells. He'd driven by them a million times and never paid the slightest bit of attention. Now they were part of the puzzle that would keep people from starving through the winter … maybe. That maybe kept him praying quietly as he prepared for the harvest. His math said there wasn't enough corn in Jericho township to keep everyone alive through the winter, but they'd have to let God work on that problem because, near as Alex Lufgren could tell, it wasn't up to the people of Emmaus to do anything besides the task set before them this minute. Harvest the corn. Care for the stock. Prepare for ….

A shiver shuddered down his back. A memory of that man at the cooperative meeting came to mind. He'd been really insistent about Wendat Lake. Now all of a sudden, the fields were afire because ....

No, I'm not going to worry about this. That's not my job ... at least not until after I've harvested the corn. Let people like Shane worry about it. He'll let me know if I need to worry. I think.

Project Sunset

Shane leaned back in the tub of hot water, trying to relax. The news that Cai had not returned with Jacob might have rattled him if he hadn't been on the verge of passing out from hunger. Now with food in him, he vibrated like an overstrung guitar string. Every fiber of his being wanted to rush to Wichita to find his brother, but Jacob, Rob and his mother, Jill, had all insisted he use better judgment. They didn't know him, didn't know what he could do. He could find Cai if needed. He'd already texted Rigby. Still, they were right that in this situation, finding any one man in this chaos might not be that easy. With the possibility that the USDA was coming to confiscate the crops, it would be really poor timing for his dad's hired gun to disappear. He was the rope in a tug-of-war. No wonder he vibrated.

He nudged the hot water faucet with his toe, but the trickle turned warm headed toward cool. He kicked it off and rolled up out of the filthy water. He rinsed the tub down and ran a squeegee around the soap line. He'd missed a spot under the curve of his chin, so he wiped the mirror down, applied a little shaving crème and willed his hands not to shake while he removed the whiskers. Just to be sure, he looked at his reflection. The bruises from Thursday's tumble had nearly faded. A red mark in the trapezius muscle attracted his attention. A small throb of pain pulsed when he prodded it.

That's an injection site. I never blacked out before. Maybe I didn't this time either.

A dream before waking – a desperate whispered conversation between Marnie and Rob, a memory of sitting on the church steps and peeing in the bushes with .... *Dad roofied me?*

In his room, he pulled on sweats and a t-shirt, trying to decide what he should do. His phone buzzed.

-What part of scrubbed do you not understand? Your brother's DMV file doesn't even have a picture on file. D P3 at least around the dial.

Damn. Cut off from intel for twenty-four hours. *I'm wasting that resource being stupid.* A soft knock came on his door. Rob eased the door open.

"I have a confession to make."

"Ya think?" Shane pulled his collar away from the injection site. "What was I doing?"

"Taking Ren's plane back to Wichita, convinced you could find Cai."

"Yeah, because it makes perfect sense to fly a plane I've never flown before into unknown territory at least one sheet to the wind. What did you dose me with?"

"Ketamine."

"Well, that explains the weird dreams and amnesia."

"I apologize. I didn't have a right to drug you. Pa's pissed at me."

"Naw, it's fine. I was being an idiot. I am way too bold when I drink. Thank you for stopping me being stupid."

"You sure?"

"Yes. I need some sleep. You have my word that I won't go haring after Cai, but I do need a photo of him so I can transmit it to my handler so he can search for him."

Rob opened his wallet and handed Shane a photo of Cai. Shane's hands were shaking too hard to get a decent snap with his phone, so Rob did it for him. "Jill, Dad, Marnie and I are headed to Alex's to help clean out the old silo. Please be sensible, stay here and get some sleep."

"I will. That horse tranq kicked my ass and then this morning ...." Shane held out his hands to prove just how shaky he was.

"I may have had good intentions, but I really shouldn't have. I could have tried to talk you out of it."

"Neither of us believes that would have worked out well." Shane sighed. "I usually stick to one drink because I hear that bold voice then, but I am still in control. It gets harder after. I might seem to still be in control, but I look back and think 'Why did I do that?' See, I was listening when you lectured me when I was a kid."

"I wasn't trying to lecture."

"Oh, sure you were. You were scared for us. And right to be. Cai has it too. He ended up in bed with a teenager after about three beers."

"He's repented of that. We don't talk about it after."

Shane snorted. Ridiculous notion!

"I'm not bound by those rules, Dad. Does part of that repentance have to do with never drinking again?"

"I can't answer for him. I know that's what I counseled. You always seemed to keep your morality intact when you were drinking. You're bold anyway. The booze just pushes you over an edge you recognize is a bridge too far. So, what happened last night?"

"Older men plying me with liquor to find out what you have planned. Maybe a little stressed out over what's happened the last few days. Maybe wanting to celebrate that I'm alive when others aren't."

Rob chuckled.

"It doesn't sound like you need my advice. You are much more self-aware than I ever was. Any attempt to control your mood in there?"

Shane snorted.

"Yeah. I had to make some hard choices and – yeah – easing that ache is in there."

"That's the hole lurking, son, because there's lots of ache in our future. Better consider that maybe you want to take up running or just about anything else rather than drinking to take care of that stress and the sadness that comes after you make hard choices."

Shane yawned. He'd said enough.

"What did you tell them?"

"Them?"

"The older men? And who are they?"

"Stan Osimowicz and Anders McAuliff. I think I stopped before I said anything you will regret. My memory's a little swiss cheesy, but I've had ample opportunity to test the theory that drinking makes me gossipy and it never has before."

"I'll trust that. Get some sleep, son. I'll ask your mother to leave a plate in the fridge. Okay?"

"Yes, sir." Rob left. Shane lay down. The sun was still up and he wasn't a napper, but he knew his body needed rest.

You shouldn't be sleeping. There's stuff to do. You need to sleep. You're no use to anyone like this. Close your eyes. Breathe slowly, deeply. No, keep your eyes closed. Relax. Okay, spread your toes and fingers. Deep breath. Let it out slowly, relax your toes. Breathe. Relax your legs. Breathe. Relax your fingers. Breathe. Relax your arms. Breathe. Relax your spine. Let your spine touch the mattress. Let your shoulders relax. Open your jaw. Breathe. Just breathe. And breathe again. And ....

Although Shane didn't open his eyes to look at the clock, an hour passed and the sun moved toward the west while he breathed and tried to relax his body. Finally, he opened his eyes, groaned and rolled off the bed. It had actually been two hours, so maybe he'd napped briefly in there. Belle the cat stared disapprovingly at him from the landing as he headed down the stairs. He ate the food Jill had left for him. His hands were still a little shaky, but much better. His mountain bike still hung in the garage, but the tires were flat. Cai's, however, were in good shape, so he cycled over to Callahan's, which closed early on Sunday nights. Spying Jason Breen's truck next to his Jeep in the deserted parking lot, he stowed the bike in the Jeep before letting himself in by the kitchen entrance.

"I was wondering when you were going to come pick your rig up." Maggie and Jason sat in one of the booths. Maggie lived upstairs, but often entertained in the bar when it was closed. They had been on-again-off-again for as long as Shane could remember. They were sitting on opposite sides of the table, which meant ...? *I'm not dating Marnie anymore. I shouldn't care about the marital status of her parents.*

"Things got a little hectic this morning." Maggie stood up from the booth, sliding a cigarette free of the pack and palming a lighter. She wouldn't smoke in the bar, but she would grab a butt outside the back door before wandering off to do something bar-related.

"We need to talk." Jason remained as tact-challenged as ever. Maggie headed for the door with her cigarette and Shane sat down in the booth across from Jason.

"Jacob asked me to go to Salinas for lye. I'm leaving first thing in the morning. You want to ride shotgun?"

"I can't. Other plans for the day. How are you paying for it?"

"Andrew Bennett's giving me corn."

"Ask him to give you more. Tell him I'll reimburse him. Get as many bag silos as you can manage."

"Bag silos? What for?"

"Cover." Jason frowned. "I'll explain after you get back."

"Your grandfather mentioned he'd make it worth my while ...."

"We will. We'll pay you in corn and lye which you can trade for whatever else you need."

"You have corn that is yours to make those promises with?"

"I do." Jason raised an eyebrow. "You know the things I would lie about and that would be off-limits."

Jason snorted.

"It would. I've got a lot of mouths to feed since the crew brought their ole ladies and kids to the compound. You know, though, we can't live on corn alone."

"If you find other grocery items, I'm sure Mae would love to restock. Maybe you should talk to her on your way out of town."

"It comes down to how she's paying me."

"That's between you and her."

"You got any rules on this expedition?"

"Did my dad or Jacob give you any?"

"No and that's got me curious."

"It's the apocalypse, Jason. Rules are for civilized times. Come back alive and with lye and bag silos and I won't ask any questions the town wouldn't want to know the answers to."

"The apocalypse needs realists. You hear anything from your brother?"

"No. I'm thinking something hit the fan in Wichita, but don't know that for sure."

"And you aren't going to go find out?"

"You got a problem with that?"

"Don't particularly like Cai. My daughter thinks she loves him, but now that things are cracking up, she'd be much better off with someone like you."

Shane stared at him for a moment.

"That's never going to happen, Jason. Ever."

"You don't still love her?"

"My heart moved on a long time ago ... long before she married Cai."

"I don't believe you. You've been in love with her since you were 15 years old."

"Fourteen, and seven years later she told me to get out of her life and never come back, so I moved on. I'm also monogamous. If Marnie's looking for a man to replace my brother already, then it sure as hell won't be me."

"She's not the one doing the looking. Fathers look out for their kids."

"Good for you, but don't look my direction. Period." Shane glanced at his phone. "I should get going."

"Why don't you hang around for a beer?"

"I had enough beer last night, thanks." Are you another older man trying to pump me for information?

"Hung over?"

"Something like that. So, you've only talked to Jacob and Andrew ... not Rob."

"Right. He's busy trying to organize the community and I don't look like I need organizing, I guess."

Shane paused after the crash-bar door closed behind him. It would be sunset in half an hour. He felt wide away. Sleep would be illusive. It didn't take him long to reach Jericho Springs. The gates of the bed and breakfast were locked, but that never stopped him before. He dropped in over the top of the 8-foot board fence as Grant Rigby turned from the chopping block with an axe in his hand. Shane's hand twitched toward his gun, but Rigby set the axe down.

"Dang, kid. You still don't listen to instructions. Let's get inside before a satellite picks us up. Dylan, get a tarp over that Jeep." Rigby looked pretty much like Shane had expected he'd look in "real" life. He didn't really know Dylan and the younger man was gone before Shane had time to check him out.

The bed and breakfast had once belonged to the Sullivan family and it showed its wealth with understated grace ... plaster walls, wood moldings, lamp medallions on the ceiling, crystal door knobs. Rigby directed him into the back parlor off the gracious main hallway.

"We tell you to wait twenty-four hours and you show up on our doorstep?"

"You know how I am." Rigby grinned. He did know. He'd been Shane's handler for more than four years. Of course, he knew. "You get the photograph?"

"I did. I know you always chafe under protocols, but there's a reason for them."

"I don't doubt that, but I'm worried about my brother."

"You can't save the whole world, Shane."

"I don't want to save the whole world, but I don't include my brother in that." Dylan entered the room, closing the door behind him. They'd not met officially. There'd not been time for introductions when Dylan had plucked him out of the creek he'd tumbled into the other day. Dylan got right to the point now.

"I guess I should apologize for startling you the other day."

Shane didn't want to explain that he hadn't been startled so much as Dylan in dark clothes had looked like his PTSD "demon" from a distance.

"I'm fine. The grass was slippery." He looked at Rigby, waiting. Dylan shrugged and let it go.

"We know Cai's last known location – the banks of a river in Wichita, being chased by military personnel. But that's when the last image was scrubbed and we don't know where he is now. Dylan's pretty thorough. The military does not have Cai's image at the moment, but putting his image out there might retrigger the search." Shane sighed. He hated cyber surveillance.

"We can do the search in a safer, slower way, but there's no guarantee that we'll find him. He might already be in custody." Dylan's explanation helped, but being Rigby's son didn't earn trust from Shane, so he continued to press Rigby.

"Would you even tell me if he were?"

"No."

Shane laughed and Rigby joined him.

"At least you're honest. So, in the spirit of honesty, why are you here?"

"In Emmaus?" Shane nodded. "I needed somewhere safe to take my family. This seemed as good as any. As far as the CSA is concerned, it was decommissioned four years ago and sold to Joel Rhys about three years ago. One of my false identities – Neil Patterson – leased it from you -- er, Joel -- the day we met in the coffee shop."

"Great. How much is that monthly payment?"

"We paid for a year. If you had access to Joel's bank account right now, you'd see it grew substantially."

"So how much does Joel Rhys own? I know I didn't have enough money to buy this place or those two fields of corn and I hope I'm not millions of dollars in debt."

"Shane Delaney and Eric Faraday had ordinary mercenary incomes, but Joel Rhys is an exceedingly wealthy man. All of them have your aversion to debt."

"When did you do all this?" The room grew darker as the sun set. Dylan rose to turn on a corner lamp. This would be a lovely B&B in more sane times.

"It's a small matter to move money around electronically. Nobody can trace it to Shane Delaney. Anyone looking in county records would see that Rhys bought those fields a few years ago. They've been leased to a big corporation, but there's a clause in the contract that allows Joel or his agent to harvest the corn and own it in circumstances like this."

"You can somehow do that retroactively?"

"We're good at what we do." That's why I wasn't in Ramah. None of us were because Rigby had to keep me in the field. Shane sighed.

"So, who set fire to our fields and why?"

"A fella by the name of Rutherford operating out of Cheyenne Mountain ordered confiscation of the corn and any excess food stuff. They should get here by Tuesday … Wednesday at the latest."

"So, it's not the USDA. It's the military?"

"Maybe. There's been no chatter about the burning of the fields, just the confiscation. Rutherford used to be military, but he isn't anymore. I'm not sure who is pulling his strings. I'm more worried about our boss, the head of DHS."

"Why?"

"Because I have credible evidence that he's involved in the bombings?"

Shane leaned back on the couch.

"This just keeps getting better and better, doesn't it?"

"You have no idea."

"Enlighten me."

"You might be better off in the dark."

"Curiosity killed the cat. It died by drowning."

Rigby snorted. Dylan sat down in one of the wing chairs.

"You don't look healthy today." Although Shane no longer officially worked for Rigby, his health - mental and physical - had been the man's concern for half a decade, so Shane didn't balk at the examination.

"I overindulged at the bar last night, then fought a corn field fire without breakfast. I tried to catch some zzz's this afternoon, but I am still an insomniac. In all truth, those problems from before ... they took a backseat to the current crisis Wednesday night. I think I had too much time on my hands before."

Rigby mulled it over for about ten seconds.

"Operations Sunset. We're still piecing it together. We're pretty sure Ellerby was involved."

"It was a DHS operation?"

"We're not certain of that. It's a lot of data gathered from many sources. There's no smoking gun. No topic statement that says 'these people were involved and this agency did this or that.' Agents of the government were involved, but that doesn't mean the government itself was.

"Seems like a lot of trouble to go to in order to confiscate some corn."

"Yeah, that's just part of it. Not just your crops, but anything is subject to confiscation." Rigby stared at the carpet for a moment before going on. "You sure you want to know all this?"

"My life is going to be complicated by it, so yeah ... if you can tell me, then I want to know. Just tell me what I can't share with my father."

"You're really sure? Maybe you'd just rather worry about the town and not the rest of the world."

"Just wait for some guy with a code name to show up and ask for the flash drive? I don't think so."

"Okay. This was a multi-pronged terrorist attack using unaffiliated groups. While it appears to have been orchestrated by the Neharis Group, I think that's a red herring and it was really orchestrated by someone else. We don't know who. Dylan thinks it's the government. I'm not convinced. The government was involved in fomenting incidents around the country in the last few months – the San Diego riots, for example, flash mobs, anti-Dotson protests. Those two plots came to us from separate sources, so we don't know if they're connected."

"So, I'm holding this information because nobody is looking for Shane Delaney?"

"Exactly. That's why you cannot drive your Jeep up to our gate again. The last thing we need is anyone connecting you to us because ultimately, you are the failsafe."

"If someone named Chavez shows up?"

"Yes. What's going on with you besides your brother?"

"Mike reached out. He figured out that Shane Delaney and Eric Faraday are the same person. Apparently, he learned something about the Kanorado incident."

Rigby frowned. Shane realized that this was the first time he'd ever seen him without some element of disguise. He was average – medium hair, hazel eyes, average height and build, dressed in jeans and a t-shirt. He looked like a bureaucrat on holiday. Dylan must favor his mother. His hair was lighter with a modern cut and he needed a shave.

"I know you like the guy, but I don't think he's that smart. Do you trust that he's not compromised?"

"Yeah. Mike is a friend and could be a good asset so long as you realize that he's not me. He's not a complicated guy who sees nuances and connections. They have to jump out at him. But if I ask him to observe and report, he would. He did when we were partners. Some of the things I reported came from him. He just thought it was a game we were playing, something to keep our minds off the danger, something to make us more aware of our surroundings."

"Where is he?"

"Wichita. Which is why I'm bringing it up."

"You're wondering if you can use him to find Cai?"

"No, he's already been in touch with Cai, but he isn't anymore. First, he teased me about Kanorado and my secret identity, but then he warned me about the search. I was too drunk to do anything about it. When I got back to him this afternoon, he said he'd keep an eye out, but that it's the Army looking for Cai, not the Knights, so there's not much he can do except find him someplace to hide."

"I doubt the Army will keep looking for long. Their drones are pretty useless without facial recognition," Dylan said.

"We can find him with a grid search," Rigby explained. "We'll work out from his last location, take snapshots, upload them and then run scan software on them. That'll keep his image safe, but it could take days doing it that way. We don't have the Utah Data Center in the basement. Wait until you hear from us."

"I promised my dad I wouldn't run off, so I won't. If he's in custody, you won't tell me, so how do I know when not to believe you?"

"You'll have to rely on your own gut."

Shane snorted.

"So, will you do us a favor?"

"Depends."

"Dylan has another zip drive of information. I'd like to give it to you to put in your safety deposit box."

"Bank is supposed to reopen tomorrow, but if it doesn't – there's an old safe in our house – up in the attic. Cai and I found it when we were kids playing up there. I spent days with a stethoscope figuring out the combination, sure we were going to find treasure."

"Did you?" Dylan asked.

"If history is treasure, yeah. A bunch of old photo albums from Jericho Springs. Have no idea why they were in the safe. I still remember the combination. I used to hide stuff there from the folks when I lived there. It's not as secure as my box, but since nobody but me remembers it exists and I'm the only one with the combination ...."

"Actually, having it in that safe instead of the bank might be better. Right now, we'd have no way to get to it." Rigby stood up. "We need to get you away from our gate. If you need to visit in person, next time park up at the hotel and walk here. By the way, have you inventoried the boxes in the basement?"

"I was going to ask you about it."

"It's storage food. Enough for two people for a year. I wanted to get more, but they couldn't pull a larger order on short notice."

"Wow, you are amazing. Why didn't you just tell me?"

"I couldn't risk that someone would intercept you."

"But here you're not worried about that?"

"Here you're not Eric Faraday. I should have known you couldn't sit still and wait out the apocalypse, but I feel a lot safer with you here than in San Diego or just about anywhere else."

"San Diego no longer exists, so ... yeah. So, if they're coming to confiscate our crops ... what do we do about it?"

Rigby looked at Dylan before looking at Shane.

"I might have a couple of ideas, but first, I'm going to need that combination, just in case something happens to you."

"Sure, but I surely hope I'm still alive because I want to watch you just stroll by my folks without getting shot in the head."

"You think so?"

"Grandpa and Dad were both Army Rangers and my mother was a nurse in Da Nang, so yeah, I'd lay even odds on that one. You sure you don't want me to tell them you might be dropping by?"

Rigby grinned.

"I'll put Dylan on Project Smoke & Mirrors. We can make half of Kansas' corn disappear if need be. And, yes, you can tell your folks the bare minimum. Break it up so they can't accidentally tell someone else. Code name Clotilde and tell me the combination."

"Clotilde?"

"She was a special girlfriend."

Shane would have believed that, but Dylan snorted.

"I missed something," Shane recognized, looking back and forth between the two. He shrugged. "Not my business. You hang out in this town for a while and you start gossiping like everyone else."

"I can't imagine you chatting up the neighbors."

"No, but I start thinking like them, so ... I should just go home and continue acting like I don't know the bigger picture." Shane stood up and walked toward the patio door.

"You've got a lot to do before the USDA gets here," Dylan explained. "Someone needs to organize this town."

"Organize them? Nah. You've been living in a blue state for too long. These are red-staters. You can make suggestions, but they decide what they'll do … or not. It's kind of like herding cats … if cats had AR15s." He let himself out the patio door into the cooling dusk.

Lila Takes a Stand

The buzz of the fluorescent light echoed off the bottom of the last bin. The hastily constructed board-and-brick shelves in the fall-out shelter were full. Marnie wrote the number 27 on the line labeled Bumetanide. Lila turned back to the bin to pull out the last of the boxes.

"There's only three boxes of Atenolol."

Marnie sighed.

"Jacob said SullCorp had our list, but they could only get what was available. I'm relieved we found the Toposar and Cytoxan. Is that the bottom of the box?"

"Yeah."

"We're not doing too badly on antibiotics and insulin. It'll give us a month to get the supply lines back. No Misoprostol?"

"Nope."

Marnie ran a hand across her eyes.

"That doesn't leave us with any other choice. I need you --."

"No."

Marnie blinked at her.

"Lila ...."

"No. I told you when you first brought it up and I will repeat myself now. I won't help you abort your baby."

"It's not a baby yet."

"It is a baby. If you leave it alone, a baby comes out. I left St. Louis because I wouldn't assist in abortions. I am not changing my mind now."

"This is a horrible time to be pregnant and the risks of neural tube defects ...."

"I think you're panicking over nothing."

"I thought you were my friend."

"I am your friend. I'm also Cai's friend and he has a right to participate in this decision."

"If I wait too long, I may go past the safe date."

"Maybe. And, if I know that boy, he won't say 'yes', not after what happened with Marie."

"Don't bring that up." Marnie looked ready to cry. She'd loved her sister and probably didn't want to remember her husband's involvement in that whole situation. Marnie brought herself under control. "If Cai said 'yes' ...."

"I would still say 'no', but I might know someone who would."

"Someone?"

"That's for me to know and you to find out, but before I'll give you the name, I want to do a sonogram."

"That's not fair."

"Yeah, it is. Right now, you want to believe it's not real. You need to see that it is. And while we're at it, we'll make sure there's no neural tube defect."

Marnie sighed.

"Fine, but I'm not changing my mind."

Lila's cell phone chimed. It was her husband Vin.

"Melanie tripped going down the stairs," Vin said without preamble. Her heart caught in her throat. "Her ankle is swelling."

"Was it immediate?"

"No, it took a few minutes."

"Sounds like a sprain, but keep her off it, put some ice on it, and bring her here. We'll check on it."

She hung up.

"Break's over. We'll do that sonogram tomorrow."

"Yes, ma'am." Lila knew Marnie was just being compliant for the sake of not pissing her off. That girl knew how to do passive aggressive. She'd figure out how to get what she thought she wanted one way or another. Lila could only hope that Cai would show up before Marnie found a way to do something she would greatly regret.

In the Wind

Wichita, Kansas

A heavy truck's passage woke Cai Delaney from a jumbled dream in which he was running from a nameless shadow, clutching Marnie's hand. Just as he wrapped his arms around her, the truck shook him awake. He stared up at the vaulted ceiling of his refuge. He had never slept this rough in his life. He felt like crap. He worried he'd been sleeping in it all night. He pushed himself to sitting, back against the curving wall.

The sun had moved from the left-hand opening to the right-hand opening and it slanted to suggest afternoon. His stomach rumbled. Hungry, stiff, scared ... it had taken a supreme act of will not to move from his hiding place right at sunrise, but now he was acutely aware that he needed food and drinkable water. He planned to head out as soon as the sun went down.

To that end, he pulled his jacket to him and began inventorying what he had to his credit. His wallet's contents had taken a good dousing, but they were mostly dry now. It had been a wise choice on his part to laminate his wallet photos and Social Security card. Yeah, that was against the law. At this point, having had the Army shooting at him just last night, he wasn't inclined to care. Strange how your mind could change so much in just the space of four days. Laminating the card had bothered him a week ago and now he knew it didn't make a difference.

The otter box on his phone had not been adequate for swimming in the river. He'd opened everything up and dried it out. Now he slid the battery back in. The screen lit up and announced "Battery Discharged" before going black.

And me without a charger or an electric outlet.

He put the phone and the otter box back together and stowed it in the inside jacket pocket. He had $243. Earlier in the day, he'd stripped the gun and dried off everything he could reach, even used a shoelace to clean the barrel of grit. Dell Conopher had suggested that technique once. It seemed to work in a pinch, though without oil, he doubted he'd done more than moved the grit around. He'd put the gun back together, but he had no confidence that it would work if he needed it. How long could bullets be submerged in river water before the primers got too wet to function? He wished he'd paid more attention when the gun gurus had been talking. The weird shoelace trick had stuck, but the knowledge of primers hadn't. He'd never thought he'd need to know. Carrying a

gun made a political statement in rural Kansas …
until it became a matter of life or death.

Without a means to communicate with the
outside world, he could only wonder. Were Marnie
and the folks okay? Had the Army gone after Shane
too? Why had the drones suddenly sped off, leaving
him alone in his makeshift hiding place? Why
hadn't humans followed up?

*Why do I care more about that than I do that
they were chasing me in the first place? Maybe
because that's about what you should expect if you
were with your brother when he shot two soldiers?*

"I dented their Kevlar," Shane had said.

Cai had gone back and forth all night, trying to
sleep cold and wet in his culvert refuge, irritated
with Shane for getting him into this situation and
then grateful that he hadn't let him be killed in the
conflagration at the Kanorado state line.

*Fact is that I wish Shane were here now. He'd
know what to do.*

Cai knew he needed to make a plan and he
suspected Shane would have had one before now.
He couldn't stay in the culvert. He needed food and
drinkable water and it had gotten cold enough to
chatter teeth last night. If he left here, he needed to
get out of the city as soon as possible. But how? He
tried to remember the map of the city from his cell
screen. Assuming he'd only gone one bridge down
the river, he wasn't far from Sullcorp. If he could
get there, could he get a vehicle and get out of town
quickly? Should he risk the attempt? Maybe it

would be best to run out of the city as fast as he could.

He could get out of town on foot in one night. He'd never been the track star Shane had been, but he'd been a running back in football and he could put in ten 7-minute miles on a good day. Getting out of Wichita wasn't the problem. There were hundreds of miles to get home. He needed a vehicle. For all he knew, as soon as a drone spotted him, he'd be on the run once more. He'd know when he got up to street level whether he was near Sullcorp or not. He could make a decision then.

Last night I did what Shane does – make it up as I needed to and don't stop ever. How does he manage not to be scared?

Cai filled his pockets, donned his shoes and then the jacket. The sunlight moved up the curved wall of the culvert, taking on a ruby blush. He crouched in the opening. Was it the right time to go or ...?

Traffic was light, it being a Sunday and the apocalypse and all. Cai dragged himself free of the culvert and crawled up the slope through a tangle of scrub brush. He had never been so sore and stiff before and he could imagine what he must look like, covered in dried mud. The street lights didn't come on at dusk. While weird, it gave him cover that he appreciated. He turned slowly in a circle. Atop a tall building on the far side of the bridge he could make out a giant S on a sign. It wasn't lit, but enough light remained in the sky that he thought it was what he remembered as the Sullcorp logo.

Halfway across the bridge, he heard the rumble of a big truck far behind him. As soon as he reached the far side of the river, he turned and dropped down into a green space, hoping he'd not been seen.

That hope fled when the truck pulled into the parking lot between him and SullCorp. He turned back toward the river as a search light swept over the nearby trees. He sprinted in a general direction, but he heard boots hit the ground behind him.

"Stop. We will shoot!"

Cai dodged to the left. Cold and hungry as he was, he didn't have his ordinary speed and the men chasing him were fresh. He could see the river and he stretched to reach it, but one of the fatigue-clad soldiers tackled him. He fell face first in the water, tried to crawl away, but two soldiers caught his arms and pulled him to his feet. When they got to the shore, a third man slugged him in the stomach so hard he couldn't breathe.

"Why do you people not get that there is a curfew and you have got to stay inside during it? Load him up!" The two soldiers who had his arms dragged him through the grass. Cai managed to draw a breath, but before he could decide what to do, they zip-tied his hands behind his back and tossed him into the back of the truck.

"I want a lawyer." The heavy boot driven into his ribs suggested these soldiers were unfamiliar with Miranda. Gagging and fighting for breath, he felt warmth at his back.

"We're not in America anymore, kid," the older man whispered. "Asking for a lawyer, demanding your rights … that's not gonna work."

Cai craned his neck to see him, but with his arms behind him, he couldn't really move. The dim light filtering into the truck revealed that they weren't the only ones here. People leaned against the walls and some lay unmoving on the floor.

The truck jerked forward. A couple of people cried out. Cai shifted so his weight wouldn't be on his arms. Getting out of this truck wouldn't be easy. He couldn't very well jump with his hands tied behind his back.

Don't panic! Think! What do you know?

The Army was rounding up all sorts of people, which meant they weren't looking for him exclusively. That felt like a good thing, but a cynical voice that sounded a lot like Shane reminded him that nothing was likely to be good for a long while.

Vi Leaves a Message

Emmaus, Kansas

Everybody slept while, barefoot, Shane crept along the landing to the attic stairs. The hinges creaked softly as he slipped into the dark stairwell. He'd planned for that and sprayed some WD40 on the hinges before closing the door. He turned on the headlamp he had snagged from the hardware drawer. The intense little light sent twisting shadows across the walls and the cleaning supplies on the narrow shelves attached to the walls on either side of the landing before the stairs. Jill used the area at the bottom of the stairs as an upstairs utility closet. He had to step around a vacuum and avoid the cleaning supplies on the bottom two steps. He tried to remember where the steps might groan. He'd been pretty good at this in high school, slipping up here to smoke pot where the folks couldn't smell it. The stairs ascended over a closet in his parents' bedroom, so there had always been the risk that they'd hear him, but they never had caught him. Now he understood why. The master bedroom occupied an addition to the original house. The builders had cut a hole in the siding to access the closet under the stairs, but sound didn't carry through the thicker walls. His theory had held so far. One stair groaned under his right foot. He listened to the silence of the house, but nothing echoed back. He ducked under the lintel at the top of the stairs and stepped out into the attic.

The waning quarter moon sent a weak trail of light through the dusty window in the front gable. He'd really not thought about the attic in years. It didn't look like there'd been a lot of traffic up here since he'd been here last. Once they'd grown up, their favorite indoor playground had been forgotten by the Delaney children. It had returned to being a storage area for things people had no use for, but didn't think they should throw out. The safe rested in a knee wall, fronted by a door made to look like the surrounding drawers. There were footprints in the dust to some boxes that hadn't been there the last time he'd been up here. He felt dust ooze between his toes as he walked to the safe and hefted the boxes aside. He thought they contained his belongings from when he'd left town abruptly. He'd have to go through them sometime … or leave the past amid the dust and cobwebs. Who was he kidding? It would still be here when Cai inherited the house someday.

He hit the safe hinges with WD40 before working the combination, grinning when the latch gave on the first try. A dusty 5th of bourbon rested in the back corner behind a stack of photo albums, and a burgundy leather-bound Bible with an envelope on top. He deposited the thumb drive in the other back corner, then wrapped his fingers around the bottle. As he pulled it out, it dragged across the Bible and the envelope fell out by his feet. He picked it up. He had no idea how it had gotten into the safe. He thought he was the only one who knew the combination. The envelope and Bible weren't covered with much dust, so they hadn't been there that long. The front of the envelope bore his name written in what seemed like Vi's handwriting. His grandmother had died just last year, so it was possible she'd put this here, but how had she known the combination? When he flipped over the envelope, he saw that she'd written across the flap.

-Take the Bible with you, stubborn one.

Shane sighed. The old woman pestered him even from the grave. He pulled out the Bible and closed the safe. The house echoed with the sounds of sleep. He avoided that creaky step on the way down the stairs and the hinges didn't complain this time. He paused on the landing as bed springs creaked in Jacob's room. Somewhere in the house he heard the jingle of Belle's bell. Glister's head appeared at the top of the stairs. He ruffled the yellow Lab's ears and wasn't entirely surprised when he followed him into his room. While Glister sniffed around to find a comfortable spot on the braided rug, Shane set the Bible and envelope on the dresser.

Her hair had been unbound, flowing past her hips. "Shhh, don't tell them."

That had been a Ketamine hallucination … right? Lately, reality mixed liberally with the Miristan memories, but he'd hoped at least Kansas would stay normal. Why would his dead grandmother invade his dreams except as a result of a sedative known to cause hallucinations? Had he ever seen her with her hair unbound? He must have.

He looked at the bottle. Why would he not have opened an expensive bourbon? He didn't remember why he'd put it in the safe, although he might have been hiding it from his parents because he'd not been 21 that last summer he'd stayed here. He and Marnie had moved into the spare room at Callahan's the summer after college graduation, when he'd been working undercover for the feds. Maybe he'd just forgotten it was there. But then why hadn't Vi dumped it when she'd put the envelope and Bible in there? That would have been exactly what she would have done. That woman hated alcohol.

Rob's reminder that he might not want to numb his pain with alcohol in a circumstance where things wouldn't be getting better flashed through his mind. He could dump it easily enough. But aged bourbon was a smooth treat from time to time.

He nestled the bottle into the back corner of the closet shelf behind the extra blankets and pillows, eased the door closed and turned toward the bed, stepping over Glister who had decided on a spot to bed down for the night. He stared at the Bible on top of the dresser. Should he read the letter now or later?

Yawning made his decision for him. He turned out the light. He'd left the window open an inch. He could hear katydids just beyond the screen. The radioactive rain hadn't killed the insects, just the birds and squirrels, though he'd seen fleeing prairie dogs while fighting the fire this morning. He guessed the soil of their burrows had protected them as concrete and soil had protected the townspeople through the rain. Rob had reported the reservoir by the college was registering only slightly above normal radiation. They'd been lucky. The memory of a family of travelers who had tried to weather the storm in a storage shed flitted through his mind. He shoved the unwanted image into a dark corner of his mind labeled "forget it." Of course, that wasn't going to work.

Far off, barely at the edge of his hearing, he thought he heard a semi out on the interstate. The mine guards had reported seeing a handful of semis headed east on the interstate. Where were they coming from and where were they going? More importantly, what were they carrying? A chill made the hairs on his arms stand up, but not for long.

Glister's quiet breathing dragged his eye lids downward. He slid between the sheets and settled the pillow under his head and shoulders. It had been a long day and he felt every moment of it. He had almost drifted off when he heard Cai's door open and Marnie enter the bathroom. Glister's head

came up. Shane's eyes opened. A bright light out
the front window caught his attention. He leaned an
arm on the night table to stare out at the southern
horizon as a flare briefly lit the night. That was a
long way off, the other side of the interstate. What
was going on out there? The toilet flushed and
Marnie went back to Cai's room.

*This is a little stalkerish. She's not your girlfriend
anymore. She's Cai's wife. She's none of your
business.*

Shane rolled back onto the bed, settled on his
left side and tried to relax into the mattress.
Tiredness dragged his eyelids downward .... What
about the envelope? How had Vi gotten into the
safe? He yawned. Scenes of the corn field fire
flickered across the back of his eyelids. Could flares
have ignited them? This could be the last night for
the katydids. It ought to be cooling off here soon.
He wondered how long it would be before they
heard birdsong again. A flush of warmth curled up
around his torso and between one breath and
another, he slipped into sleep.

MONDAY

Five Days after the End of Life As They Knew It

Warnings

Casa Blanca Hotel
New York City, Times Square

The Casa Blanca usually laid a lavish breakfast, but today they offered a selection of day-old bagels and cream cheese with coffee. Katharine Sullivan hadn't slept well and gratefully sucked down the caffeine as she shredded a bagel and chewed resolutely. Julian Raines slid into the chair beside her.

"Did you catch the news?" he asked.

"No. Why bother? It's the same footage over and over."

"This was new. They're setting up food stations."

"Well, that makes sense, I suppose. People in apartments can't store much."

"I tried to speak with the manager about it and he dismissed me."

Katharine stared down at her bagel. Was the hotel running out of food? With one-and-half million people in Manhattan, food shortages were expected.

"I'm sure they'll clear it up today." She glanced at her watch, feeling odd that it wasn't her phone. She'd decided to leave it in the safe because it still had no service.

Julian chewed his own bagel.

"They taste okay for day-old," he remarked, slurping coffee. "Do we want to walk together as we make our circuit?"

"It might be safer that way, yes." They had planned to collect enough money to escape the city in the near-future. They'd agreed not to include anyone else in their plans. Katharine hoped that they'd do all this planning and then her husband Joseph would show up to whisk her away to Kansas. Amazingly, she wanted to see Podunk Emmaus again. Allison must be so worried by now. She was supposed to get the cast off last week. Would Joseph take care of that? Or Ren?

She needs her mother for this. Someone to assure her she is still healing.

The news was still running the brief swearing-in ceremony of President Anna Byers from yesterday. They paused in the lounge to watch it.

"Does that pink bit of fluff look presidential to you?" one of the hotel guests gathered there demanded of his wife.

As if to highlight the point, the camera shifted to Marshall Ellerby, addressed as Acting President, talking about food stations and national defense. He seemed to be ignoring Byers entirely.

"I wonder if that's his wife," one of the women asked.

"Who?"

"That woman with the great posture to his right."

The image had already moved on, but Katharine had a memory of her. She had looked like she was … well, in charge … like a chief of staff. *Maybe she was his vice president. The country's probably ready for a female VP.* Ellerby did look presidential. He wasn't trying to garner attention for himself. He was working to fix things. Julian touched her elbow, asking with his eyes.

"Let's go." She led the way through the lobby. Gillam, the hotel manager, was the only front desk staff at the moment as they were working in shifts to keep the hotel running. Katharine leaned in to keep her comments private.

"We noticed the news is talking about food pickup stations. How is the hotel fixed for food?"

"I'm working on it, Mrs. Sullivan. Don't you worry about it."

Katharine felt he might be lying, but life as the daughter-in-law of one of the richest men in America had taught her how to be subtle. She merely smiled and followed Julian out the door. The military appeared entirely absent now from the streets, though there were black-clothed mercenaries every few blocks. Katharine had made a successful round of several banks on Saturday, gathering a hundred dollars at each. She hoped today they would do even better, but she still had a cold ball of ice in her belly as they passed those mercenaries.

Frightening Math

Emmaus, Kansas

His beard hadn't been this short in years, but to get it all even after the singeing, he hadn't had a choice but to make himself look like a professor. He'd been that once ... in a life far away.

Dick Vance finished brushing his teeth and left the small bathroom to the boys who were already lining up to get ready for their day.

He ordinarily would have already been out in the fields on a harvest day, but his corn had been hastily harvested during yesterday's conflagration and now was the time for weighing and measuring.

Trisha, his bride of 25 years, was already deep into the math when he entered the small room off the living room that they called their office. She hit total, sat back and sighed.

"You should run the numbers," she told him. "I'll go make breakfast."

She left the adding machine right where it was, the computer open to her verifying math. Dick saved her document and tore off the adding machine ribbon to run the numbers himself. Even with the fire, it wouldn't have been a bad harvest. He would have made another profit to continue another year. He wished profit were his problem this year, but no ... the only profit he needed to worry about this year was the calorie count of his family's needs for the next six months divided into the caloric value of the corn and other crops he had on hand. Never in his life had he regretted speaking his mind so much as he wished he'd stayed silent Saturday night when the USDA representative had offered to help relieve the community of its corn.

Trisha came in with a plate of bacon, eggs and toast just as he finished. His bride was tall and lanky, still slim after four children. She kept her curly black hair short and didn't worry about sunscreen or makeup. Some people might have thought she was plain, but he'd fallen deeply in love with her the moment he'd laid eyes on her in a college classroom.

"Well?" she asked.

Dick stared out the window where their daughter Kitty was transferring eggs from her basket into the washer which was just inside the barn door.

"If we don't find another way to procure food, we're going to go hungry by January."

"We'll still have chickens, eggs, the goats ...."

"Yeah, come January when the feed runs out, we'll start eating them, which might stretch starvation out until February, but ... those fields represented four months of food. If we keep enough feed back for the animals, we can eat the eggs and drink the milk, but if we're not selling eggs, we will struggle needing whatever they would have bought.

For a long moment, they just sat there while his eggs congealed.

"It'll be fine," Trisha finally said. "We'll figure it out. It always looks darkest when you first enter the tunnel, but there's light at the other end."

Dick sighed and drew her toward him, enveloping her in a close embrace.

"God knows what we need."

He believed that. God had been guiding him all his life. When his dream of teaching chemistry hadn't panned out because the tenure board objected to his political and moral beliefs, he'd been worried for half a second, but then his brother-in-law had called to report that he'd been diagnosed with cancer and asked if Trisha wanted to take ownership of the family farm so her parents would have a place to stay for their retirement years. Paul had gone into remission after treatment and Dick had made some great business decisions. God had guided him where he needed to go. So why was he scared now?

"The math doesn't lie, but you're right, God might yet intervene." He sighed again. "Assuming the USDA doesn't confiscate the corn. If they do that ...." He growled. "Got stop being worried. Delaney and his kid seem to be pondering that.

Meantime, I'm going to get the boys working on those old bunker silos. We can hide half what we have there, cover them with sod and maybe the USDA won't see through it. Then we only have to figure out how to hide the other half."

He took a deep breath, let it out slowly and released her from his embrace to reach for this plate of food.

"You want me to warm that up for you?"

"Nope, but I'd like it well enough if you brought a plate for yourself and some coffee and sat out on the porch with me for a while."

She smiled and nodded. Dick set the plate on the small table they kept out there for evening meals on hot summer nights. The sky was azure blue without a hint of cloud from horizon to horizon. The smell of char from the fields tweaked his nose, but realistically, burning the fields added micronutrients to the soil that should boost his harvest of winter wheat and next year's corn. The math was frightening, but your perspective all depended on your attitude. They'd figure it out and look back on this time like folks who had survived the Great Depression did. Yeah, it had marked them for the rest of their lives, but they'd lived through it.

Thanks, God, for reminding me of that.

He tucked into his plate and smiled when the most beautiful woman in the world sat down across from him.

Disobeying Ren Sullivan

Missouri near the Mississippi River

Perry Carmichael admired Joseph Sullivan's adoration of his wife. The man would do anything to get to her and bring her to safety. Perry had once loved a woman like that ... a long time ago in a galaxy far far away. He didn't really remember why they'd broken up, but he'd never connected with a woman like that before or since. Maybe he'd agreed to take Joseph Sullivan to New York, come hell or high water, even if Ren fired him for it in the memory of true love.

They weren't making a lot of progress, unfortunately. Nuclear radiation from Kansas City and St. Louis had forced them north. They'd had to sit out two days of rain in Chillicothe, Missouri, then discovered that someone had drained the fuel out of the helicopter. Not that Perry had thought the helo would take them farther than Wichita. It drew too much attention. Joseph had convinced a local farmer to keep the helicopter as collateral for a truck and they were now, just past dawn, headed along Highway 36 almost to the Mississippi River.

I'm impressed with what the Sullivan name can do. Money does indeed talk.

Joseph studied the map intently while Perry drove.

"Looks like we'll connect to I72 just past the river, which takes us to Indianapolis and then Columbus. We have a hub there. I can commandeer a plane."

"I don't think that's necessarily the best way there. We limit ourselves to having to stop for av gas and finding airfields. The roads are slower, but they're guaranteed."

"Can we make Columbus by tonight?"

"I think so. We'll see how the river crossing goes. Be prepared to flash around Sullivan money and your father's name."

"I've never had any problem with that," Joseph said with a laugh. "I just want to thank you again for being willing to do this. If bribing people were all that was necessary to get halfway across the country, I wouldn't have asked."

"Don't worry about it. Mrs. Sullivan should be in your arms by the end of the week."

"You haven't said why you're doing this."

"I get paid very well for shuttling Sullivan family members where they want to go."

"My father may not be very happy with you for doing it this time."

"Ren Sullivan loves his family ... even Mrs. Sullivan ... and he will forget all about my indiscretion when I bring you and her back alive and well."

They entered the outskirts of Hannibal and traffic slowed before coming to a halt with a long queue before them. One of those black-kevlared mercenaries tapped on their window.

"I need to see your ID and registration."

"My name is Joseph Sullivan of SullCorp. I'm traveling east on urgent business."

"That right?" the mercenary drawled. "Still need to see your IDs and registration."

They turned them over and he walked over to the side of the road to process them at a makeshift checkpoint. Joseph opened the door and got out. Mercenary rifles swiveled his way.

"Get back into the car, sir. Now!" someone ordered.

"I'm just trying to explain ...."

"We won't warn you again. Get back in your car, now!"

Joseph hesitated a moment longer and then obeyed.

"We're going to be stuck here all day," he complained.

"When he comes back, offer him money."

Joseph sighed, running a long-fingered hand across his perfectly styled hair. Perry relaxed as the rifles went back to neutral positions. Ten minutes passed before the mercenary returned with their IDs.

"I checked with SullCorp. sir, and Ren Sullivan himself has waved you through at the request of the Kansas governor's office."

He handed them a red placard.

"Hang that from your mirror. It should get you past most the checkpoints going east."

"Thank you," Perry said. Joseph mumbled something appropriate sounding as well, perhaps bothered that his father was now involved. Perry wondered what it felt like to be dependent upon your parent at 40. Joseph worked, of course, but he worked for his father and that seemed to Perry to be less than a grownup life. The mercenary waved them into the left-hand lane and they sped past hundreds of cars waiting to cross the Mark Twain bridge. Below them, it seemed as if every barge on the Mississippi waited at the banks.

"They can't get past St Louis," Perry explained when he saw Joseph staring at them.

"My god. It's chaos. Those cities are going to poison the rivers."

They had the truss bridge largely to themselves as they crossed with only three other cars. A fan of truss bridges, Perry wished he weren't so distracted by world events that he couldn't enjoy the engineering. The early morning sun reflected off the girders and made the whole structure glow silver-white.

"If this is how they treat us, we'll make Columbus by nightfall," he said. "Though I won't promise further than Indianapolis today. It's just so unpredictable right now."

"I understand. So long as we keep moving eastward … I'm going to try texting Katharine again. I don't know why she's not replying. I'm worried."

"Don't be. With the attack foiled in New York and the designated survivor there, they're probably just keeping a tight rein on communication."

"Thank you. You are kind to remind me."

"Of course, sir."

"Joseph. I think we've spent sufficient time together over the last few days to consider ourselves friends, don't you?"

"Certainly, sir. Joseph."

Now they neared a stream of cars headed east and the traffic slowed to about 40 mph. Perry didn't say anything, but he mentally revised their travel schedule. They'd be spending the night in Indianapolis.

On Being Human

Allentown, Pennsylvania

Javier Chavez woke to bird song, rolled over and blinked at the gray light of dawn. His legs were cramping from sleeping in a confined space. He wriggled up against the wall and the back of the front seat. He could almost straighten his legs if he sat diagonally. The air felt cold to his nose and the windows were dripping with condensation. He cranked the passenger window to allow some ventilation. A long way off, he heard a big rig slowing down on a highway. The trees glowed orange as the sun came over the horizon.

It had been cold last night and the trees had turned. He ought to have a beautiful drive this morning ... or not. He'd expected to only spend one night in Allentown, but the Army had needed to clear his identification and that had taken an entire near-wracking day. He knew Rigby created iron-clad identities, but that didn't mean every checkpoint didn't make him nervous. The sun had been going down when he'd received the clearance, so he'd run up against the curfew. This wooded area had remained private and quiet for 36 hours now.

He had eaten a pork chop dinner at a diner last night and now he dreamed of bacon and eggs. He'd kept halal for his cover for so many years that he'd actually felt guilty as he ordered last night, but now he could happily eat a pig. That diner looked like it had a great breakfast menu.

Turning on the heat to warm the car faster, he saw he had half a tank. It wasn't worth risking being unable to fill up later; he'd refuel before heading out. Pulling his jeans off the back of one of the seats, he stepped out of the car to don them and take care of nature.

His toes curled in pain for a moment, but his heat warmed the grass quickly. He donned the rest of his clothes, slipping his back holster under a blue jeans jacket. He really wanted some coffee. He opened the trunk and began to put his things away. There'd been a time in his life when he would have left his camp set up until he knew he was leaving town, but he hadn't felt that safe in years and he certainly didn't want to trust to circumstances now. He had just zipped his bag closed when he heard a car door slam and a woman's stifled scream.

It really wasn't any of his business, but he couldn't really avoid it either. He could see the scene through the screen of bushes. The warming sun filtered through the trees as the white man in the red baseball cap threw the woman to the ground. He dumped the contents of her purse and began rifling through it.

"Where the hell is your money?"

Javi couldn't hear what she said, but then Red Cap pulled back a foot to kick her in the ribs. It had been a long time since he'd been able to act on basic human decency. The few times he'd witnessed spousal abuse in the Muslim community he'd infiltrated, it had not been in his cover's best interest to intervene. It felt good to step out of the shadows, even as the air whooshed from her lungs.

"You need to stop that."

Red Cap startled, staring at him. He had that look ... a small-minded man with a quick temper who would use a massive tragedy like this to take advantage of people who couldn't fight back.

"You need to get out of here, buddy. I'm warning you only once."

"I'm not the one who needs to be warned, *pendejo.* "

"It's just a disagreement between man and wife."

"That true, ma'am? You want to stick around to see if he kills you?"

She still gasped for breath, but shook her head vigorously, her dark curls bouncing.

"Looks like the lady isn't interested in continuing the relationship. You can save yourself a whole lot of trouble by getting in your truck and driving away."

All the while, Javi moved closer, hand on his gun in the back holster, gauging his opponent. Left-handed, knife at the belt, gun in a shoulder holster under his jacket. Javi never broke eye contact, but he was aware of the woman in his peripheral vision, aware of the narrow road that led back to the country road, aware of the tiny scar on Red Cap's right ring knuckle as he pulled his knife. Training took over. Javi stepped sideways, his hands moving down and under. He grabbed Red Cap's wrist to bend it at an acute angle, forcing him to drop the knife, then continued moving so that his elbow connected with Red Cap's jaw. Red Cap stumbled backwards and went for his gun. Javi twisted around and before Red Cap got it free of the holster, Javi had slid behind him, twisting the bully's head so his neck flopped like a dead chicken. Red Cap dropped limply at his feet, no longer breathing, his eyes wide open. Javi leaned down and whispered "You should have taken the warning."

The woman grabbed the knife. She knew how to hold a knife to do some harm, but she barely weighed a hundred pounds and Javi judged that he could disarm her easily if it turned out she was Red Cap's significant other rather than his victim. Javi fished around in Red Cap's pockets, found his wallet stuffed with bills, but not the keys to the truck.

"Jerome Gettinger. World probably will not miss this puke." He found another wad of cash in Jerome's right front pocket, held with a rubber band. He rolled the wallet cash together with the other and tossed it to the woman. "He leave the keys in the truck?"

"I...I don't know." She still held the knife as if she thought she might use it on him, but she crawled forward to check Jerome's pulse.

"He's fading," she reported. Javi rocked back on his heels, observing her practiced movements. "He's not breathing. There. His heart's stopped." She closed Jerome's eyes, then returned Javi's stare boldly.

"You don't seem too unhappy that Jerome's no longer with us."

"I didn't know him. My car ran out of gas. He offered me a ride to a gas station." Her full lips twisted wryly. "I stupidly believed him."

"This happen today?" She was beautiful with a fountain of shoulder-length black curls and nut-colored skin. Javi turned to remove Red Cap's shoulder harness.

"Earlier, yes." She moved away from Javi and Red Cap, set the knife on the ground and began to prod her own ribs, grimacing, but still talking. "I tried to get gas in Harrisburg, but my card wouldn't work, so I estimated I could make it to Allentown. I miscalculated."

Her accent was multi-layered. She'd been in the United States a long time, but under her accent were hints of a native-flavored English accent.

"How are your ribs?"

"Sore. I don't think he did any permanent damage. I thank you for coming to my rescue."

Javi slipped the gun holster free of Red Cap's body and set it aside so he could remove the knife holster.

"Where were you headed?"

"I lived in Chicago, but I had just left Philadelphia when the bombs hit."

"So where were you headed?" There was really no easy way to say this. "Chicago's a nuclear wasteland, by the way."

"I know." Her eyes hardened a moment, but grew sad. "I didn't when I left Philadelphia. In Akron, they declared martial law and I was there until last night. They told us to go east."

"Philadelphia isn't safe either. There's a radiation cloud from DC. They're evacuating."

"My god! Do they know yet who did it?"

"Not that's being said. So, that money will come in handy for buying gas, but this gun will go a long way toward keeping you safe. I'll help you get it adjusted. Ever use a gun before?"

"A boyfriend took me to the shooting range a few times." She stood, stuffing the money into her sweater pocket. He ejected the magazine and cleared the slide on the 45 while she did that. He told her to take the sweater off, so he could help her don the shoulder holster rig. Thoroughly adjustable, it just needed straps pulled to make it fit after he anchored it with Red Cap's knife belt around her waist, tucking the extra length in behind her back.

"Generally, people don't mess with the armed," he explained, handing her the gun. She fumbled a bit, but managed to get the mag in and lock it. He always carried his cocked and locked, but he wasn't going to be the one carrying this gun, so he didn't give her a lecture. "They'll see you wearing it and assume you know what you're doing and not bother you. But don't hesitate. You run into another one of these idiots, put one center of mass."

She nodded as if she'd already known that. The truck keys were hanging in the ignition, but it didn't do her any good because, she explained, she couldn't drive manual. That lecture was on the tip of his tongue, but necessary life-skill or not, most Americans couldn't drive stick.

"I don't have time to teach you, so we'll have to take my car and get you gas for yours."

Red Cap didn't have a gas can in his truck. In fact, he didn't seem to have much of anything in there. Apparently, he lived in the area and had been trolling the roads to take advantage of people like ….

"Ami. Thank you for helping me, …?"

"Javi." They shook hands. Her grip surprised him. He couldn't believe he'd used his real name. Must be slipping. "Well, actually Martin, but Javi's a nickname."

"Mine's short for Amisi. Where am I delaying you from getting back to?"

"I live in White Plains, but I was headed to visit my kids when this happened. Do you have anywhere to go to?"

"No. I had friends in Denver. I went to school in Baltimore. I don't know where I'm supposed to go." Her huge toffee gold eyes misted briefly and then she blinked the tears away. "He was a total creep, but should we leave him like that?"

"I'll drag him into the woods to give us some time to get away."

"How'd you learn to do – do that?"

"In the military."

Martin was a sheetrock worker who had never been in the military. He'd successfully managed to keep Francis Xavier's cover story sacrosanct for four years, but he couldn't manage five minutes with a normal human being. Maybe he was tired of being someone else.

Javi deposited Red Cap's body in a shallow depression between two trees and pushed several seasons of leaves over him. It didn't really conceal the body, but it might not attract casual glances. He returned to the truck to find Ami still there, having collected the spilled contents of her purse and just finished wiping down the truck.

"Don't worry that I'll tell anyone," she assured him, "That's why I wiped down the truck. He deserved it."

"Car's this way and I wasn't worried." She didn't seem afraid of him, which she probably should have been, given what she had just seen him do. "Are you legal?"

"Oh, yes. I've been an American citizen for more than a decade. Most people don't catch that."

"I've got a good ear for accents. Egypt?"

"A long time ago."

He moved to start the car, but her stomach growled and his answered. They laughed.

"I was going to get breakfast at a diner. Do you want to stop before we go to your car?"

"I would love to have breakfast with you. I think the creep should pay."

New Assignment

Wichita, Kansas

Commander Crispin strode into the mess tent at 0530, just as Mike Biurrarena y Sanchez poured his second cup of coffee. Crispin didn't head for the chow line, but stepped up on a bench of an otherwise unoccupied table.

"My unit, we have new orders. NORAD has requested our assistance with routine security of needed food stuffs."

"We're confiscating food, sir?" Jacobson asked.

"We are facilitating transportation of food from rural communities to the cities where the majority of the population is. It's the harvest. Rural communities have plenty of food, but there are already short rationing occurring here in Wichita and other larger towns."

Mike sat down to finish his coffee. Jacobson's cheeks were bunching.

"Something up?" Mike asked.

"We did this redistribution in Miristan too. Sometimes those rural communities fell all the way to the bottom of the list and starved because there wasn't enough food to go around."

"They can always move to the cities if their rations aren't enough," Kriczek said.

Mike nodded, but he had something else on his mind. He headed to his tent to gather his gear, but on the way, turned into one of the Porto-pots and pulled his cell phone out, swapping the sim cards.

-They're confiscating crops/groceries, amigo. Don't know how long before they're in your area, but you should be planning for it.

He replaced the sim card and dialed his wife's number. He held his breath waiting for Alicia to answer the phone.

"How's it going there?"

"You woke me. Um, lots of Army activity yesterday. There's rumors they're doing house to house searches."

"For what?"

"I don't know. Mama thinks they're looking for guns and food, but that's only because she has guns and food."

Do I risk it? Do I love her?

"They might be. That, uh, room you told me about. Can you guys get everything in there, including the freezer?"

Silence trickled across the miles. He thought he heard the squeak of bed springs.

"Should we be worried?"

"Cautious. They're starting to confiscate crops here."

"Dios mio."

"Leave something for them to find, so they don't look too deeply. And if they tell you that you can sign up for rations, do it. Don't give them any reason to go looking for places that aren't on the building plans."

"Okay. Can you come soon?"

"Not now. I'll talk to my CO, see if I can get transferred that way, but for now, this is the best I can do."

"Have you heard from Ric?"

"Yeah. Can't talk now. I'll text you."

"I just would feel better if he were guarding your back."

"Me too, but he hasn't volunteered for that. I gotta go, *mi corizon* . Remember what I said."

"I will."

Mike severed the call before he could be tempted to desert his post and take a bullet in the head.

When he got back to the command tent, Crispin told him that a National Guardsman would be joining their team.

"Why?"

"Army request. They appear to be the sacrificial ensigns, designed to give us legitimacy, but entirely expendable."

"Okay. Where is he?"

"In the barracks tent, stowing his gear. You've got Trucks 87, 88 and 95 for the trip. These are the towns you're supposed to go to and then you take your collection onto Hutchinson. They've got a warehouse center set up there at the Fairgrounds. You're expected there on Wednesday."

"Yes, sir. What's the National Guardsman's name."

"Kristoffer Lawson. I think you interviewed him the other night."

"Oh, yeah! Glad he survived that. I'll collect him and get on my way." Mike strode through the mess tent hollering for his guys to get their gear and to mount up in 20 minutes.

Bio Fuel

Emmaus, Kansas

Alex steered the truck down a gravel road between two of his fields. They'd cleared the one on the left yesterday and Mark now drove the harvester around the one on the right. He'd picked up the basics extremely quickly, though he claimed he'd not done it before. The Ramirezes had been lifesavers in the rush to harvest all the corn. Shane's fields made the harvest that much larger and longer, ending in an unknown deadline. Any moment, the USDA could come up over the horizon and they'd all be waxed.

The sheared field glimmered in his headlights ahead of the first blush of dawn. Dust plumed up behind the truck. He loved this time of year because it felt like reaching a finish line or scoring a touchdown. The radio played a song about partying in a corn field and Alex remembered that phase of his life with a smile. Shane had such good ideas and when your parents couldn't hear, you could throw a party in their backyard and they'd not wake up. Well, that hadn't worked out so well. The song ended and a voice he didn't recognize came on.

"Good morning, Emmaus, greater Jericho Township and whoever else has their ears on. This is Click Michaels coming to you on KERB, the voice of Beulah County.

"Yesterday, I was busy just passing informational messages back and forth and I'm told that the phones are working today, so I'm not needed any longer, but here's the thing …. I came off a commuter to Chicago that had to set down here in the emergency and … well, I don't have anything else to do. This radio station reaches a whole lot further than anything else might, so I'm going to use it while I can. I'm going to try to entertain you and, if the people I love somehow weren't in Chicago when the bomb went off, I can hope they'll hear me and come find me. We're in Kansas and I'm sleeping in the radio station for now. Come find me, please."

Michaels paused and cleared his throat before continuing with a slight rasp to his speech. It made Alex think about a couple of family members who had moved to Chicago. Were they still alive? Would he ever find out?

"So, a bit about me. A week ago, I was a reporter for the Chicago Tribune. I deejayed to put myself through college, so it made sense when the mayor needed a way to communicate that I would end up behind this microphone. And, yeah, the name is Click. There's a legal one too, but I don't answer to it. I'll be here until someone who owns the place comes and tells me to go, I guess."

He cleared his throat again.

"I promise not to be so emotional in the future. Rough week ... for all of us. So, the Internet is sort of back and I collected some news, which I'm going to read. I don't vouch for the veracity of anything. I don't know that we're there yet. But at least some news is floating about and we can maybe know more than we did yesterday."

The unelected president/Secretary of Homeland Security Marshall Ellerby presided from New York, which had managed to stop the bomb attack there. He assured the American people that normalcy was within sight and they needn't worry.

The unelected president/Secretary of Education Anna Byers presided from Cheyenne Mountain and asked people to please cooperate with authorities as they secured supplies against looting.

"How did we get two presidents?" Pete asked. He sat in the passenger seat.

"Um, I don't know. I wasn't sure how we got the last one."

"Yeah, that one was complicated."

Alex slowed and stopped in front of a barn. It had once been painted a deep barn red, but he'd neglected it in recent years so that the paint almost acted like camouflage against the ripened fields.

If there's a next year, I'll paint it. God, for Poppy's sake, I sort of hope there's a next year ... not that I'm telling You what to do.

Alex glanced at Pete, who seemed to be waiting for instruction. Of course, he waited for instruction. The kid was his employee ... or, er ....

"You're home-schooled, yeah?"

"The advantage of being raised by vagabonds."

"Explain to me how Dotson became president."

"The vice president died of a heart attack and President Meyer selected this guy ... a businessman .... A total unknown. People objected, but he did it anyway. Then someone assassinated Meyer. Dotson's been president about a year, year and a half. My dad says he'd have lost the election because nobody liked his policies. What do you think?"

"I don't pay that much attention to politics. I just wanted to test your civics."

"Did I do well?"

"You did, but we've exhausted my knowledge of modern politics, so .... Grab your gloves, we have a lot of work to do."

Alex planned to put the dump truck of cobs in the barn.

"Aren't they just waste?" Pete asked as they chucked the cobs into a wheelbarrow to ferry them back into the barn.

"Not entirely. I've been selling my cobs for years for biofuel. This year there's no buyer, but I suspect my neighbors will want cobs for burning come later this winter."

"So, you'll leave them in here and share when they need them?"

"Well, if I can get something for them I will." Pete snorted. "What?"

"What happens if people have nothing to buy them with? Will you let them freeze?"

"I'll probably offer them credit. You do realize that the world revolves around voluntary exchange, right? If I start giving stuff away, my family starves and your family right along with us. I can be generous only to a point. Nobody's getting fat this winter, but I'm not letting us starve so others can eat."

Pete glared at the ground for a moment.

"I know how the world works. What happens to us if you run short?"

"Then we all starve together. I don't go back on my promises. But I've got enough ... if I can hang onto it. So, let's get these cobs stacked. Hopefully, if the USDA finds anything, this will be what they find."

"This barn seems pretty conspicuous, out here away from everything else. Why's it so far from your house?"

"This was another farm at one time. Some ancestor bought it."

"Them being deaf, how'd they negotiate that sort of thing?"

"They could read and write and when you're good farmers, other farmers want to know your secrets so they learn to talk to you. When most of the other young men were gone to World War 2, Lufgrens were a large percentage of the town. If they hadn't been deaf, one of them probably would have been elected mayor."

"So, all your family lives around here?"

"I've got five cousins in the county." Alex watched Pete glance southward. "You worried about your grandparents?"

"Yeah. They live in del Rio. Houston and Dallas are a distance, but still .... I don't know why my parents aren't just headed back that way to make sure. You know?"

"Yeah. But your folks want to keep you and Lisa safe and there's a lot of miles and a lot of unknowns between here and Texas."

"I know. I'm still worried about my grandparents though."

"Well, you heard the news. Sounds like they've contained Denver, Dallas and Cleveland and maybe Washington DC. They're probably okay. Our goal has got to be to get through the winter."

"You really don't think the government is coming to help us, do you?"

"I think when the government thinks it's helping we're probably in trouble. The telex Shane saw said they were confiscating everything more than two weeks of food per household. That's less than I'm comfortable with."

"But, if they catch us, won't that get us into trouble?"

"I think we're probably already in trouble. Choose your flavor. Starvation or the wrath of the government?"

"You seem like a rule follower."

"I am or was most of my life, but I believe Shane when he says following the rules is not going to work out for us this time." Pete bit his lower lip and then snorted. "What?"

"Who makes these rules anyway?"

"Exactly."

Pete nodded, pulled his gloves out of his back pocket and got to work.

Awkward Situations

The sound of the toilet flushing woke Shane. He blinked at the clock. The power had gone down while he slept. It was not yet dawn. Who would beat him to being awake before sun up? Probably Jacob. Was that puking? That had better not be Jacob.

The toilet flushed again and then whoever-it-was began brushing their teeth. The movements were too fast to be Jacob. Shane estimated by sound that the person in the bathroom was taller than Jill, shorter than Rob. That meant Marnie. *It's none of my business why Marnie is puking.*

He rubbed a hand through his short hair while checking his phone for the time. Getting up at 5:45 probably represented a happy medium between his insanity and his parents' normality. He reached for his sweats, taking his time so that she would go back to her room. When she did, he headed downstairs to take Glister out to pee.

Because of the dead radioactive squirrels and birds that were everywhere, the yellow Lab had to be leashed for outdoor activity. He gave Shane a

look like "I'm a good dog. What is this leash crap?"
You couldn't explain to a dog that the church youth
group had been organized by someone to clean up
the streets, but it would take time to get into the
woods and fields. Shane didn't babble this to the
dog. He concentrated on the peace of the morning.

Shane watched the sun come up mauve to
scarlet as the dog sniffed around at the end of the
leash and finally selected the just-right spot to
poop. Shane headed into the house to see what he
could find in the kitchen. After a brief stop in the
powder room, he'd toasted some bread and started
coffee when he heard her behind him.

"How are you feeling?"

He turned and stared at her. She was still a
beautiful woman even if she was married to his
brother. She wore jeans and a blue t-shirt that set
off the color of her eyes and stood in sharp contrast
to her loose dark auburn hair. It also clung to all
the right places. Yeah, he remembered that body.

"I could ask you the same thing. My room
shares a wall with the bathroom."

"I'm stressed out." She stared at the refrigerator
door. "Way too many people relying on me as the
only doctor. Speaking of which, I heard you almost
passed out yesterday at the fire." One good lie
deserved a half-truth. He *knew* her. He didn't know
why she was lying, but he knew she was and he
remembered that she lied way too easily. He
wondered if Cai knew that.

"I didn't eat breakfast." He willed himself to ignore the dark-robed figure that materialized behind her.

"And Rob dosed you with Ketamine."

"Yeah, I let him get the drop on me. But I'm fine."

"Maybe you ought to let a doctor evaluate that."

"Mom's a nurse and she checked me. And didn't you check me before?"

"She's hardly an unbiased judge. You remember that, huh?"

"Like a weird dream. And, you are unbiased?"

He stared at her and she giggled, shrugging, blushing.

"Not likely."

"Which is why I think it's best that we just stay away from each other."

He turned to continue with his breakfast.

"Are you going to go find Cai?"

Now that's an odd segue.

"I have someone looking for him."

"Jill said you worked for the government."

"I told too much. I have connections. I'm using them. That's all you need to know."

"What if ... what ...?" He glanced at her. Marnie didn't do inarticulate. She looked distressed.

"They'll find him and I'll go get him. Not for you, but because he's my brother."

He took his coffee and toast upstairs to end the conversation. When he looked at his phone, there were two messages. Mike warned of food confiscation. He remained a good friend. Shane wished he could tell him how to find him. There was also an unknown number call … a text message that hadn't come through. Should he forward it to Rigby? No, this time he would respect the protocol and not make contact until the afternoon. He copied the call to a packet for later transmittal. His toast done, he headed for the shower. A characteristic knock sounded on the thick wood door while he shaved. Rob stood outside.

"How are you feeling?"

"Tired of that question."

Rob snorted.

"I take that as 'fine as frog hair'. This came across the telex yesterday." Rob held out a folded piece of paper. Shane swiped the last of the shaving cream from his face before taking it.

(Text) By Order of President Anna Byers, officers of the United States Department of Agriculture have been tasked with securing necessary supplies for the long-term support of survivors of the recent terrorist attacks. While I recognize that giving up control of crops, groceries and equipment may be frightening to an independent part of the country, I ask you to cooperate with these efforts for the good of the nation. I promise you that supplies will be available to you when needed. President Anna Byers. (End Text)

"If you're asking me to help round up people's crops, Dad, you might wish your other son hadn't gone to Wichita." He pasted his toothbrush.

"I'm hoping you have some bright ideas for hiding our crops and equipment."

Shane grinned.

"Lots of them. Already got Alex and the Deaf community started on them. Bennetts and the Conophers were already ahead of me. We're going to run out of storage space though, the equipment's going to be harder to hide than the food, but I think Anders McAuliff might have an idea or two about that."

Rob gave him a skeptical look, then snorted.

"Yeah? Do tell."

"Let's go down to the office and I'll lay it all out for you ... over coffee."

"Masterminding rebellion against the government always goes better with coffee," Jacob said, rubbing his hands together enthusiastically. Rob jerked, apparently unaware that the old man had walked up beside him.

"Nobody better than an anarchist for it either," Rob agreed. "You done making yourself pretty?"

"I'll join you." Shane started brushing his teeth. Rob watched as Jacob apparently walked away.

"You know, you can put anything in that safe you want. You don't have to sneak around in the middle of the night." Shane brushed while he talked. "I figure you have secrets you need to keep safe."

Shane spat, but he never rinsed.

"I do. Speaking of which, will the bank be open today?" He rinsed his brush, put the cap back on his tube and dropped both into his kit.

"Could be. Brandon said they would be." Rob hesitated, then shrugged. "I shouldn't ask, right?"

"No, but if something should happen to me, a guy might show up using the name of Chavez. Mom will know the other half of the code. Don't you tell her yours. He'll know the combination. Let him take what's in there. Does anyone besides me know that combination?"

"No. Vi took that secret to her grave."

"So, she had it. You know where she got it?"

"She never said, but a few weeks before she died, she wrote letters to all of us and said yours was in the safe, so Cai couldn't go reading it before you did."

"She knew him well."

"She knew all of us well ... soul-deep well." Rob smiled. His must have been spot on. "Have you read yours yet?"

"No. I'm not ... I'm not sure I'm ready to read her take on my soul."

"That worried me for a moment too, but she meant it for good and it was." Rob stared at him for a moment. "I'll see you down there."

Shane rinsed his face one more time and as he straightened, *she* stared over his shoulder in the mirror. He felt an icy hand against his ribs. He grabbed his shaving kit and fled. Belle the cat hissed as he entered the room, then sprinted away from his pillow, disappearing into the hallway as Shane swept the door closed behind her arched and twitching tail. He set his kit beside the burgundy Bible and white envelope.

I don't have time to read her letter now. I don't need any more ghosts right now.

Shane pulled on underwear and clothes and pushed his feet into his boots. He flipped his blankets back to the top of the bed so at least Belle couldn't fur his pillow while he was gone. He set aside the past and headed downstairs to deal with the present.

M.O.A.B.

Grant Rigby stood in the back yard of Sullivan B&B with a Geiger counter in his hand. The radiation detector still measured higher than normal background radiation, but well within acceptable limits, though that didn't alleviate the tension that grew in his gut when he thought of his children being exposed to it.

He turned off the counter and entered the kitchen, closing the door behind him. His wife Emily stood on the counter, an orange-and-blue psychedelic scarf protecting her hair while she wiped out the cabinets.

"Your coworkers apparently never thought to clean. It was all show, I suppose."

"It wasn't. We ate off those dishes. Where are the girls?"

"I sent them downstairs to play like you said. I hate that we have to treat them like moles."

"I know, but the levels are continuing to drop. They're just so young. They have decades more than we do to develop cancers and other problems from exposure now."

"I know. You don't need to tell me again. Dylan poked his head up a bit ago and said to send you down when you came back in."

Grant stashed the Geiger counter in the cabinet by the door and headed downstairs. The girls had taken over the large room at the bottom of the stairs, using sidewalk chalk to make a hopscotch pattern on the concrete floor. They didn't seem to even notice that the world had gone off the rails. He touched Kalena on the head as he walked by. She giggled.

Shelves lined the back wall. Kneeling before the second bay from the left, he reached back behind a box and slid a panel aside to access a keypad. The code he entered triggered a latch and then he stood and slid another panel aside at the back of the fourth shelf to release the bookshelf from the wall completely and pull it open like a door. That revealed an actual door, which had a four-digit cypher lock. Beyond that was a concrete bunker consisting of four rooms, including a telemetry center with a dozen computers and a bank of servers. It wasn't the Utah Data Station, but it was a fully functional CSA field center hardened for just such a national disaster.

"What's up?" he asked Dylan. Their son was fifteen years older than Miranda, a testament to Grant and Emily's complicated history and a lot of perseverance by her long-suffering parents. Jim and Madelaine were at the B&B too. Grant enjoyed that he'd done the right thing and told them what was coming. Mostly, he was glad. Today, he was glad. He and Madelaine sometimes had trouble forgetting their complicated past.

"Some odd movements in the Middle East." Dylan typed something into the keyboard and pulled up a menu. While a video played, he sipped some coffee, grimacing and setting it aside. The still satellite shots showed a runway at Bagram Airfield, empty as of 12 hours ago and then updated this morning.

"Three C-130s? Three? What could they possibly be carrying?"

"I wondered and I've got searches running now. That's a lot of something."

"Could be anything. Dignitaries. Military personnel and equipment. What do you know about aircraft?"

"Not much. They had me reviewing traffic cam footage. This week is the most actual high-level surveillance I've done."

"Seriously? Watching Shane's back at Fashion Valley was your first field op?"

"I did a van thing outside a consulate, but pretty much, yeah. So, what is it I'm supposed to be seeing here?"

"Don't know. Forward the photos to Shane. As a pilot, he may see things we don't."

The computer dinged and the screen refreshed. Dylan cast the photos up onto multiple screens.

"They arrived within an hour of one another. Same mission then?"

"Most likely. Not a lot of people got off. Refueling. Pilots burning butts and confabbing. See?" Grant indicated three small figures ahead of the first plane.

Dylan's tablet beeped. He showed Grant Shane's reply.

-So you can reach out and touch me whenever you want, but it's not reciprocal? I see how you are. I haven't got x-ray eyes, so I don't know what they're carrying, but the payload is heavy and about the same in each plane. You can tell by the skid marks on the runway.

Shane had attached a photo with the skid marks circled and numbered.

-It might be nothing. Al Udeid handles a dozen C130s a day. Could be going to Afghanistan, Iraq-Syria, Miristan or just refueling. The only thing odd about it is that they aren't unloading the cargo, which seems to be about equal in all aircraft.

"Impressive." Dylan grinned at Shane's analysis. Grant typed into one of the other stations.

"He studied at Embry and he flew several of C130s over the years."

"I was actually admiring his ability to recognize Al Udeid from a close-up."

"He's flown in and out of it often enough. I'm running a scan for any orders that might have gone out."

Dylan's screens refreshed and Grant glanced at him when he gasped.

"I hijacked base surveillance cameras. Two of the planes have taken off in the last 10 minutes. Third one's taking off now. They're flying with fighter escort toward Miristan."

They spent several minutes in silence, typing search queries. Grant gasped.

"We just dropped three MOABs on Shalamar Province in Miristan."

"Three. What are they trying to do? Blast a hole to the other side of the planet?"

"The Shalamar Valley is a major rebel stronghold in Miristan. Whole families were living there."

"Why? We've no evidence that Miristan was involved in the attacks on the cities."

Grant ran a hand through his hair.

"Forty million ... mostly civilians -- died a few days ago and the chief suspects are those terrorists. Their families are immaterial to that. The people will want to see Ellerby doing something ... or Byers. One of them"

"But if the US government was entangled in this ... why would they attack Shalamar if they weren't involved."

"Distraction. The whole world wants to know who did this to us and was waiting to see what we would do when we found out. You and I know it's not as straightforward as that. There are no quick patsies. But Marshall Ellerby is under intense pressure to look competent, especially with Anna Byers nipping at his heels, so he picked a target and prosecuted and condemned them. That sends a message to the world that you still can't mess with the United States."

Dylan stared at him. Grant waited for him to shift his gaze, but when he didn't, he finally asked "What?"

"You still say 'we' as if we're part of the government and not outside looking in."

"As far as anyone knows, that's absolutely true."

Dylan sighed. Grant frowned.

"What opened your eyes?"

"That night that Shane left San Diego ... I had to kill the B&W operative who was following him. He was moments from blowing Shane's cover."

Grant blinked at his son.

"They wanted to bring Shane in to force him to work, but his cover wasn't blown yet. What was your evidence?"

"He was in the process of texting his HQ, saying Eric had escaped him and he thought he might be more than just a pilot." Grant didn't reply immediately. "Did I overreact?"

"Maybe not. At this point, it doesn't matter. I don't second-guess what happens in the field. And what happens in the field stays in the field. If you need to talk about it, just say so. Otherwise, I don't need to know."

"I'm fine. It bothered me that first night, but it's faded. I can still feel him writhing in my arms, but … is that normal, to be over it a week later?"

"Given the magnitude of what has happened in the world since … yes. But still, if it ever starts to bother you, don't suffer alone."

"Then you've … have you …?"

"Yes."

Dylan nodded, then turned back to his screen.

"The world is already starting to react. Here it goes."

Herding Cats

"It's our corn. *My* corn. What you want to do with it … how are you any different than the USDA?" Dell Conopher tugged on the brim of his cap so hard that he pulled his own head forward. Conophers had been banes to Emmaus' mayors for almost as long as there'd been a town.

Rob stared at Dell and waited for the babble to die down. They mostly agreed with Dell, but some of them also liked and respected Rob and trusted his judgment. The council chamber held a standing-room-only crowd. He'd been surprised that so many people would show up in the middle of the harvest on a moment's notice, but with no television and spotty Internet, KERB was apparently the entertainment de jour.

"I'm not telling anyone what to do. I'm making a *suggestion* for people who haven't got the means to hide their corn and other crops. If you want to do things your own way, that's fine. The offer has been made. It's completely your choice to use it or not."

"How do you know it will work?" Hiram Schoenfeld asked. Hiram had been a few years behind Rob in school, but they'd been friends for forty years now.

"I don't. I'm not making any promises here. We're going to do what we can and hope for the best, but the government could clean us out. They're less likely to do it if we can hide the corn."

The door at the back of the chamber opened and closed. Stan Osimowitz was one of the tallest people in the room. He leaned against the door since there was nowhere else to stand.

"What are you going to do to stop them?" Ted Murdock asked.

"Me? By myself, I can't do anything. I'll protest, they'll push past me or shoot me in the face and they'll take the corn. If you stand with me, however, there's hope they'll be intimidated by our resistance."

"How do we get organized for that?" Sharon Laughlin asked this.

Rob had to grin. Sharon was short, gray-haired and tough as nails in a soft grandmotherly sort of way. He felt for the USDA if they ever met her on Main Street.

"Shane has agreed to organize a resistance."

Nobody openly questioned Shane's ability to be resistant. They knew who he'd been as a teenager and they hadn't seen evidence that he'd mellowed. He'd tossed Rance Conopher, Dell's brother, out of Nick's Pizza Bella on his first day as a dishwasher.

166

He'd been fourteen. Rance had been twenty four. Drunk, but still ten years older and a barroom brawler too. Shane had been born to organize a resistance.

"Where is he?" Ted asked.

"Harvesting fields. He'll be here in this chamber at 6 pm tonight. Bring your weapons. Give him something to work with."

"You're drafting us into a militia?" Dell Conopher asked.

"Not at all. I'm *suggesting* some of us volunteer to join a militia for the defense of our town. If you prefer to go your own way or turn your food over to the USDA, I'm fine with that."

"Why don't I believe you?"

"Because you forget that he's a libertarian," Sharon said.

The crowd laughed. Instinctive individualists, they weren't comfortable with collectivist solutions, but Rob couldn't offer better ones in this circumstance.

The meeting's goals had been accomplished, so people began to sort themselves to file out the door, which Stan made easier by graciously opening both sides. Some townspeople a few generations ago had wisely installed the doors to open outward.

Rob stepped down off the platform and joined Stan where he was shooting the ceiling bolt into place. Rob got the floor bolt and they closed the doors on the public. The mayor of nearby Mara Wells had bags under his eyes and his biker mustache might have been grayer than even a week before.

"How much corn did you lose?"

"Two farmers lost about a month's worth each. You?"

"My folks are opting for a more collective approach. We lost about two weeks' worth."

"It's up to my folks whether they help each other out or not. We were all going to go hungry by January anyway."

"Yeah, that's about our math too. Had some folks show up yesterday … family of residents … two of them. You have that?"

"The mine guards reported some folks who lived here or were related to folks who live here. But we also had about 100 people from that commuter and the interstate who stayed through the rain. Some of them have left. I don't know how many."

"That's going to matter when the winter closes in. I'd be shooing them on home."

"A lot of them no longer have homes to go to. We let them know if they find places to stay, it's up to their hosts to feed them."

"What about the folks at the motel?"

"Donna was in City Hall. She didn't have kids or a husband. She left the motel to the church, so it's up to Brad to decide what to do with the motel and, by extension, them."

"Donna's dead?" Stan broke into a string of filthy language. "Sorry, I know that offends. I have lost too many people this week, but you lost more."

Rob blinked, swallowing the lump in his throat.

"That didn't need to happen. If I'd just thought to tell Maintenance ...."

"Shut up! You'll never get through all of this if you blame yourself for everything you didn't think about."

"Why do you think I chose to make my people responsible for themselves?"

"Because you're not a cat herder? Me, I'm 'here, kitty, kitty.' By the end of this, I'm going to be more than ready to retire. So, I meant to tell you about Beulah, but I never caught up to you Saturday."

"You caught up with Shane though."

Stan laughed.

"I saw his Jeep in the parking lot and I figured he'd know stuff or tell you what I reported."

"That didn't work out so well."

"He didn't give me any information. Why didn't he tell you about Beulah? No head for drink?"

"More complicated than that. So, what was it you wanted to tell me."

"Remember Gus Hornsby?" Rob frowned before the image of the short, muscular man with the permanent brush cut slowly dawned. "He's holed up at the Courthouse with what's left of the National Guard that tangled with the Army out at Kanorado. He's going to run telemetry for us. He recommends we don't cooperate with Rutherford. They served together. Sounds like a Melei situation."

"Does he know if the USDA is under Rutherford's control?"

"Don't know. I'm headed that way. I'll ask, but I think we should proceed that we don't trust any of them."

"That's what Shane says."

"That kid … he tell you what he's been doing the last few years?"

"Broad strokes. Military contractor in Miristan and, I think, South America. What's the vibe you get from him?"

Stan stared at the hardwood floor for a long moment. He'd been an interrogator in Nam and interrogators knew how to read people.

"Haunted. Dangerous if you corner him. Basically, a good guy transferred to a dark place. He chooses his kills." *Breathe!* "He's a soldier, Rob. No different than we were at that age … maybe a little less ruthless."

"You think our war was nastier?"

"We followed orders. I gotta hope contractors can say 'no'."

"When I look in my boy's eyes … I don't think it makes a difference." Rob wiped his eyes. Stan sniffled.

"You should talk to him."

"You ever try to get anything out of him?"

They both laughed.

"I'll report back. Gotta get used to using that landline again."

"Your cell not working?"

"Is yours?" He whipped his out of his pocket.

"Yeah, since Saturday."

"Tower out our way must still be down. We got power yesterday." He held up his cell. "Yeah, it's working. I'm off. I'll see if Gus will give me a number so I don't have to drive there for reports."

"Good idea. Way Twenty-first century."

"You think?"

They stepped out into the hall. Stan slowly scanned it. You could leave the field of battle, but it never really left you. Rob scanned too.

"I gotta get to work."

"Your feed store is open in this?"

"I think Pa's sold some stuff when he's there and people show up. I'm running a harvester on my dad's allotment. Corporation never showed up, so he decided this morning that the corn is his."

"Wise man. So, JD's place still standing?"

"Pa had it rented for a while, but it's been boarded up for a few years. I guess I should check on it while I'm working."

"He gave me my first job." Stan stared at the floor, moustache fluffing as he smiled to himself. "Whatever happened to your uncle?"

"Which one?"

"The one that lived there when we were in high school."

"Which one was that? Never mind. It had to be Lai. He died while we were gone to Vietnam. The Greyeyes who drank didn't have long lives. When you talk to Gus, ask him to be on the lookout for Cai."

"You haven't heard anything from him?"

"Shane's got contacts looking, but ... another pair of eyes can't hurt."

"I'll tell him."

They walked down the stairs together, then split to go to their respective vehicles.

Prisoners

Wichita, Kansas

Cai lifted his head off his knees. After hours of hearing only distant sounds, he could hear voices and bangs closer to hand. He moved his tongue around his mouth, trying to encourage any saliva. He had no idea what time it was, but it had been at least two nights and a day since he'd eaten or drank water. His muscles were cramping and his head and stomach hurt.

The soldiers had questioned him last night – name, address, what were you doing out after curfew. He'd opted to pretend not to know the military had been looking for him. He identified himself as Malacai Delaney, City Attorney for Emmaus, Kansas, come to fill a pharmacy order for the town. He got separated. He invoked Ren Sullivan's name in hopes of getting some grease there. Far as he could tell, he was being held for vagrancy. That was better than attempted murder of soldiers, but given his current circumstances, not really. The soldiers on the first night had been

173

shooting to kill. Why were these holding him instead?

Bang! There was a sound of someone being dragged from another cell and escorted down the hallway. Cai stretched. His ribs were sore, but not broken. He needed to get some water soon.

He'd given up trying to make sense of what was going on. At some point in the long dark night, he'd asked God to explain it to him, but so far, He hadn't gotten back to him. *Where is God in all of this? I will never forget you or forsake you should mean He's here, but ….* Cai wasn't feeling it.

The door to his office/cell rattled, then bright light blinded him as dark figures swarmed toward him. They pulled him to his feet, but his legs buckled beneath him as they dragged him into the hallway and held him up while he sucked from a water fountain. When he gagged, they pulled him over to puke in a garbage can. When he finished purging, shivering with reaction, they zipped-stripped his hands in front of him, pushed a bottle of water at him, and dragged him out into a garage area and up into a panel truck. The door closed, leaving him alone.

He braced the bottle between his feet and cranked off the cap. Instinctively, he sipped water, forcing himself not to drink it too fast. Toward the end of the bottle, his hunger returned. He used the last of the water to wash the puke off his face.

He heard voices and objects being moved outside of the truck while he waited. When the truck started and jerked forward, he spilled over onto his side and smacked his head on the bulkhead. He pushed himself up into the corner and braced his legs so he could respond to turns, stops and starts.

He lost track of time as the journey went along. The truck stopped and he could hear the driver talking to someone. The door opened and soldiers in Army fatigues dragged a man and woman up into the box. They were given water and then the door closed again.

"Don't drink it too fast," he advised.

"How do you open it?" the woman asked huskily.

Cai told them how he'd done it. They all sat quietly while they rehydrated.

"Where are we?" the man asked.

"Not sure. Still in or near Wichita, I think."

"Why are you here?"

"I think vagrancy. You?"

"I told them they couldn't search my house."

"I was walking my dog ... in my back yard," the woman whispered.

"This is crazy," the man said after a moment. "Less than a week and it's all going to hell."

Cai didn't reply because he had no good counter argument to reality. A hundred people had died at Emmaus Townhall Saturday morning. Soldiers had tried to kill him later that day. He was beginning to wonder if he'd ever see his wife and family again. *If I get my hands on Shane … no. He didn't do this.* The world was clearly spinning out of control. This was the collapse of order the survivalists talked about.

The truck stopped again and three more thirsty hungry people were dragged into the box by soldiers, who at least distributed water to everyone. The new prisoners had their hands zipped-stripped behind them, which meant they needed help to drink, not an easy task in the uncertain light inside the truck.

"I can't believe our own Army is doing this," the woman Cai helped said after he propped her up in the corner.

"Power goes to people's heads," the first man said. "It'll all get straightened out once the government sorts itself out."

"Will it?" someone asked with a hint of sarcasm in his voice. "Maybe this is our new normal."

"People will fight back," a woman said in the darkness. "They can't do this to everyone."

The truck slowed and came to a stop. A half dozen people were added to the truck this time. By the time everyone had drank the water provided, the truck stopped again … and again … but this time the new prisoners had been given water before they were put in the truck, so nobody got any extra. The fifth time the truck's door opened, Cai felt the rush of fresh air and enjoyed it. The sixth time, he realized there were too many people in the truck. Fortunately, they didn't add to their numbers after that, but set out on a long, winding trip while the sun baked the box and turned them all into starving, sweating people. Moans of suffering began to rise with the body odor.

When the truck stopped again, Cai planned to argue that there were too many people already and that they needed water and food, but this time, the soldiers began to pull people out of the truck. He slid to the ground inside a building, where a folding table held a stack of sandwiches and bottles of water. Nobody said anything for several minutes, just stuffed their faces and drank water, though a couple of people had to puke because they drank water too fast.

With blood sugar finally restored, Cai recognized that there were only two soldiers now, but a whole cadre of personnel in blue uniforms with some kind of government patch on their arm. It featured an eagle anyway. These civilians appeared to be in charge, but the soldiers had rifles at the ready. Several trucks were pulled up to a loading dock, their doors open, awaiting cargo. He could sense a large space beyond the interior doors. All the unused garage doors were closed and the man-door was guarded. A woman in a blue uniform stood before them.

"I'm Helen DeWald of the Federal Emergency Management Agency. Most of you have been picked up for petty crimes that will be addressed tonight when we get to the warehouse, but for now, we need you to help us load needed supplies into these trucks. Anyone here have any experience running a pallet jack?"

Cai had worked in a Walmart all throughout college and law school, so he held his hands up.

"Good. How about a forklift?"

Two of the men indicated they did.

"Any inventory experience?"

Two of the women had apparently done inventory before. One of the soldiers whispered something into DeWald's ear. She looked surprised, then nodded.

"You should understand that this is martial law and these soldiers will mete out harsh punishment should you resist or attempt violence after your cuffs have been removed. You are here to do a job, to pay the penalty for your crime. None of you has done anything to warrant the death penalty, but attempted escape does carry that punishment under martial law, so please, just do what you're told and make the best of a difficult situation."

"When will we be allowed to go home?" one of the women asked.

"When your sentences are complete."

"But we haven't had a trial," one of the men insisted.

The FEMA commander glanced at the soldier who spoke.

"This is martial law. There is no right to trial or habeas corpus. A provost will hear your case tonight at the warehouse, but you should know that is merely a formality. You will be sentenced according to your crime and you will serve out your time in service to your country. Then and only then, you will be released to go back to your lives."

"I was walking my dog in my own backyard."

"Ma'am, I won't argue with you about this. Get to work or my men will be forced to provide you inducements to do what you're told."

She opened her mouth. At a glance between the soldier who had been speaking and the one standing near the door, Cai grabbed the woman's forearm.

"Don't! You're going to get yourself shot."

Tears ran down her cheeks.

"Sir was a good dog and they shot him."

Cai tried to look sympathetic. He would feel the same way, but right now, she endangered them all.

"They didn't even let me stay with him while he died. They just left him bleeding on the grass."

"Shut up about your stupid dog. You're going to get us all killed," another of the women hissed.

The woman sniffled, but she didn't say anything after that. Cai moved away from her when a sneaking thought suggested she might be the first object lesson. Instead, all of their cuffs were removed and they were ushered into the retail space of a Walmart and told which aisles to clear and what trucks to put things in.

And so, the work day began.

Bad Idea

Allentown, Pennsylvania

She had coffee and a bagel while he ate eggs, pancakes and a double order of bacon with coffee. A doctor, Ami turned out to be a very smart woman, who kept lifting a raven eyebrow at his answers to her questions. Javi doubted his cover story fooled her. Maybe it had something to do with his knowing how to kill a man with his bare hands.

By the time they finished breakfast, there were semis backed up in front of a nearby market with blue-clad personnel taking boxes from the store into the trucks.

"What's going on there?" she asked.

"Looks like they're confiscating the food. We'd better get going."

She bought a gas can and fuel at a Gas N Sip and he filled up, then they drove west to where she'd left her car, but the turnout was empty.

"Did you leave the keys in it?"

"No." She showed where they were hooked to her purse. "Could the cops have towed it?"

"Possibly, but I'm thinking they're too busy for that right now. Red Cap might have been working with a group." He had already forgotten the dead man's name. He'd not killed a more meaningless human being ever.

Now Ami misted up.

"We passed an old tow truck as we were driving away. I remember feeling lucky that I didn't have to shell out big bucks just to get gas. Stupid! My first decent car and I just paid off the note. What am I supposed to do now?"

"I don't know." *This is a bad idea!* On the other hand, if the authorities were looking for Francis Xavier this far west, they were expecting him to be alone. They'd be less interested in a man traveling with a woman ... though the fact that she looked Middle Eastern might ....

"You can come with me if you like ... until we find somewhere safe for you to stay."

She responded oddly, almost like she hadn't heard him. She slid down the embankment to catch a red bag and a blue cloth briefcase out of the bushes. She stuffed a couple of stray bits of clothes back in the red bag before scrambling back up to him.

"My overnight bag and this. I guess they just tossed it since there was nothing valuable to them. That doesn't sound like something the cops would do, does it?" She unzipped each to check the contents.

"No, which means the car is gone."

"I don't think we wanted to go to the police station anyway." She smiled at what she found inside of the briefcase. "Yes. I'll travel with you until I find someplace to land. Thank you."

"I'll enjoy the company."

The odd thing was, he thought he would enjoy having her with him. It had been so long since he'd been able to just be human.

Why Did They Blow Up Our World?

Emmaus, Kansas

Emmaus High School echoed emptily even at 10 am. The teachers had decided last night that they would open school today. Mike LaRoche would have wanted them to carry on. The first two hours Jazz Tully had been alone, except for the occasional coworker who stuck their heads in to report the same lack of students. She'd been about ready to break out her lunch for something to do when the three Vance brothers showed up at 11 am.

"You are in three different classes," Jazz greeted. James, the oldest boy, grinned at her.

"We're harvesting corn. That's the first priority. But Dad said we ought to come to one class. You got lucky because you're my favorite teacher and they don't drive."

"I'm flattered. You might be on to something, reducing classes to just one. Have a seat. It's going to be a casual discussion."

"Just the three of us?" Jonathan asked. A young freshman, Jonathan seemed mature beyond his years, similar to James, who was already over six-foot-two and growing facial hair, though he hadn't grown a beard yet.

"Unless someone else shows up."

"Ours was the only car in the student's," James said, but he took a seat.

"In 1742, a young surveyor for the British crown encountered a band of Frenchmen in the Ohio River Valley."

Kim Randolph entered just as Jazz started speaking. By the time she'd finished the sentence, two others had joined her. The now-six students stared at her blankly. Jonathan shifted.

"Can we talk about what happened last week?" As the youngest student in the class, Jazz wouldn't have expected him to be the one to speak for the entire group.

"Instead of the French and Indian War?"

They all nodded.

"Why would someone nuke all those cities?" Kim asked. Her left arm was in a cast, which Jazz would have to ask about later.

"Who did it?" Jos Osimowitz asked.

"I don't know."

"Does anyone know?" Maranda Callahan, Marnie's cousin, asked.

"Maybe someone in the government does, but I don't."

"Dad says the USDA is coming to help us by taking our corn." Normally a class cutup, David, the middle Vance brother, had a somber expression today. "Do you believe that?"

"I think so."

"Why would they want the corn?" Maranda asked. "I think everybody is just paranoid."

"My grandma thinks they're coming for the food in the grocery store." Jos looked like he hadn't been sleeping.

"Why would the government want to hurt us."

"I don't think they think they're hurting us," James said. "Governmental authority can get out of hand in these circumstances. My mom says, anyway. What I want to know is, how did we get here? Last week at this time everything was normal and now ... it's like a meteor took out the world." Tears brimmed in his brown eyes. He covered by adjusting his glasses. "I'm trying to figure out why someone would do this? Do you know, Ms. Tully?"

"No." It was disconcerting to see a 6'2" senior blinking back tears. She thought about the last conversation on this topic she'd had. "You know ... I think I might have someone who can answer those questions. Not about who did it specifically, but the reasons behind it. Do me a favor? Tell your friends that I'm holding class tomorrow from noon to 2 pm only and as many people who show up will be the class. If you show up, you get an A in the gradebook. I'll try to have answers for you."

She took a deep breath and considered what to say next. The inadequacy of her lesson plan for the circumstances they were living in today stared back at her blankly, so she did the only thing that came to mind.

"Class dismissed."

They looked surprised before exchanging questioning glances and then filtering out the door.

Pragmatism

Mae "Huffy" Osimowitz hung up the phone and sighed. Alice Ramirez glanced over from updating the inventory on the computer. She'd just pitched right in ... one of the best employees Mae had ever had. You couldn't teach that sort of work ethic.

"Someone is answering at the glass shop now, but there's a waiting list. I hate that plywood, but ours isn't the only store that had windows smashed."

The door alarm sounded and Mae stepped out of the office to see who it was. Jos had intercepted her nephew Paul as he entered. *Why is Jos here? School's in session for another couple of hours.*

"What do you want?" Jos demanded.

"Get out of my way, little cousin. I need to talk to Aunt Mae."

"She's busy. Maybe you need to make an appointment."

"I'm not afraid to talk to him," Mae said. "What do you want, Paul?"

"Can we talk private-like?"

Jos' jaw tightened. At 15, her grandson had become quite protective since the bombs. It didn't suit a kid who wasn't old enough to shave yet and still had that long-limbed clumsiness of an adolescent. Besides, she didn't need protection from a child she'd diapered.

"Jos, watch the store. Come on, Paul."

Her nephew followed her into the warehouse area, which looked barren since they'd hidden everything.

"What do you want?" she asked.

"It's more like you want. Can I trust you?"

He rubbed the back of his neck, peeking at her sideways.

"Paul, don't waste my time. What have you done?"

"Why do you think I've done something?"

"I know you. Humph! Let me guess. You want to sell me the Cosco shipment."

His mouth dropped open. She laughed.

"Shane Delaney couldn't have taken it without Jos seeing, so it had to be you. Which is completely your character. What do you want for it?"

He brightened.

"50 percent of the take."

She chortled.

"I'm buying your stolen goods, child. I'll give you 5 percent of the take."

"I took all the risks. Give me 40 percent."

"I won't go higher than 10 percent. That'll make up for your friends smashing my window."

His eyes shifted back and forth. *Dumb, dumber, dumbest.*

"I won't go lower than 30 percent."

"Fine. Let the USDA find it in your house and get nothing, except possibly a bullet since hoarding is supposedly a death sentence."

His Adam's apple bounced up and down. Mae waited.

"All right. Ten percent. I'll have Chuck deliver it this afternoon."

"No. When the USDA comes through, they'll confiscate it. Take it to the Wolf's Head mine. Jos will go with you to store it there."

"The Wolf's Head has been closed for years. It might be collapsed."

"It isn't and it has a new lock on it that I have the key to. Jos will be there at 2 pm."

"Fine. When will I get my cut?"

"When the goods sell. I'll pay you weekly until that order is used up."

"How much do you think?"

"I haven't inventoried it yet."

"Well, you can pretty much charge whatever you want, right?"

"No. I can charge what the market will bear, which is determined by what the customers will pay. Just because it's a crisis doesn't mean the laws of economics can be set aside. Once the USDA passes on, we'll bring it here and inventory it and start selling it. I've made a deal with Jason Breen for other items as well, so I'll be able to mix the Cosco shipment in so nobody will know."

"I'm surprised you are willing to do this, actually."

"I'm a businesswoman, Paul, and without resupply, I can't keep the doors open. I'd rather sell the shipment myself than have the USDA confiscate it and take it somewhere else. So, 2 pm. You can go now."

Jos said "goodbye" as Paul went through the door and then slipped into the warehouse.

"You're really going to do this, Granmae?"

"There should be plenty to pay Cosco back after the goods are sold."

"You really going to pay him 10 percent?"

"Your grandfather's side of the family are not the brightest – well, except for Stan and Randi. Paul never asked for gross or net, so he'll get 10% of the net ... if I feel like it. After all, he's trying to sell me stolen goods."

"This is a whole new side of you, Granmae." The smile Jos gave her said he didn't mind, which worried her a bit.

"No, not really. I used to have to be a lot more practical when your grandfather was alive. You just haven't seen this side of me. Why are you home from school so early?"

"When only two or three students show up, the teachers get through the lesson plan really fast."

"Uh-huh." That didn't sound right to Huffy, but she didn't have a definable reason to argue. A lot had probably changed in the years since she'd been in school. "Let's get back to work so you can be at the mine to meet him."

"Yes, ma'am. Do you think I should go armed?"

"Of course." One eyebrow raised. "Did you think I would object?"

"No. I guess not. We've moved into different times, haven't we?"

Mae sighed, nodded and gave him a brief hug before heading back to the office to check Alice's inventory figures.

Western Approach

Sergeant Major Gus Hornsby, late of the Kansas National Guard, asked the young soldier to "show us the western approach". With a few keyboard entries, the technician pulled up a screenshot of I70 headed west from Mara Wells.

"How old is this?" Stan asked.

"This morning. We ran it for you because we knew you'd be coming."

Stan stared at the blackened pavement as the camera moved past the Colorado Stateline sign. There were no cars visible, but it clearly a large amount of gasoline and plastic had burned there recently. The camera kept advancing westward.

"That looks like Burlington." Stan kept expecting to see something horrific at any moment, but the camera kept moving westward. There were no signs of anyone in the fields, though crops had been recently harvested. In Strasburg, a sign suggested not going any further, but nothing stopped further westward travel until just before Aurora when it paused at a solid wall of cars stacked up well above the overpass and a sign that read "STOP! Nuclear radiation zone. Do not enter."

A flaring on the camera distracted Stan.

"What is that?"

"The radiation levels there aren't at lethal dose, but they're high enough to affect the cameras," the technician explained.

"Do you suppose those are cars from the containment zone?" Stan asked Gus.

"Seems likely. We saw a pile of bodies being burned on Saturday and there's a lot of military movement in the area. In fact, what I want to show you is this."

The technician pulled up a shot obviously taken earlier in the day because of the acute angle of the sun.

"That's Limon, right?"

"And that's where 24 heads off to Colorado Springs. Wait for it."

Stan wanted to be impatient, but moments later a dozen heavy-duty trucks turned from I70 onto 24, headed west.

"Somebody's stocking up."

"That's what we think too. Unfortunately, there is no way to get a drone anywhere near Cheyenne Mountain."

For a moment, Stan felt angered about that and then he remembered his mission.

"No. And, it's not any of my business. I've got a town to protect. Where is the USDA?"

"Everywhere. They're working to strip the whole state of Kansas. There are towns that are resisting, but unless you can hide your crops and your harvesting from satellite footage, you're not going to have any more success than Sharon Springs did."

"What happened there?"

"The Army burned it to the ground yesterday. That's where we saw the bodies being burned."

Stan sighed, swallowed and tried to remember that this was America, despite the evidence that it wasn't.

"What's Beulah doing?"

"We haven't seen USDA yet and when we do, we'll pretend to be on their side. The farmers have hidden as much as they can. There's an old underground bunker from World War 2. We're hoping it's no longer on anyone's radar."

"Where's all this food going to?"

"Some to Cheyenne Mountain. Some to Wichita and other larger communities. A lot is going to a distribution center at Hutchinson."

"Wendat Lake?"

"Yeah, some. Why?"

"It doesn't matter, but if you get a drone over it, I'd be interested to see what's going on there. You didn't happen to catch any footage of who set the corn field fires, did you?"

"Middle of the night. Can't fly drones and we can't redirect satellites, only review what they photograph."

"Well, Gus, thanks so much for the help you've given us so far. You've been a lifeline."

"I hope we'll be here to help you some more. Now that we've exchanged numbers, we can talk more easily."

Stan paused before getting into his truck. Having exchanged contact information with Gus, he no longer needed to come here every day, but still .... Why did he feel comforted by the snipers on the roof and the checkpoints on the approaches? Maybe it was because they were on his side ... as long as he was standing next to Gus. Or was he just feeling nostalgic? Hard to know. He just knew he was glad Gus had rolled up into their area. It felt like a good omen and they certainly needed some good luck right now.

Stretching for Redemption

Casa Blanca Hotel
New York City, Times Square

It had been a successful outing. Katharine had managed to hide $900 in her bra by the time they had hit all of them. The Sullivan name worked wonders. Julian had fewer solid gold connections, but he still had $500.

"At this rate … we should be able to leave by Friday. How well do you know New York?"

"I grew up in Queens." She felt grubby, even after all these years, admitting her origins.

"Really? You don't have the accent."

"I lost it a long time ago. I really only know Manhattan as a tourist. Stanley, the doorman, seems to know a bit about the city. I'll ask him about routes. It's means that has me concerned. I haven't seen a privately-owned vehicle since this started."

Julian nodded. They were passing two black-clothed mercenaries … guns at the ready, faces unreadable behind their masks, eyes hidden behind tactical glasses. Katharine shivered. Julian put his hand on her arm.

"You're thinking of Lillian?"

"What happened to her was ... I just can't believe it. It could so easily have been me."

"These are vexed times we're living through. Let's get back to the hotel. I just don't feel safe out here."

At the hotel, a delivery van parked in front of Tony di Napoli's, being unloaded by hotel employees.

"I guess we won't starve just yet." Katharine and Julian smiled at one another. Inside, the manager Gillam spoke in low urgent tones to a couple who were surrounded by their suitcases. Tamara Michaels burst into tears when she saw Katharine.

"Can you help us? Our card has been declined. They're going to take us away somewhere."

Katharine turned to Gillam. The lines on his face had deepened in the couple of hours since she'd seen him last.

"You can put their room on my bill." The words were out of her mouth really before she'd thought them through. She was Ren Sullivan's daughter-in-law. She could afford to buy the hotel if it came to that.

"And what will you do about the three others who will be declined tomorrow?"

"This is not right. I have the resources."

"Are you certain your husband would agree?"

"Yes." *Well, not entirely, but he won't say no after the fact.* "I'll cover their room through the end of the week."

"Very well." Gillam seemed stunned that she had stepped forward and frankly, she had surprised herself. The memory of Lillian loomed in the back of her mind. They'd just gone for a sauna at the gym and overstayed the curfew by minutes. The mercenaries who seemed to be in charge of the city's security now had gunned down the California vintner in the street less than a block from the hotel. Katharine had barely escaped with her life.

Tamara thanked her profusely while her husband looked miserable. Men didn't like to be rescued by women and Katharine had learned that people were often embarrassed by Sullivan wealth. Ren had told her she would get used to it, but it wasn't like wearing silk blouses. It always felt odd when she used their wealth to help others. Treating herself well felt less odd.

"It's the least I can do." Tamera had helped Saturday night when the soldiers had been on her tail after killing Lillian. It really was the least she could do.

Alone in her room, she pulled the hundred dollar bills out of her bra and felt around behind the desk vanity until she found the envelope with the other bills. She counted the thousand dollars. It would be the end of the week before they could hope to leave ... unless Joseph showed up before then.

Oh, my love! Where are you?

Weapons Cache

Seattle, Washington

Geo Tully scowled at the gloomy sky that obscured the emerald mountains. Such a beautiful city Seattle ... when it wasn't raining. The other 300 days a year could get a little depressing. Duke the black lab ran around the yard checking out his territory, lifting a leg to a favorite spot. The radio in the breezeway chirped on the edge of Geo's consciousness as he sipped coffee and ate toast. He perked up when the word "alert" preceded the report.

"City officials from Tacoma to Bellingham are recommending residents stay indoors during the rain today and to keep their pets inside to reduce the risk of radiation exposure. The weather system from the south could be carrying radioactivity from Portland. Currently, radiation levels are within safe parameters, but taking precautions is recommended. Keep your radios tuned to this dial and we'll keep you informed."

Geo whistled for Duke and blocked the doggie door. Wes Marcus, his provisional ops partner, yawned and poured himself a cup of coffee while Geo told him about the alert.

"We should just keep inventorying supplies and looking for your uncle's guns."

"I think Fred must have sold them ... or Joyce did, but sure, let's do another circuit of the house before we settle down to do something useful." They had different definitions of "useful", but Geo chose not to fight about it.

Geo ducked his head under the lintel going up the stairs into a craft room. Would a woman who was afraid of guns allow them in her space? Doubtful, but Geo figured he'd look before they started tearing out walls. The room would have driven him crazy because the ceiling was really the dressed underside of the slanted roof, which meant he couldn't stand up straight, but there were all sorts of nooks and crannies to explore. If he'd been looking for quilting material, it would have been a fruitful search.

After thoroughly inspecting the window seat in the front dormer, he sat down on it to view the space. A mass of cubbies occupied the opposite wall ... nothing out of place, everything open. He sighed, closed his eyes and tried to remember everywhere he'd been in this house so far. As he mentally walked through the rooms, a question arose. Plumbing. There was the kitchen, bathroom and laundry room. The laundry room was an addition.

How did the water get from the house to the breezeway? Under the wood floor.

Geo smacked his head in his hurry to get down the stairs to the basement. Marcus stared at him as he hastened by. He'd lost interest in the search and returned to scanning the radio stations. In the basement, Geo located the water meter on the back wall, where the house's distribution line came in from the alley. He followed the lines up the wall, across the ceiling and to the bathroom and kitchen. The drainpipes met in the northeast corner, ran down the wall and disappeared into the floor, obviously headed north. Of course, the laundry tapped into the original cleanout. The shelves beside the drain pipe seemed sturdy enough. Geo shifted the boxes stored there. It looked innocent enough, just a panel of Masonite painted white like all the others, but when Geo pulled on the battenboard, it moved. He pulled down some of the boxes to give him free access and the panel lifted away nicely, revealing a narrow space between floor joists that neatly held a plastic wrapped AR15, a SKS and two 9 mm and a cache of ammunition.

"I never would have found that." Marcus shook his head upon answering Geo's shout. "It's almost like he expected something like this."

"Some people do. My dad is a gun collector and he buys them without registration for just this reason. He's got a special room in the basement for reloading bullets and storing guns."

"You're from out in the flyovers, right?"

"Kansas. And we don't like being called the flyover states. We're the people who provide the coasts and cities with resources."

"Yeah. Sorry. That was rude. Given what's going on now, you seem a lot smarter than we here were. Speaking of resources … besides the ancient MRE's, we don't have a lot of food. Any ideas on how to get some?"

"We've got enough for a few days. We should just monitor the airwaves and figure out the lay of the land for now. Our IDs will just flag us as military and those black-suited bastards don't look like they appreciate us, so we shouldn't move too quickly to stand up in the free fire zone. Speaking of which, what do we have on the airwaves?"

"The weather report is pretty much the warning to stay indoors and then they go to old music. The CB is picking up scattered chatter. Knight Industries mostly. It's just patrol chatter. We're too far from their base to pick up anything important."

"We need a shortwave."

"Fred must have had one once because the antenna is ham capable, but I don't know what he did with it. Maybe he wasn't really interested in hearing stuff in Idaho or Hawaii. He just wanted to know what was going on around Seattle. This is the best I've got. At most we have a 20-mile range, but in the rain, it's less. I think their base is Seattle Center."

"If it wasn't raining, you should be able to pick that up, right?"

"There's buildings in the way. I'll keep trying."

"I'll clean these weapons and inventory the ammo."

"Sounds good."

He and Marcus had met quite by chance during the massacre at the shopping center on Saturday. Gratitude for the shelter of the house did not extent to seeing Marcus as more than a grunt who relied on others to tell him what to do. He knew radios, but he wasn't Special Forces, trained to think for himself.

Geo sat down at the kitchen table and began stripping the weapons. Duke came over and rested his head in Geo's lap. A young and healthy dog and a sweet breed, they'd have to decide what to do with him when they left town. Maybe Marcus knew a neighbor who would take him.

Adjustment

Emmaus, Kansas

The underground complex made day and night irrelevant ... a great deal like prison. Dan's bed had been covered with plastic, so hadn't collected the dust that he'd flipped onto the floor, but the sheets smelled of disuse. Patterson said the power generation equipment needed some work before it could be used as intended, so laundry would have to wait. So would heat. He'd never realized how damp and chill an underground facility without heat could be. Dan snapped on the light, not quite dispelling the oppressive weight of concrete and dirt. The light bounced off the floor to ceiling shelves. He assumed Anders had been the one to demand the return of his books and papers after the trial. They all seemed to be there, just out of order ... even what the government had deemed his manifesto – the rough draft of his book on political philosophy.

Others stirred in the rooms around his, their voices and sounds of their movements echoing off the concrete and slipping in under his door. In the Communication Management Unit, he'd spent weeks and months only able to hear the guards who brought him his food three times a day. To hear others felt like a violation that caused his jaw to tighten and his pulse to pound in his ears.

Dan went into the bathroom. The water still ran cold, but he brushed his teeth and shaved. The shaving cream was kind of flat, but he had had less sharp razors in prison.

A knock on his door startled him. Monahan waited outside. They sat down on the couch. It had been covered in plastic too.

"Do you want to see the inventory?"

"I trust you. Just give me the big picture."

"They left the storage food in place. We can get this group through the winter."

"Good. What are we missing?"

"Meds. They cleaned us out. What we snagged from the prison pharmacy will help, but none of us had better get really sick. Unless, of course, you want to order we resupply."

"No. Our best bet for surviving this thing is to lay low. Do we have Internet yet?"

"Patterson's working on it. Power's still the issue."

"Then we continue with what I said last night … clean the place up, put things to rights, maintenance what needs maintaining. We'll decide our next move after Patterson gets things up and running again."

"Sounds good. Kowalzcky's lining out a security patrol schedule. A couple of the guys asked if they can contact their wives."

"Who?"

Monahan gave him the names.

"Yeah. Tell them to keep it on the DL. If their wives come, they need to bring food and meds."

"Will do." Monahan hesitated. "How you doing?"

Lying occurred to him.

"It's noisy out in the world."

"Compared to the CMU?" Dan nodded. "I had more time to adjust to regular population. It takes time."

"How long?"

"I'm still overwhelmed by it sometimes, so I'll let you know when it stops. None of the others were CMU, so they don't know. Do you want me to explain it to them?"

"Don't know yet. What time is it?"

"It's midday. That's another problem with winter coming. We're not going to know day from night down here."

"Ask Patterson to consider a way to work around that. Brighter lights during the day or something."

"Taking the plywood off the solarium would ...."

"Tell the whole world we're here. Not yet. Let's just see what happens with the world outside before we expose ourselves like that."

Monahan snorted.

"We thought we'd be leaders when the system finally fell."

"I didn't. I hoped we'd be inspirations."

"Can we still?"

"If we don't alert the authorities, maybe."

"I'll reiterate that. There's lunch in the mess if you're hungry. I'd better get back to what I was doing."

Monahan left and Dan sat listening to the sounds of the complex. The subterranean shelter of the decommissioned missile silo had seemed like a good idea before. Now the concrete walls reminded him a great deal of prison. He felt tons of earth pressing down on his face, squeezing the air from his lungs.

He stood up from the couch. Time to go find something to distract him from the damage that institutional slavery had done to him.

Kingdom of Jeriko

The muscles in Shane's arms reminded Jill of the cables and rods in the Terminator. He set the wire basket beside the freezer here in the well pump room and she started unloading the contents back into the freezer.

"Thank you for doing all of this. You were so clever with hiding the storm shelter. And how you got it all in, I'll never know." He grinned.

"It's just a giant game of Tetris. Hopefully, the creepy basement and the lack of light will keep them from looking too closely."

"That was brilliant, disconnecting some of the lights. Where'd you learn that?"

"Electrical work? Dad showed me that when I was in high school."

"No ... never mind. You won't answer me anyway."

He didn't answer. Instead, he took a deep breath and wiped sweat from his face.

"You okay?"

"Still claustrophobic. You owe me for spending the morning down here."

"Can't we just count it toward the pregnancy?"

He laughed as he walked to the old-style hand pump. After a couple of pumps, he drank some water and washed dust off his face. Far off on the ground floor, the doorbell rang and Jacob answered the door. Friendly tones filtered down the stairs.

"This the last of it?" Shane asked as he picked up the wire basket they'd been using for transport. It was. "I gotta get out of here."

He ducked under the low entrance. She held the flashlight while he moved an old cupboard in front of the entrance. She helped him to sweep up around the basement, hiding where they'd moved things to conceal their hiding places.

Upstairs, Jazz and Jacob were leaning over the dining room table looking at a hand-drawn map, but Jacob had already put his lunch on the counter by the steps to the mudroom, with his truck keys on top.

"Where you headed?" Jill asked. He straightened.

"Spray seeding one of Alex's cleared fields. I'm catching one of yours today too, Shane."

"Thanks, Jacob. I defer all that to Alex."

"It's making room for other stuff, you know. You'll have to fly two fields yourself this afternoon. I can't do more."

"How you fixed for avgas?"

"I'm not low yet, but I wouldn't object to more."

"We'll work on that."

"You know Stan Osimowitz' grandfather used to have a big still. They made all sorts of alternatives with it, using corn."

"Yeah, I sipped a bit of aged white lightning from that still once. It gets smoother with age, but holy cow, it was high octane."

"There's more uses for a still than that. A little tweak of that and you have av gas ... or rocket fuel. I should see whatever happened to that old gear."

"I keep learning more and more about people here that I never would have suspected," Jazz said to Jill.

"We all live different lives when things are safe."

"I gotta go," Jacob said, heading to the door. "So, the map is there for you."

"Thanks." Jacob disappeared down the steps and they heard the screen door thump.

"What's it for?" Jill asked.

Shane finished filling a water bottle and chugged a long drink.

"I'll show you."

"The Kingdom of Jeriko" looked remarkably like Jericho Township.

"Jacob got as far as saying it was a D&D map," Jazz offered.

"Yeah. Jacob was our dungeon master and he drew this map of the township for us based on the actual typography here."

"Did you LARP?" Her gently teasing tone won a twinkle from Shane.

"Without the silly costumes and role-playing, yes. We called it exploring. It's amazing what you can learn by wandering through the woods and recording your adventures." He set a forefinger on the map and Jazz leaned in to see the details. "This is where the well house is and here's Jusilla's Creek and you can see how it flowed this way and there are the old falls, the mill race."

"Is there still a building there?"

"Fifteen years ago, the stone foundation of one still existed, but I haven't been back there since. Over here to the west is Wolf's Head silver mine and then Jericho Salt at the east. Sullivans owned both, which is how he ended up owning Mission Ridge."

"Ren Sullivan owns the Wolf's Head? But I thought ...."

"No, I said he did own it. Past tense. His family owned it, but back in the day, they used to pay their workers with script. The Huffmans collected so much paper that they eventually foreclosed on the mine ... which was fine with the Sullivans because it was playing out by then. What was left was enough for Mae's grandparents to replace their old general store with the market and then sink back into being middle-class."

"And here I thought you weren't paying any attention when Vi would talk about town history," Jill remarked. Shane laughed.

"You'd almost think the cellars of the Shack connect to the Wolf's Head." Jazz used her two fingers to show how they were practically on top of one another.

"That was Cai's theory when we were kids, but I could never figure out how to get into the tunnels. I think Dad was on to me, had Mae's husband upgrade the locks."

Their arms touching, Shane pointing out various draws and old roads that nobody used anymore.

It wouldn't be the worst thing in the world if they started to like one another.

Jazz blushed as if she had read Jill's thoughts and for a moment, Shane's gaze dwelled on her face. No, on the soft curve of her throat where the blush started. The angles of tension on his face eased subtly and then his gaze shifted toward the china cabinet and he stepped back, tension bunching muscles in his jaw.

What does he see? Galina Greyeyes or a more personal specter? And what do we do to help him?

"So how come the north part is less detailed?" Jazz had a crease between her eyebrows. She'd noticed Shane's momentary lapse. He shook himself free of it.

"We grew up, moved on to other interests. But now it's important to finish it, so I'm taking it to the meeting tonight."

"Great. I gotta go. Jacob asked me to be a point of contact at the feed store. I'll see you there."

Jazz let herself out the front door and Jill put a hand on Shane's arm.

"You okay?"

"Yeah. Why wouldn't I be?"

"You just seemed a little distracted."

"She was the one who was distracted. And, what she was thinking is really not a good idea."

"Why not?"

A dusky flush darkened his cheeks as his full lips thinned. She remembered that expression from his teen years and braced for an explosion. He swallowed, lowered his eyes.

"Gotta go," he said. "Dad asks, I'm pumping diesel out of the tanks with Vin to put in the medical center tank, so it won't be confiscated and then I'm apparently flying fields for Jacob before the militia meeting tonight."

He closed the door behind him with a measured finality.

Jill sighed as he headed out the door. How do we help him if he doesn't want to be helped?

Lemons & Lemonade

Marnie Callahan supposed you eventually learned not to feel too deeply for your patients, but she wasn't there yet, having only been a fully functioning doctor for a year. She waited for Abigail to give her assessment. Abigail and Lila were the only medical team she had with Dr. Vashon gone to Wichita and Dr. Morton dead in the City Hall bomb shelter.

"Bone overgrowth on the fixation apparatus, there, there and ...." She looked at the film of the lower leg. "... there."

That confirmed what Marnie had found in Allison Sullivan's cloud file. The granddaughter of one of the richest men in the United States and a home-grown Emmaus scion, Allison had received the best medical care after she'd been tossed from a horse and dragged by her foot, but what she needed to complete her healing wasn't available in Emmaus, Kansas during a national emergency. Marnie considered herself and Allison lucky to have the information they did. Apparently, Joseph

Sullivan wasn't as snobbish as his wife and had provided Dr. Vashon with access for local consultation. Dr. Vashon had even noted his suggested course of treatment as a full-leg brace.

"Damn," Abigail muttered, scanning through the file. There'd been plexus damage. "These are not good circumstances for her."

"You tell me. Should I remove the cast or not?"

"You're the doctor, honey. Clem would say that overgrowth means the bone is strong. Of course, he says that about horses and dogs, but the principle is the same."

Abigail, wife of the local veterinarian, was the only nurse besides Lila to show up since the bombs. Two of them had died when the air handling system went down in City Hall and no one had seen the other three. Marnie didn't know how she was going to pay Lila and Abigail, so she supposed it didn't matter that the others had decided to take vacations.

"I could do a walking cast. It would give her the ability to do some weight-bearing."

"That's not a long-term solution and if this file is correct, she won't have the strength to advance the leg with a plaster cast."

Of course, Abigail couldn't make the decision. As the only doctor in Emmaus at the moment, Marnie had to decide. Maggie would say "Put on your big girl panties." Marnie strove every day not to be like her mother, but sometimes Maggie made sense. She went into the examination room where Allison waited.

"We're going to remove the cast today, but you should know there's been some nerve damage."

"Yeah. My mom said it would get better with time and therapy." Allison read Marnie's expression. "My dad told me I'd need another surgery."

"There was damage to the nerves as they come out of your spine. The muscles might strengthen with therapy, but you're going to need a nerve transfer."

Allison stared at the cast resolutely.

"Do you understand what I'm saying?"

"Yes, but I don't believe you. Or I don't believe them. The doctors in Denver."

Marnie sighed.

"Okay. Well, maybe they were wrong. Let's take the cast off and see. This is the third cast you've had, so you know it's not pretty, right? There's scars, the leg is atrophied and casted legs always have skin peeling and stuff."

"Yes, I know that."

"Good. Let's get started then."

Allison's leg had that gray, dead-ish look to it that every casted limb had, but it also looked skeletal. The neurological exam showed exactly what the file had prepared them for. Allison had no or reduced sensation throughout her leg and no movement. Abigail brought in a splint to hold her ankle and foot straight.

"You won't be able to walk with this, but it'll prevent deformity until we can take better measures," Marnie explained. "If you hear from your parents or grandfather, please ask them to call me."

Allison sniffled, but she wiped her eyes then and, using her good foot behind the other ankle, she lifted both legs off the table and gathered her crutches.

"You going to be okay?"

"Sure. Nothing's changed except ...." Allison choked up. She swallowed audibly. "I was just hoping for a miracle and I didn't get it. But I'm good. Thank you for getting that awful cast off. I'm going home now to take a real shower."

"Lemonade out of lemons," Abigail encouraged.

Allison smiled without meaning it and then swung out the door. Marnie leaned back against the counter, sighing, suddenly exhausted.

"Why do I feel like this is just the start of having to tell people I don't have a magic cure in my hip pocket?"

Abigail patted her on the shoulder.

"Because it is. I hope I'm wrong. But I don't think I am."

Abigail left the exam room, leaving Marnie to wipe her own tears and lift a short prayer for Cai's speedy return. She needed him and his hopeful perspective more than she had at any time since Shane had brought their lives crashing down on their heads five years ago.

Fuel Redistribution

The hose under his hand grew cold to the touch, so Vin Barrett dropped back onto his haunches and gave Shane the thumbs up. He got the same gesture a moment later, so he straightened to join Shane at the fuel truck.

"Thanks, Vin ... for being willing to do this."

"Your father is very persuasive. I didn't want to at first, but he pointed out that under martial law, he could just confiscate it and the USDA probably will anyway. The town's going to need it."

"If it soothes your conscience any, SullCorp owns this station and I can't imagine Ren firing you over it."

"No, especially after I tell him you put a gun to my head."

Shane laughed.

"You're welcome to if you want. He'd believe it."

"Yeah." An awkward silence ensued, broken only by the swish-swish of the diesel flowing into the tank. Shane's gaze drifted behind Vin, who glanced over his shoulder, but saw nothing. "You know, this town's lucky that you were visiting your folks when all this happened."

"Yeah? How do you figure?"

"You have experience in the outside world."

"So do you. Didn't you and Lila live in St. Louis before you moved here?"

"We did. It was a nice neighborhood. Kind of like this town is a nice town. Most folks here say they distrust the government, but they aren't rule-breakers by nature, so you're really valuable. You may be noticed your father keeps dispatching you on things that are borderline."

Shane snorted.

"He's letting me do what I already want to do. Which is a big switch in our relationship. My whole life has been a testament to free will and rebellion against good parents."

"I remember ... when we got here my nephew told me that you were the most reliable pot connection in town."

"Nah, just in the high school. How is Trey these days."

Vin spoke around the lump in his throat. "He moved to Kansas City a couple of years ago. Tyron hasn't heard from him, so ...." *It hurts to admit that.* "You heard from your brother yet?"

"Not yet." Shane frowned. "Ren Sullivan got caught in the Governor's web in Wichita, so maybe Cai is with him and just not able to get hold of us."

He cocked his head, listening. "Check the pump. I think we're getting to the bottom."

The pump cavitated, so Vin cut it off and pulled it out of the diesel tank. Shane disconnected the hose, closed the inlet and climbed down from the truck.

"We got one-thousand-and-two gallons. That's five hundred for the clinic generator. You got a preference of where I put the other five-hundred-and-two?"

"Um, Brad Snow said he's prepared to turn Emmaus Road's fellowship hall into a shelter if need be. Take it there."

"Sounds good. Ren supports giving to non-profits. I don't know if that includes churches, but at least we can make a case for it."

"Ask you a question?"

"Sure."

"If Cai doesn't come back … what happens to Marnie?"

"That's kind of a personal question, Vin. Lila wondering?"

"Yeah."

"She and I were over a long time ago and that's not changing under any circumstances, so if Cai doesn't come back, she'd better figure out how to take care of herself. I'd say being a doctor gives her plenty of valuable skills in a world gone crazy."

"So, you don't care about her at all?"

"I wouldn't go that far, but I guess I'm not John Folgerberg. I run into my old lover in the grocery store and we ain't ending up in the car feeling nostalgic. Especially not when it turns out they're married to my brother."

"You didn't know about that?"

"My parents were afraid I'd never come home if I knew, I guess."

"Would you have?"

"Oh, sure, eventually. Probably after they were no longer living at the house. *That* is awkward."

Vin didn't mean to laugh, but Shane seemed to invite it and he joined in.

"Well, I'd better get to rolling. How much gasoline do you have left?"

"Maybe 100 gallons."

"Good. Better if they find a little bit. It makes them think we're not hiding stuff."

"You hope?"

Shane grinned.

"Yeah, but it's worth a shot."

He swung up into the cab of the fuel truck and left Vin to contemplate his future after giving away his job.

Hutchinson

Wichita, Kansas

Cai slid the jack forks under a pallet of flour and lifted it free of the floor. They'd been working for hours without a break and he needed water in the worst way, but the last time someone had asked for water the vehemence of the denial had been frightening. He wiped sweat off his brow as he steered the jack toward the trucks. Lana, the woman with the dead dog, stood by with a clipboard, ticking off the loads that went by her while one of the men, Carl, called out what truck it should go into. Cai's eyes scanned the shelves.

He'd never stripped a Walmart bare before, but he'd been a night stocker for five years. He estimated they had another hour of work and then they would go wherever they were going to face whatever judgment had been predetermined for them.

He unloaded and turned back toward the retail space. Lana no longer stood where she had been and the clipboard lay discarded on the ground. Lester looked distressed and Angie, one of the other women, wept.

"She said she had to go to the bathroom," Lester said.

"And?"

"Two of them dragged her off that way."

It might have been in the direction of the bathrooms. That they were actually thinking they'd not see Lana again would have been unthinkable a few days ago. Everybody scurried back to work. Scurried was the right word for it. They resembled field mice hoping the hawk wouldn't see them before they made it to the next tunnel.

Cai literally felt like bursting into tears when Lana was again standing with clipboard in hand.

The FEMA workers finally allowed them to use the facilities and get water, then loaded them into the truck with a flat of water, that disappeared quickly as the truck rumbled along. Exhausted and worry-worn, nobody spoke. They just waited to find out what happened next. Cai's stomach rumbled, but he dreamt of a shower more than food.

After about an hour, the truck slowed to a stop, but didn't turn off. People talked outside the truck, which rolled forward a few feet, stopped again for a few minutes, then rolled forward once ... twice ... three times. Then the truck powered off. Cai's group sat there for what seemed like a really long time. People called back and forth outside the truck. And then, at last, the tail door opened and a soldier ordered them to get out.

The sun dropped toward the horizon, long shadows illuminating their surroundings. At first, he didn't know where they were, but then someone said "Fairgrounds" and relief washed over him. Though still some 300 miles from Emmaus, Hutchinson lay a lot closer to home than he'd been this morning.

There were many more FEMA workers here and also many more soldiers with their guns at the ready. They herded Cai's group into the Encampment Building and then into Dillon Hall where several rows of still-folded cots awaited them. A FEMA worker instructed them to set up their cots with men on one side of the columned room and women on the other. They issued two blankets each – one for the bottom and one for the top – and no pillow.

"When will we go before the provost?" Cai asked one of the FEMA workers.

"In the morning." His name patch said Jared. Cai tried to remember that and his face since he didn't seem unfriendly. "I know this stinks, but it's better not to rock the boat. It'll be over soon enough."

Cai didn't argue because he wanted to keep Jared on his side ... if he was indeed on his side.

Once their bunks were set up, they filed by the commercial kitchen for a bowl of stew and a couple of slices of white bread with another bottle of water.

They sat on the floor while they ate. A few people tried to talk, but a FEMA worker who said his name was Larry Wincott ordered them to silence. When they finished their stew, they had to remain sitting on the floor until instructed to put their bowls in a big bin and then file back to their bunks.

Stripping off his filthy clothes felt divine, even without a shower and needing to keep his underwear on. Horizontal felt odd because he hadn't lain in a bed for at least a week. He wondered when they would turn the light out, but he was asleep when they finally plunged the room into pitch blackness. That woke him up and he laid there for at least half an hour, disoriented and trying to remember where the exit was should there be a need to escape.

An Appropriate Movie

Pennsylvania/Ohio

Old Route 22 wasn't the interstate and with everyone on it, the traffic oozed along bumper to bumper between small towns and harvested fields. Occasionally, the old route would be above I 78 and they could see military transports, but otherwise, they poked along on the two-lane within sight of the deserted multilane.

Traffic ground to a halt just before Harrisburg. Ami watched Javi as he sized up the black-clad mercenaries working their way from one car to another, searching as they went along. He wasn't what he pretended to be. He had certain tells, very subtle, that spoke of anxiety. She'd known he wasn't just a sheet rocker who'd been in the military when he'd dispatched her attacker this morning, but now, seeing the knowing look in his brown eyes and how his thumb gently rubbed the steering wheel, she figured he had been some sort of special forces or

Or maybe I just want a hero.

Ami didn't like handing over her driver's license when the mercenary asked for it, but Javi turned his over without hesitation, which didn't give her much choice. Even after becoming a citizen, interaction with authority figures scared her. The mercenary asked to look in the trunk and Javi got out to open the hatch. Ami stared off to the south where a pall of smoke drifted above the roofs of the buildings. She could hear Javi speaking with the mercenary, the cadences suggesting they'd lapsed into Spanish.

Javi got back into the car, returning her driver's license.

"We have to take a small bridge across the river and then there are only small roads going west for quite a distance. We have to avoid Pittsburg. That'll put us up toward Cleveland, which is a radiation zone, so we're aiming for Canton. He thinks we can make it to Columbus by nightfall."

"What's going on over there?" She nodded toward the smoke.

"Looting. He tells me it's happening in a lot of the bigger cities and towns, those remaining ... it's just happening all over. Whatever we see on the way through here, we've got to pretend we don't see it. You understand?"

"I do. What happens after the river?"

"The farther west we go, the fewer cities, so it should be less dangerous. I guess they feel DC and Cleveland have been contained."

"How?"

"A lot of concrete. These were suitcase nukes so once they cover the hotspots, the radiation should be contained."

The car in front of them started moving and Javi followed.

"Like Chernobyl?"

"I guess." She saw him opt for a lie. "I wouldn't know."

Ami tried not to stare at the mercenary troops standing at deadly at-ease along the road, rifles casually ready to deal death at any provocation. She shivered.

"This isn't good, is it?"

"You don't need to worry with me with you."

"I know that. I'm talking about the government. They're losing control."

"Looting happens during power outages too."

"Not in Harrisburg, Pennsylvania."

As they proceeded down the main road, Ami saw knots of soldiers standing guard over groups of civilians. Somewhere a big building burned beyond the bombed-out cars in sight of the highway. The queue inched forward, then ground to a halt. Ami rolled her window up almost to close. Not a minute later, a young man burst from cover and began banging on the glass.

"Let me in," he demanded. Ami glanced at Javi, who shook his head. Three mercenaries jogged out of a side street. The young man sprinted toward the river and they sprinted after. On the edge of hearing, they heard a gunshot. Ami stared at Javi.

"Best to pretend we didn't hear that."

The queue started moving again and Javi followed smartly, gaze fixed firmly ahead. Clearly, he hoped to reach the other side of the river and whatever new danger awaited. When they left the bridge, they weren't allowed to go south and were forced onto small feeder roads going west and north at 15-20 mile per hour for many hours.

"It's Columbus," Ami announced when Javi handed her the map as a skyline came into view. "I've been here before. Could we find a motel or do we just keep pushing forward?"

"I'm seeing double and starving." They'd stopped midday to make sandwiches from his cooler, but the sun hung low on the horizon now. "Besides, there's probably a curfew and I don't have a second sleeping bag."

Columbus seemed peaceful enough. A mix of National Guard and mercenaries patrolled the streets, but they didn't seem hostile. Most carried only side arms. A few had rifles slung across their backs. A traffic control sign informed them of the 10 pm curfew, so they found a Best Western. When Javi asked for two rooms, the jovial innkeeper whose name plate said he was Barry Clarke, shook his head.

"Sorry, folks, but we're full up, what with all the people on the road, trying to get home and all. I have a nice room around back, faces the woods. It's got two full sized beds."

Javi glanced at Ami, who shrugged, so he agreed to the double room.

"If you're not married, you both have to sign the register." He turned the register around for them to sign. Since he didn't ask for identification, Javi signed "Juan Rivera". Seeing that, Ami signed "Amanda Sierra." When they got into the car, Javi grinned at her.

"Before you were a doctor, you were a secret agent?"

"No, but I did come to America as an asylee. I've met people who had to take precautions. Why did you?"

"More or less the same reason. It just feels like a really good time not to leave breadcrumbs wherever we go."

Their room faced the woods across a narrow parking lot. Family-owned, the motel offered a pleasant room with floral print drapes and matching bedspreads and the cleanest bathroom Ami had seen outside a hospital.

"I'll arm wrestle you for the shower," Javi joked as he checked the windows and door.

"Let's not and say we did. You can have it first. I wonder if we could order a pizza."

"You don't keep halal?"

"I'm a Copt ... or was when I left Egypt. You?"

"Don't know. Haven't really cared much. Keep the door locked and the curtains closed. I won't be but five minutes."

"About food ...?"

"I saw a diner back a couple of blocks. It appeared to be open. But if you want to call the front desk and ask the odds of getting a pizza during Armageddon – it's not pizza without pepperoni."

"Got it."

He dropped his overnight bag and jacket on the bed closest to the door and disappeared into the bathroom, his gun still stuck in the back holster. Funny how they had known each other only about 12 hours, but it already felt like they'd traveled together for days, so that she wasn't at all surprised that he took it into the bathroom with him. Whoever, Martin "Javi" Pulgarin really was, he wasn't a sheet rocker from White Plains. At one point this morning, she'd thought maybe a drug lord, but now she was leaning toward witness protection.

She shrugged out of her sweater and then the holster, setting the gun on the night stand between the two beds. As an after-thought she unsnapped the restrainer for easier access. She found a pizza delivery posted in the guest folio on the desk. Someone answered the phone and joked "You're in luck. We just reopened today. Unfortunately, the credit cards aren't working."

"That's fine, we have cash. Double pepperoni with black olive, large. At Clarkes Castle, Room 127. How have things been here since ... you know?"

"We didn't have power for the first four days and we keep being ordered to seek shelter on account of possible radioactive rain. But we decided to open today anyway, so we'd make some money. Anyway, I've put that order in and it should be to your place in about a half hour."

"Thank you so much."

"How about you folks? You doing okay?"

"It's been a mess, but we're headed west."

"I hear it's better out there, fewer cities."

"I hadn't thought of that."

Javi came out of the bathroom, bare chest glistening damply, a towel in one hand and his holstered gun in the other. The mystery of why he took it with him immediately evaporated as she stared at his manly form. He moved with animal grace, his muscles taut. He had body hair, but not so much that he looked like a troglodyte. His skin was lighter than hers, but here and there creased with shiny scars, kind of what she would expect to see on one of those mercenaries. Another possible answer, she supposed.

"We'll see the pie in half an hour or so."

She hung up and watched Javi don a clean t-shirt, white cotton skimming his hard abs. As he turned to pull sweats out of his bag, his glutes bulged under the fabric of his boxers.

"Not closed on account of Armageddon?"

"No, they're open. Pizza places ... like cockroaches ... will survive."

"You seemed chatty."

"The end of the world changes people, I guess. He asked me how we were doing. It seemed rude not to answer."

He shrugged.

"I'm going to catch that shower before they get here."

She came out as he accepted the pie. She'd had the good sense to take her sleeping shirt with her. It covered her from her collarbone to just above her knees while she blotted water from her ringlets. He set the pie on the end of one of the beds and turned on the television, before settling his butt on the floor.

"I'm starving." She joined him on the floor, lifting the pizza box down to set between them, then gratefully accepted an ice-cold bottle of root beer. "I didn't order this."

"I called them back and asked them to add a sixer. They had beer too, but I'm not feeling comfortable enough to take the edge off."

Javi shrugged in a go-figure sort of way, flipped through several channels and got nothing. Finally, one of the New York channels was playing the intro to the first Terminator movie.

"You've got to be kidding me."

"Someone has a sense of humor. What would Sarah Connor do when the world blew up?"

Javi gave her a sidelong glance, a slow smile developing. He wasn't truly handsome. His nose had been broken sometime in the past, his eyebrows were too heavy and his jaw putative. His full lips looked like they would caress a woman though.

"Well, first she has the smart idea to hide somewhere far away from cities." He popped a loose pepperoni into his mouth. "I never really bought the whole tries-to-blow-up-Cyberdyne-ends-up-in-a-mental-hospital shtick. The second movie had more action, but this one has more … the characters are more believable."

"And Kyle Reese was so lovely back then." It was the scene where the future soldier comes through time naked.

"I'll have to take your word for that."

"You don't think he's handsome?"

"Heterosexual male." Javi pointed to his own chest. "She was hot. Swartznegger was impressive. Reese was the guy who got the girl and then got dead."

They watched the director's cut all the way through, making occasional comments.

"That always bothered me, about the dogs being able to tell the terminators. How?"

"Dogs can hear really well. Maybe they hear the servo-motors. Or maybe they smell the chassis."

"Smell it?" That seemed unlikely to Ami.

"Why not? They can smell cocaine through coffee."

"Can they?"

His eyes twittered for just a second.

"That's what I hear."

"Uh-huh." What is it that he's lying about? It can't be everything.

Ami had never before seen the edited scene where Reese freaks out over the flowers.

"You'd think he'd be more overwhelmed with a world of cars and living people than the flowers."

"You've never known war, have you?"

"No. I missed the Arab Spring. Baltimore General's ER has some war-zone-like qualities though."

"I'll bet, but war ... you know, like Syria or Miristan – that's the sort of thing that if you live through it, you're surprised to discover that anything lives beyond it."

For a moment, he looked far away as if caught up in a memory of blood and fire. He shook himself. They watched until Linda Hamilton drove off into the Baja storm, then he turned off the TV and picked up the empty pizza box to put it on the table, corralling five empty root beers in one large hand.

"We should probably turn in. I want to get an early start tomorrow. Have you given any thought to where you want to go?"

"I have, but I haven't come up with anything. My sister was in Chicago. I don't know where else home would be."

"I'm sorry for your loss."

Ami blinked at him. "It's odd. I grieved when I heard the news, but then someone got a call from someone they thought would be dead. I started to think ... Christine was supposed to come back from a trip that night, so maybe ... but I have no idea where to find her if 'maybe' occurred. Her cell phone hasn't picked up."

"Keep trying. Maybe it'll connect."

"What about you? You haven't' mentioned your kids at all."

"I think they're safe with their mom."

I think you're lying. . She didn't feel a problem with that. Somehow, he didn't scare her. Like I'm such a great judge of character after this morning.

"I'm going to go make sure the car's locked up. You can turn out the lights and hit the rack. I'm going to take a few minutes."

He donned his holstered gun and jacket, but walked out barefoot and left his bag. *That's for me to feel like he's not going to abandon me. But if that's not it, then why is he really going out.*

He closed the door on her questions and left her to wonder.

Dead Limb

Emmaus, Kansas

Allison Sullivan sighed and renewed the page to continue with the stupid marble shooting game she'd been playing all afternoon. It helped keep her mind off her leg, which currently rested on a pillow. The bath had gotten rid of a lot of the dried flaky skin, but it had also proven the reality of the paralysis to her. She couldn't feel the water and the leg had a tendency to float.

Like a dead body.

She startled when her phone vibrated in her hand and for a second couldn't remember how to open the call screen. Then she hit "Accept".

"Granddad?"

"Yes, it's me. How are you, sweet pea?"

At the sound of his pet nickname for her, a lump formed in the back of her throat.

"I'm trying to get back to you, but the situation here is complicated. How is it there?"

"The mayor says the USDA or FEMA or someone is coming to confiscate food and stuff." Tears overflowed from her eyes.

"I know about that. I tried to get hold of Rob Delaney, but he didn't pick up. What are you doing at the house?"

"We're taking things down into the cellars. Once the bookcase is in place, they shouldn't be able to find it."

"Good, good. So, the staff is sticking in?"

"So far. Pay day is Friday, though." That was one of Ren's favorite sayings. He always seemed to have a great relationship with the men and women who worked for him, but whenever someone complimented him on the loyalty he inspired in his workers, he'd joke "Pay day's Friday." He chuckled now.

"Right. I'll be back by then. I heard from your father ... well, sort of. He's fine and headed to New York to find Katharine."

Allison sobbed.

"Now, sweet pea, you tell me what's going on with you."

"I-I-I had Dr. Callahan remove the cast. I just couldn't take it anymore."

"It'll be fine, darlin'. We knew getting the cast off wouldn't be the last of it. I've already spoken to some doctors here in Wichita. It won't happen immediately, but soon. By year's end."

"In the meantime, I'm stuck on these stupid crutches."

"They were supposed to make a brace. That's probably gone. I'll see what I can do about that, try to get you walking instead of swinging. I'll see if Dr. Callahan will answer her phone. You just keep your chin up, sweet pea. The future won't look so dark if you're not looking down at the ground."

Allison sniffled. That was another of Granddad's favorite sayings.

"I'll try."

"You call me if you need anything. And I'll call you tomorrow night around this same time. Now, I have some other calls to make. I'm also sending you an email that's on care of your leg. Your mother insisted we not burden you with it while you were healing, but you have to take care of yourself and I've had this on my docs for a couple of months now."

"Thank you." Allison wiped tears and snot off her face with a tissue. "Have you tried to get hold of Mom?"

"Circuits are still busy going east. I heard from Joseph by a roundabout way. Perry better bring him back alive or I'll kick his flyboy butt."

"You know Dad was the one driving Perry to do what he wanted, Granddad." Allison laughed thinking of how adamant her father had been that he was going to find Katharine.

"I know. I gotta go, sweet pea. I love you. You ought to have some of that chocolate fudge ice cream you love so much. Celebrate this stage of recovery as a victory because you are that much closer to being well again."

Allison nodded, said "yeah". She promised she would take care and then he hung up. She glanced toward the bedroom door. She would have to negotiate two flights of stairs to get to the freezer and then get a quart of ice cream up to the kitchen, but it would be worth it. She grabbed her thigh with her hands and lifted the dumb leg to the floor. Five months of crutches had definitely built up her arm strength. She had even learned how to go up and down stairs, though she didn't need to because Ren had installed a lift after her grandmother's stroke several years ago. In fact, it went all the way to the cellar, which would make getting the ice cream so much easier.

Prepping a Defense

Shane scanned through the notes on his phone as people began peeking into the council chambers. He ignored them. If they were truly interested in what he had to offer, they'd walk through the door. He could hear folks murmuring in the hallway, but again ... he wasn't dragging them into anything they were hesitant to do.

Keri broke the ice, glancing over her shoulder as she entered the room. She had retrieved her 9 mm from Jazz and now wore it under her arm.

"You got two dozen people hanging out in the corridor," she reported. He supposed he loved his sister, though it had been some time since he'd had the luxury to entertain such notions, but the thought occurred that she really needed to have her judgmental ass kicked. Was that unbrotherly? Probably.

"I don't bite on Mondays. If they want to hear what I have to say, they can come in here where I am."

He didn't speak louder than normal, but he knew how to project his voice. A handful of people entered, followed by the other three handfuls. While they tried to figure out what to do with themselves without chairs, Jazz came in, her AR-15 slung over her back.

Great. Now she's stalking me.

He knew that probably wasn't true. Lots of women found him attractive ... at least until they saw him shoot people for the "crime" of having radiation sickness ... but he was also prickly and prone to paranoia these days. Jazz and Keri didn't fear guns and held the egalitarian belief that guns made women equal to any man. They were right and Jazz would have shown up if she didn't like him as a male. Sharon Laughlin was the third woman in the crowd, twice his age and rumored to be a closeted lesbian ... not that Shane was brave enough to ask for confirmation.

"All right, folks. Welcome to ... what do we want to call this?" He gave them half a beat to respond and then moved on. "A week ago, nobody thought we'd be doing this, but the USDA is coming. The more other towns resist, the more likely they'll have the military or Knight Industries mercs with them when they get here. That's why I asked folks to show up here tonight. My experience in Miristan was that towns that resisted usually got creamed unless they were organized in their resistance."

"That's why I'm here," Ted Murdock said. "Your father seemed to think you know what you're doing."

"Maybe. By now, most of you know what we're doing to secure what's important to the community ... food, seed and equipment. Hiding it won't do us a lot of good unless we can hang onto it. That's where resistance comes in. The USDA are civilians, but they are authorized to carry weapons. If they come with the military or mercs, we're going to have to let them have what they want because we won't be able to scare them off, but if they come alone, we have an opportunity."

"To kill people?" Keri asked.

Kick her judgmental ass.

"I hope not. I don't think any of you have been soldiers or mercenaries, and I am not equipped to train people to pull the trigger on another human being. That's not as easy as you might think. But shooting holes in buildings or asphalt ... I can teach you to do that, which is still very effective in instilling fear. Fear is more useful as a control technique than leaving dead bodies all over the place. There are people in town who do have experience as soldiers. You notice they're not here. That's because they don't need my instruction in how to kill people."

Shane swallowed. *She* stood right beside Jazz.

"So, what's your plan?" Jos Osimowitz asked. Shane ignored *her*.

"We're going to make the cow police feel like cats in a room full of mouse traps."

He unrolled the LARP map onto the council table, which he'd pushed up against the wall to make room for physical activity. At his invitation, people gathered round. Within 15 minutes, his plan had been laid out and folks were haggling for sniper assignments. An icy hand slid up Shane's back as *she* moved closer to him than ever before. Shane started inspecting weapons to distract himself.

"No, he's right," Jazz said to James Vance. "At Walmart, I popped a shot into the asphalt and they immediately took us more seriously."

"Killing their friends will piss them off," Shane added. "Pissed off people who have had friends martyred are much more dangerous than scared people who think they'll catch a bullet if they jump in the wrong direction."

James nodded. Shane asked to take Jazz's AR ... a sweet weapon that had been well-maintained.

"So, when are you going to make good on the promise to teach me how not to have my gun taken away?" she asked.

He grinned at her. *She* still stood by the door, far enough away for him to ignore. Jazz wore her 9 mm in a modified shoulder holster so that the gun fit in the small of her back. She was small, even compared to Keri who was willowy.

"Why are you here, Jazz?" She raised an eyebrow. "Really?"

"A woman can wield a sword or die upon it."

He snorted.

"Okay, Eowyn. Clear your weapon and I can show you right now. In fact, I'll show everyone." He called for people to pay attention. "Jazz asked an important question and so I promised to show her how to do it, but I figure everyone ought to know this."

He asked Jazz to demonstrate with him.

"Tiny little girl. Big strong man. I've got the advantage. I've got reach, weight and strength. If I want her gun, is there anything she can do to stop me?"

Generally, the group didn't think so ... except Keri, who had been trained by Rob.

"Concealed carry generally prevents grabs of holstered guns because if it's concealed ..."

"Nobody knows it's there," the crowd said with him, about what you'd expect in rural Kansas.

"If someone does figure it out, you can keep control of it by putting your hand over theirs and not allowing them to draw it." He put his hand on the butt of Jazz's gun in her holster. She pinioned his hand with her left hand, hooking her ring finger in the holster and pinching his skin between two fingernails. "Crap, girl! You're deadly," he gasped. Then the crowd laughed because she had come around with the blunt end of her belt knife into his rib cage. "Okay, I'm bleeding on the floor. I didn't think she'd be so tough."

He sucked his pinched finger until blood returned to it. At least it wasn't bleeding.

"Having to fight for your weapon while it is in hand can be avoided by using mindset, awareness and sound tactics. We don't have time to learn how to clear a building, but never lead with your weapon around corners or through doorways." He demonstrated how to tuck the gun in close to their chest. "Don't let someone get within an arm's length of you. Bring the gun up to their face and order them to backup. At this point, your life is in danger, so be prepared to shoot them."

Jazz demonstrated with the unloaded gun, but like most demonstrators he'd seen, she drifted off his face after half a second.

"If someone does get his hand on your weapon when it's in hand ... and why wouldn't they if they see you're not willing to blow their face off? ... your response should be immediate and decisive. Jerk sharply while stepping back to regain control." He grabbed her gun with one hand and she demonstrated. "Here's the problem with this, though. Jazz likes me and she doesn't want to kill me, which means I still have the advantage. If I want the gun, I'm going to take it unless she's prepared to shoot me." They demonstrated it, Shane taking the gun away from her on the third pull, although she held on better than she had when he'd taken it away from her for real. If they ever had a repeat of that, he'd have to hurt her to break her grip. "So, when pulling away fails, drop to one knee while attempting to direct the muzzle into their midsection and then fire. This lowers your center of gravity and throws your opponent off balance. Even if you can't aim it at them, firing the gun might scare them into letting go. If firing the gun doesn't dislodge your attacker, fall on your back while dragging him with you. Place your foot into his midsection and use his momentum to flip him over you."

Jazz grinned like an idiot and asked "Really?"

"Uh, you outweigh her by 60, 70 pounds," Ted Murdock said.

"Jazz, you ready for this? Keri or Jos could demonstrate if you prefer."

"No, I want to learn." She took a guard stance, he advanced, grabbed the gun and refused to let go. She dropped to her knee and dry-fired into his middle, at which point he started trying harder to get the gun away. She rolled onto her back and slammed her foot up into his side, then flipped him. Shane lay on his back, breathing hard, while she rolled to her feet and pointed her gun at his face, her smile triumphant.

"Most attackers will let go once they start to get off balance. My kickboxing and wrestling experience means I'm more skilled than most attackers, plus I know the gun's unloaded, so I can be very logical and proactive in my attack. Generally, if you do something unexpected, most opponents will be forced to react to your actions rather than plan their own." Shane stood up. "If you're carrying a long gun, wrap the sling around your arm or keep it across your shoulder. You can fire the weapon numerous times and that should scare your opponent into letting go or make the muzzle so hot he'll have no choice."

"So, at some point, we're going to have to be willing to kill someone?" Keri noted.

"I hope you don't, little sis, but that's the world we live in now."

Some of the men were nodding.

"You going to continue these lessons?" Sharon asked.

"If we live through this week ... yeah."

"Well, aren't you just a ray of sunshine," Ted said.

"That's the world I've been living in for the last five years," Shane acknowledged.

Acknowledging that fact made everyone look someplace other than at him ... except Jazz, who somehow looked sympathetic without even a hint of pity or judgment.

Or am I projecting that?

As everyone filed out and Jazz reloaded her weapon, Keri slid up beside Shane.

"Who is Joel Rhys?"

Shane stared at her, trying to find a polite way to answer her.

"Me and I have documentation to prove it."

"So, you're like Jason Bourne?"

"Yeah, but I can't blow up an apartment with a toaster."

Keri laughed.

"You and I are going to need to talk soon," she warned and headed out the door. Jazz pulled her jacket over her holster and settled the AR over that. Then she helped him close up the council hall.

"Tell me the truth. Could I really have kept my weapon?"

"You had me when it was in the holster. My hand still hurts." They started down the stairs. "The other technique would only work if you were willing to shoot me ... or at least discharge your weapon in my direction. Concealed carry courses are great, but they don't really transfer to a war zone."

She nodded. Here in the confines of the bottom of the staircase, he could smell the strawberry scent of her shampoo. He pushed through the crash bar and let the door close behind them. A light wind lifted her pageboy away from her face. He wondered why she went through all the trouble to straighten her hair. He had liked the dripping-with-sweat look. It had reminded him of Saadia. That thought threatened to bring a visiting by *her* , so he moved on quickly.

"You are surprisingly strong," he complimented. "And, not afraid to be physical, which would surprise most men. Small women usually cower, but you surprised me the other day when you came up with that gun. Reflexes took over at that point for me, although if I hadn't known you, I would probably have shot you as a threat. So, you ought to wrap your mind around the fact that, given the times we're living in now, you will probably have to discharge your weapon into someone at some point. You're a small woman who doesn't cower. Sooner or later, someone is going to call your bluff, so it's better if you're prepared to pull the trigger."

She swallowed audibly, then nodded and strolled away toward her apartment. He considered volunteering to walk her home, but she was well-armed and he was prickly and paranoid, so he went to his car and headed home.

Tuesday

Six Days after the End of Life as They Knew It

Running from Dawn's Demons

The convoy of trucks rumbled down the gravel road. Movement on the heights caused Shane to glance that way, but it was only a goat herder driving his herd to forage. Mike's gaze remained out on the austere landscape. They were coming up on an incline that featured a hairpin curve. Shane downshifted to gain the necessary torque even as the trucks in front of him slowed.

"I have got to talk to Crispin about not putting newbies at the front of the convoy. We've already lost an hour ...."

A roar accompanied a fountain of dirt as the first truck suddenly flipped up on top of the second truck. Both burst into flames. Shane slammed on the brakes to avoid rear-ending the third truck that was quickly engulfed in flames. A human torch stumbled off to the side of the road and set off another IED.

Shane jerked awake, heart pounding painfully against his ribs. He lay as if frozen for a moment, listening to the silence of the house while he recounted the dream. It hadn't happened exactly that way, but close enough. He inhaled, exhaled and glanced at the clock. Five am. He'd not be going back to sleep.

He disentangled himself from the damp sheets. Glister lifted his head, his tags jingling. He'd climbed up on the bed after Shane had dozed off. Shane heard him wag his tail, so he dropped a hand on the dog's head while he waited for his own breathing to return to normal. Glister licked his hand.

He shouldn't be awake. He'd been up before dawn and not to bed before midnight for days. The house echoed with silence. The world still slumbered. Sleep wasn't an option for him now, so he donned sweats and tennis shoes, left Glister to finish his night's sleep and let himself out the back door. The chill air reminded that fall hovered stage left, but Shane could tell it would be another hot day. That worked well for harvesting, according to Alex. The less water in the corn, the better ... for some reason Shane didn't really care enough to know.

Memories of the dream kept floating to the surface and he kept pushing them back down. Jacob would say he should grieve those memories, but he didn't have time to let them drag him down into despair. He had to keep them at bay so he could concentrate on the objects in view.

After stretching his legs for a few minutes, Shane jogged to the nearest cross street and turned north toward Mission Ridge, kicking up the speed as he went. This being rural Kansas, most of the townspeople still slept, though the farmers were probably headed out to their fields already. He ran for several blocks without seeing anyone until he spotted the reflective tape on the jacket of another runner a few blocks ahead. He lengthened his stride a bit to close the gap.

When she slowed to remove her jacket and tie it around her waist, he recognized the runner and poured on some speed to catch up with her. She startled when he drew even with her.

"This a race?" she asked. She was a little out of breath, but clearly not laboring.

"No. I just saw it was you and decided to catch up."

"You're not even breathing hard. I saw your trophy yesterday."

Trophy?

"Which one?"

"State track. There's more than one?"

"Regional wrestling. And I have a couple of belts for mixed martial arts, but that was at college and overseas."

They turned up the Heights road. He could tell this was a standard run for her because she didn't slow down. At the top of the road, she stopped, panting a little bit. He circled her once and then stopped too. She pointed east where a purple line had opened up along the horizon. They didn't talk at all while they watched the dawn slowly develop from purple to scarlet to gold and then the sky blushed blue.

"I'd forgotten what a prairie sunrise feels like," Shane murmured. He turned to look at Jazz and flinched. *She* stuck her veiled face over Jazz's shoulder, her brown eyes accusing him. "I should get going."

"You want to tell me what's wrong?" She offered him a drink from her water bottle. He shook his head, momentarily afraid that *she* might get upset.

"There's too much going on. I don't have time … time to …."

Her lips were so damned kissable, but *she* was never going to let him find out.

"Sorry. My timing sucks. Gotta go."

He left her behind at that point, running full-out, feeling the burn in the back of his legs and the rush of air past his ears. As he swerved into the driveway, Jacob stepped off the porch. So far, he'd outrun *her*. Too bad he couldn't run forever.

"Whoa there, Speedy Gonzalez. Don't go using up all your energy so early in the morning. I'm headed to fly a field and a couple more, but three's my limit for a day, so I'll need you to fly two this afternoon. I'm no spring chicken, you know?"

Shane turned on the garden hose and sucked water, nodding, breathing heavily. Jacob stayed by his truck, waiting.

"Got it. Alex and I will be at the airfield today anyway. I'm storing corn in a couple of the hangars."

"Right. I'll see you then. You know, talking helps more than running."

"Since when did you earn your counseling degree?"

"Since I went to Europe and killed people whose only crime was not wanting me to invade their country. But, you know, go on being stubborn because that's working out so well for you."

Jacob got into his truck and started the rig up before rolling down the window.

"Rob would say the same thing."

"Yeah, and I'd still grab the bit and go my own way."

Shane headed up into the house as Jacob backed out of the driveway. Marnie pushed past him with a cup of coffee in her hand. Jill turned from the stove and laughed.

"You need a shower before you sit down in my chairs."

"Yes, ma'am. You can feed Dad first. I'll be back in five."

"Um, what's with the wrecked bed and the sweat-soaked sheets?" Rob asked as they met on the landing. Glister pushed past them, knowing his own morning routine.

"It's called a nightmare and I can do my own laundry, thank you. And, yes, I know … talking will help. Maybe it did for you, but I don't choose that."

"What the hell are you running from, kid?"

Shane saw the flicker of black out of the corner of his eye. There was no denying it.

"I guess that's exactly it … hell."

Then he turned to head up to the shower, hoping that keeping himself busy would keep *her* at bay for another day.

Fresh Fruit

Wichita, Kansas

Ren Sullivan wondered if everyone was eating a breakfast with sweet bread, crispy bacon and fresh fruit. Newly-minted Kansas Governor Crystal Lewis set a lovely table for every meal. Ren now knew the extent of the supply route destruction. Not everyone could be doing so well, especially not with the federal government having ordered confiscation of "excess" food.

Lewis had been Lt. Governor just a week ago, but she'd looked very gubernatorial as she'd offered a convincing argument to Cheyenne Mountain for why they shouldn't confiscate food "surpluses" in Kansas, but when she'd failed, she'd quickly become a loyal supporter of "supply redistribution."

"They promise us that the supplies will be available to us when we need them. Regional cooperation is the key to avoiding hunger during this time of recovery."

"You sound like a freaking PSA."

"As I've explained, I have to look to what is best for my people. Wichita is already experiencing shortages. We need to take care of the population centers first. UN assistance will be coming, so rural people will be seen to when it does." Ren thought that might have been a lovely speech coming from someone with a soul. Yes, she'd gotten Phil out of lockup, but that didn't mean anything other than she wanted access to what SullCorp could provide. If Ren hadn't been suspicious of government before all this, he would be by now.

As if Phil had read his mind, his head of Wichita security appeared at the doorway and signaled that they needed to speak. Ren stepped with him into an alcove near the front windows.

"Commander Crispin is detailing one of three trucks to deviate to Emmaus after they complete their circuit of town and pick up supplies at Hutchinson."

"What's at Hutchinson?"

"A newly minted distribution center."

"Do we trust who will be delivering it?"

"Crispin put Sanchez in charge ... you know, the guy that tipped us off that they were looking for Delaney."

"I talked to Cai's wife last night on another matter and I don't think he's there. Have we heard from him?"

"No, sir. I can only hope he got away. He'd have shown up at SullCorp HQ if he hadn't."

"Unless they got him. Keep an eye out. I haven't been able to find out why they were looking for him. It's as if they don't know themselves."

"Too much reliance on technology if you ask me. At least phones and Internet seem to be back on. You got hold of your granddaughter last night, right? "

"I did. And I got a shop in Hays making something that needs to be delivered there. It'll be ready this afternoon."

"I'll let them know. I like this guy Sanchez. I'd steal him from Knight Industries if I thought you'd pay him as much as they do."

"I think that might not be legal at this moment." Ren watched as Crystal looked up from her laptop. Governor Lewis had become quite accustomed to her right-hand purse since acquiring him only Saturday.

"Ren, darling, do you think your staff could begin working on the fuel situation?"

"I've already got folks working on it, Governor. Securing supplies isn't the issue. I own the supply, but finding routes to get it here isn't easy. We're working on it." He turned back to Phil. "How do you feel about Crispin?"

"Good commander. Ex-military."

"He concern you?"

"Not necessarily. Mercenaries work for money, so are amenable to the sort of reason you can offer. It's the military and FEMA that worry me. That whole rah-rah-storm-the-beaches zeal can be hard to dissuade from taking over small countries ... or Kansas towns, I'm afraid. I just have a bad feeling about this. Things turn out badly during martial law."

"I hear ya." He'd served in wartime, but pilots didn't see what they'd done to the population until they got home and watched the documentaries. He didn't want to be one of those guys this time around.

"Ren, I need you," Crystal sang out. The two men exchanged sympathetic glances before parting company.

One Sentence Fits All

Hutchinson, Kansas

Law school had taught Cai to observe his surroundings and he quickly sized up the layout. At the far end of the columned room, stood a table with three seats. He wondered if there would be a tribunal panel or just a provost.

He didn't have to wait long to find out. During the next five minutes, more groups joined Cai's group. Nobody talked, intimidated by the armed soldiers, or exhausted by a hard day's work. Just when Cai began to think they should settle down for a wait, two E-5s and a lieutenant entered. One E-5 opened a lap top while the other opened a file folder. They flanked the lieutenant at the table.

"So, opens the provost court of provisional base Hutchinson this date October 2." The female E-5 cleared her throat before continuing. "Please come forward when your name is called."

"I want a lawyer," someone called out.

"This is not a civilian court of law, Lawrence Campbell." Although the E-5 spoke, the provost pinned Larry with a bright look, as if lit from within by some inner glow. "Please refrain from interrupting these proceedings further."

At the E-5's words, one of the soldiers waiting around the perimeter shifted. The man who had demanded a lawyer subsided into silence.

The hearings followed a simple order. Respondents were called forward in alphabetical order by last name, the provost's assistant read the charges, then the provost imposed the sentence. Hearing concluded, guards fast-walked you out a side exit. Delaney was at the early end of the line, but not so early for Cai not to know the rules. He'd already seen two men who had resisted being sentenced roughed up using stun guns.

"Malacai Delaney. I see you're a lawyer." Lieutenant Wilkins stared right at him.

Did being a lawyer bode well for better treatment?

"Do modern law schools not teach the provisions of martial law?"

Cai stared at Lieutenant Wilkins, uncertain if he was meant to answer. His court training said this was a trick question.

"I asked you a question, counselor."

"Sorry, sir. I wasn't sure .... We studied it, but only cursorily."

"Would you care to explain to the rest of my guests why this is not a trial?"

"Because this is martial law and the constitution has been suspended."

"Correct. So why were you wandering around the streets after curfew?"

"I got separated from my group. I was trying to get to SullCorp when I was stopped."

"You, sir, are guilty of vagrancy. The sentence for that is really as long as I choose it to be. Thirty days' minimum We'll reevaluate then."

"I have a family to get back to." The words were out of his mouth before he even thought about the folly of them.

"They'll have to wait. You owe your government 30 days minimum and if you open your mouth to argue again, it will be more."

Cai so wanted to object, but those rifles were at the ready and he knew that any sort of rebellion would be harshly punished. He stood and moved toward the exit.

"Aren't you going to thank me for not imposing a longer sentence?" the provost asked.

Cai turned back. The hairs on the back of his neck felt like Belle's tail when she was pissed.

"Thank you."

Lieutenant Wilkins smiled as if this had been a pleasant meeting at the post exchange.

"Dismissed."

Cai moved toward the exit again, almost relieved to get through the door without further incident. A guard on the other side of the door directed him down a corridor and through an outside door. As he exited, he sensed someone move up slyly behind him, and then he felt the prod touch his side.

Electricity coursed through his body, temporarily wiping away all thought as every muscle went rigid. He couldn't even step away from the stun gunner. When the electricity ceased, the pavement rose up to smack him in the face. The pain eased in waves as he lay helpless on the ground, sucking air in gasps. The man who had tasered him leaned down and grabbed his innervated arm. Someone else grabbed his left arm. They dragged him to his feet and then the man on his right hissed in his ear.

"You're not in Kansas anymore, boy. You don't argue with any one of us or discipline will be swiftly meted out."

They heaved Cai into the bed of a truck with other moaning people. As he fought to right himself, the truck doors slammed shut, sealing out air and light, and then the truck jerked forward ... headed somewhere.

Raising Anarchists

Wichita, Kansas

Jazz's class was almost its normal size, doubling the students she'd had yesterday. All the students who had demanded answers yesterday had returned. She'd been fortunate her guest speaker didn't like the afternoon heat either.

"Thank you for coming. Yesterday's discussion got me to thinking about some of the questions you asked. We talk a lot about theory in this class and theory can leave us unprepared for reality. I don't have all the answers. I'm not sure anyone does, but it occurred to me that someone with more life experience than me might know more than I do. So, I have a special guest today."

She nodded at Jacob, who came forward and put his work-pants-clad butt on the edge of her desk.

"Lot of you know me. I'm Jacob Delaney. I used to be mayor of this town and I'm here because I'm as old as the hills. Grew up during the Depression, served in World War II, lost a brother there and a son to Vietnam. And this is what I know from all those years of experience. Fact is, our country has been on a constant war footing since 1942."

They shifted, their young faces growing suspicious.

"Bear with me. If Ms. Tully will write this on the board. Those new-fangled white board markers give me a headache, but it'll help you to see what I'm talking about. Do a timeline – 1935 through this year."

He briefly outlined how World War II ended with a Cold War between the United States and Russia, which had led to the Communist Revolution in China, which had led to the Korean War and the Vietnam Conflict.

"Of course, we call it a war because there were soldiers shooting at one another, but the government never actually declared war, so they call it a 'conflict' or a 'police action.' It's still soldiers killing one another, which is war."

He briefly explained about detente and the fall of "communistic socialism" in the 1980s.

"Communism and socialism aren't the same thing," Kim Randolph protested. In silent testament to the new world they lived in, there wasn't a single autograph on her cast.

"Yes, they are. In fact, communism and fascism both have their roots in socialism and the theories of a man called Hegel, who saw the world as a series of conflicts between two extremes leading, he thought, inevitably to a synergy ... a compilation of the two conflicts that gets rid of all the bad and retains all the good. Although it existed before that, Hagel's theory formalized the idea of government as a conflict between two extremes that are struggling against one another to a common middle ground. That's called dialectics. This is all very brief. I have a library of books on the subject. I recommend reading highly. When you're my age, you've read a lot of books."

"You haven't answered the question," Kix Conopher said.

"I'm getting there. Us old folks tend to talk in circles." They laughed because he laughed. "In socialism, the government controls the economy, occasionally with electoral input, but it will overrule the electorate if the voters get it 'wrong', so it's a pretense of democracy. We had calls for that a few years ago, so we're no better. Communism is simply socialism at gunpoint. Sometimes it pretends to democracy, but it will overrule the electorate if the voters get it 'wrong', they just do it at gunpoint instead of by the action of legislators or judges."

He let that sink in for a moment. Some of them looked stunned. Others were still skeptical.

"Benito Mussolini invented fascism. He created the word, so we know what that ideology means. People use the term incorrectly a lot, but it had a meaning in the 1930s before we started to misuse it. In fascism, the corporations control the government, but ultimately, everything is bent to the will of the State. Do you see what all these systems have in common?"

Some of them did, but they were intimidated by Jacob's age and clear knowledge, so they weren't saying. Others were staring at their desks in clear opposition to what he said. Jazz remembered when she'd been like that. Jacob answered his own question.

"If you follow any of those systems, you eventually end up with totalitarianism because only a total state can achieve the goals of socialism. Right socialism, called fascism, or left socialism, called communism, or central socialism called social democracy ... all tend toward authoritarianism, the culmination of which is totalitarianism, because only a total state can achieve the goals of socialism, which is to coerce everybody onto the same path 'for the good of society' as defined by the central planners."

He glanced at Jazz's notes on the board and grinned.

"You were listening, I see." Now he turned back to the students. "She's my student today too. So, centralized power is the real issue, regardless of what shape it takes or what label we put on it. The United States used to have a great system. The federal government was small, just mostly dealing with national defense and common diplomacy. Power was distributed among the states and the federal government generally had to ask for advice and consent from the state capitols. But starting with the Civil War, more and more power was sucked into Washington DC. We moved closer and closer to a socialized democracy rather than the individualistic system that was the Founders' vision. The people allowed it because they were being trained in dialectic thinking as per Hegel in schools like this one. We – and that includes me because I went to public school too -- were trained by well-meaning teachers to view history as a struggle between extremes that needed to be moderated into some form of socialism, though they didn't call it that. Most of them probably didn't know they were doing it. They had been brainwashed by their teaching colleges, so they brainwashed us with stories about Pilgrims and George Washington chopping down a cherry tree and then they lied to my son and you kids about World War II, then Korea, Vietnam, the Middle East … all lies to convince us that some others are enemies and others are allies, but you can't be neutral, by gum. Neutrality is suspect. Worrying about your own life is selfish. And we were trained to believe that what happened out there, overseas, was so much more important than what was happening right here. Whatever our government did here was justified by whatever was happening across the sea. What happens in DC is more important than what happens in your Podunk town. That's another lie. Question. How many of you know the name of the Kansas governor?"

They all looked stunned.

"How about the State legislative representative for this area?" Nothing. "Anyone know who the mayor is?"

Kim giggled and said "Your son?"

"You're cheating because you know him." She returned Jacob's genuine smile. "Did everyone in the class know that? You don't have to embarrass yourself by answering. Just answer the question in your head." He paused, took a sip of water and continued. "Does anyone here know who the head of the local farm cooperative is?" Nothing. "How about the CEO of the electric utility?"

"What's your point?" Jon Vance asked. He had his father's bluntness.

"These people are of far more importance to you right now than the President of the United States. Every last one of them. Dotson is dead and gone and I don't think anybody knows who is really in charge or even where they are ruling from. If they get to us at all, it'll be months. But we all need electricity and food. It's important to know who is really in charge of our lives."

"So, who is that?" Kix asked. A Conopher to the core, he probably wanted to know who to fight.

"You are, in cooperation with your parents who are working in cooperation with your neighbors. It's important to know that and to act upon it. You don't need to ask permission from anyone else. Just do what is right for you and your family and don't wait for permission from on high because it's not going to come."

The students stared around at each other, obviously not sure of their answer. Melanie Schoenfeld raised her hand. Jacob acknowledged her.

"Who did this to us?"

"It doesn't matter. The United States has made a lot of enemies over the years, and this might be the consequences. The government has, in recent decades, made the American people into an enemy and maybe someone found the means to punish it for that and we're just collateral damage. Maybe we'll never know who did this. It doesn't matter. What matters is how we get through this and that we're ready to stand up for ourselves when the time comes. By this time tomorrow, there could be blood in the streets as we try to protect what's ours because if the government takes our corn and other food, we'll starve over the winter."

"Don't they have programs for taking care of that?"

"Who? The government? You mean the people who are demanding to take what we already have? They're going to redistribute it to people who didn't have the foresight to plan ahead and when it is our turn ... well, maybe the UN will help us, but we can't count on that. We know what we need right now and we have most of it ... if we can keep it."

"I'm for standing up," Jon said. "But how do we do that against tanks and select-fire rifles?"

"I'm not saying it'll be easy." Jacob grinned and then sobered. Was he remembering war? "I've been in war and it's never easy. But we know the alternative if we don't stand up to keep what's ours. Look around this room. Look to your right and your left, in front of you and behind you. That's four people. At least one of them will be dead by spring IF we hang onto our food. If we don't, it's likely they'll all of them be dead and maybe you will be too."

Even the ones who had been staring at their desks in an attempt not to roll their eyes now looked up with stunned expressions.

"What? You didn't realize that's what this is all about?"

"Radiation?" Kim asked.

"Nothing so exotic. Starvation. Malnutrition. Lack of medicine. Running out of fuel to heat our homes. It's going to get tough even if we can hang onto our food."

"You don't think the government is coming to help?"

"No. They sent my son a telex telling him the town – the individuals who make up the town – should be prepared for confiscation of food, fuel, and equipment that they, the government, have deemed 'excess'. They'll leave us with a two-week supply and when we run out, we'll go on a list behind everybody else."

"How do you know?" Jos asked.

"It invoked an Executive Order that gives FEMA and associated agencies the authority to do just that."

Silence hung in the room like a pall of smoke.

"What do we do about that?" Jon asked.

"Yeah. Good question. My grandson is a military contractor. He and some other folks are getting together in the evenings to plan for our defense. Ask your parents, bring your own guns. They're meeting again Thursday night in the City Hall parking lot."

Jacob took a sip of water.

"Do you have any questions about what we've been discussing? We still have time to discuss some of it."

Jon shifted in his seat. Dick being a libertarian, he'd probably thought along those lines before.

"What's the alternative to this dialectic thinking?"

"Tired of the dance already? Good for you. I'm an individual. So are you. We're not enemies and we don't need to be. We can cooperate when it suits us and we can do our own thing when it works better for us. Friendly competition and looking out for your own personal interests are not selfish. It's wise. It's 'progressive', in that it leads to progress. There's no government agency behind the defense of this community. Mayor Delaney does not have a staff to plan it. Individuals are doing that for themselves, in cooperation with their neighbors."

"How can you plan it without a government?" Kim asked.

"Well, there's two different kinds of government. One is the 'archy', a structure of formalized governance where rulers ... we call them representatives in the US ... direct our efforts. The other form of government is the organic society of individuals who voluntarily gather together to do something that needs doing. There are some organic rules involved there, but no rulers. Shane ... my grandson ... is making suggestions for people who can choose to implement them or not."

"Doesn't defense require coordination?" James asked.

"It does. But there's no reason to create a ruler to conduct that coordination. We select someone for a specific period of time to be 'the leader' of that single effort, but that doesn't mean they get to stay in office for years to come because we selected them to fulfill a specific purpose and they have no more say over anything else than any other person."

"So you're saying we change the way we do elections? How do you select a president for just a specific purpose?"

Jacob grinned and for a brief moment, Jazz thought she could see a much younger man.

"Maybe the better question would be – why do we elect a president at all." They frowned, so Jacob explained. "If foreigners did this to us, why? Most likely because of things Dotson and his cohorts were doing around the world, right? You can't bomb countries without making enemies of the relatives of the dead. You understand that?" All three of the Vance boys nodded, which made the others think. "If this is domestic terrorism, why might someone be so pissed off that they would organize such a huge number of attacks?"

James' laugh got everybody looking at him.

"My dad would say you can only take people's freedom away for so long before they decide to rebel against the tyrants."

It sounded like a recent conversation in the Vance household.

"Bingo. And that flows from Washington DC. Flowed." For a moment, Jacob looked sad. "People who thought they were doing what was right pushed the buttons of people who didn't want government agents dictating to them, so .... Not saying it was right."

"We have elected officials here too," Kim pointed out.

"We do, but you can confront Rob on the street if he does something you don't like. He can't lock you up in prison indefinitely or amass an army against you. You can discuss things with him. And, generally, that's true of most local officials ... outside of big cities, anyway. They don't have the power to enforce anything without the weight of the federal government behind them."

"So, like last year, when the county was talking about PM-2.5 standards on farmers plowing their fields ... the county can't enforce that now, can they?" James asked.

"Exactly. Not that the federal government has gone away. The USDA is coming to confiscate our food."

"Can we fight back … really?" David asked.

"My grandson means to try."

"Who is he, Captain America?"

Jos snorted.

"Not your impression when you spent time with him?" Jacob asked.

"He's more flexible than that. Which is a good thing. I think."

"That's the unfortunate times we are going to be living in, yeah." He glanced at Jazz.

"We're just about done here. I'll be here tomorrow at the same time if any of you want to show up."

"Dad says we have to go to science tomorrow," James Vance said.

"Yeah? That's a good class too. But I'll still be here … unless the USDA happens to be in town and then I'll be trying to defend our food."

The students stood, but most of them gathered around Jacob and continued asking him questions. When they finally cleared out, he turned to her.

"If you want me to do this again, get more into detail, just ask."

"I would. It was like a college seminar. It was wonderful."

Jacob laughed which perplexed her.

"I was done with school in the 8th grade, you know? High school had tuition in those days."

"But you have an incredible library."

"I do. You don't have to go to school to learn. What's the quote from that movie -- why pay a quarter million for an education you could have got for a dollar fifty in late fees at the public library? I subscribe to that theory of education. Anyway, I'm flying a field this afternoon, so I should get going."

"I should get back to the feed store. People are showing up pretty steadily."

"You're keeping good records?"

"I am. A few of them have expressed concerns that the town might confiscate the corn for itself."

"That's a valid concern, which is why we're not filling the City Hall bomb shelter with corn. Gotta go, but you should know how much I appreciate your willingness to dive in and help where you're needed."

"Not a problem. I'm part of the community too."

"Someday you'll have to tell me why that is when the town you grew up in is only 20 miles away."

"Yeah, we can have that conversation sometime."

"Not today, though." He pulled out his phone. "Shane says the plane is refueled and ready to go, so I have to stop dawdling. Haven't been this busy in 20 years. Armageddon is better than advertising."

Slavery is the New ... Slavery

Someone Near Hutchinson, Kansas

"Brian," his coworker said. They were pulling canned goods off shelves and stacking them on a pallet on a jack. Brian was about Cai's age with dark skin and curly hair, but blue eyes. "You okay?"

Cai's left cheek swelled from his contact with the ground after his morning stun gunning.

"It'll be fine." Cai had seen worse bruises on Shane's face and his brother remained handsome, so he assumed it would heal. "Cai."

"My grandma used to remind me that we have it so much better than folks in past generations because slavery's been outlawed. I think it's been reinstituted ... for all of us this time."

Cai paused in his work, staring at Brian.

"They're following the court of military justice without fear of media coverage."

"So, this is what it was like in the past?"

"Yes, if the history books are telling it right.

"What happens when our sentences are up?"

"I don't know. Hopefully by that time, they'll have a chain of command and someone will find a copy of the Constitution. You got family needing you?"

"My wife was with me when we were caught. I didn't know where they had her until this morning in the hearing."

"What's your sentence?"

"They like that 30 days."

"It's probably standard."

At the end of the aisle, a soldier paused. Cai picked up the pace. Brian glanced over his shoulder, then also picked up the pace.

"No talking," the soldier ordered.

Cai and Brian exchanged significant looks and moved to the next shelf.

They worked together most of the morning, sharing their bios in whispers as they labored. Brian and April, his wife, worked at a DMV in Denver, but they'd been headed to April's mother's house in Wichita when the bombs went off. They'd managed to get off the interstate only to be diverted all over the place. They'd stayed at a motel during the shelter-in-place order and then they'd been headed south yesterday morning when they'd been stopped at a checkpoint and arrested for being "outside their district."

"What the hell does that mean?" Brian asked. "I asked and they stun-gunned me for it."

"Damned if it I know. Of course, you're not in your district. You'd be ash if you were in your district."

"I forget. What did they get you for?"

"Being out past curfew."

"They take that one really seriously."

They were loaded into another panel truck at midday and transported back to the fairground. A food line had been set up outside of the dormitory. Soldiers were maintaining order with cattle prods and the threat of bullets. Cai kept his gaze fixed on the back of the guy in front of him.

"What are you staring at?" a soldier demanded of Brian.

"Nothing."

"Don't you eyeball me! We're not taking that sort of insolence anymore."

"I wasn't looking at you. I was looking for my wife."

"Who is your wife?"

"About three rows over, blond, blue t-shirt."

"You're with a white woman?"

Cai couldn't help looking now. Fifty years of racial progress erased in one week couldn't be a good thing.

Brian snapped rigid, teeth chattering, muscles spasming. The soldier who held the stun gun smiled, his prominent nose giving him a vulpine look. When he broke connection, Brian said an explicative and slumped to the ground. Nobody moved to catch him. Everybody stared anywhere but at him, including Cai.

I can't believe this is happening. This can't be happening.

"Let's get this straight, people. You are no longer in charge. From now on, you will do as you are told or you will be punished. If you're very good boys and girls, we will allow you time with your loved ones. If you defy us, you may never see each other again."

The soldier nudged Brian with his combat boot.

"Get up off the ground, man. I'm just fooling with you."

Brian groaned, but climbed shakily to his feet. A few rows over, a pretty blond girl wept while two older women held her back from going to her husband. The soldier looked around and then walked to another area.

"How can we let this happen?" a man whispered behind Cai. They'd met in one of the trucks. Larry was a union organizer by trade and a rabble-rouser by genetic makeup. "There's more of us than there are of them. Why are we letting this happen?"

Nobody answered for fear of the guns and the cattle prods. Brian's hands were shaking too hard to hold his plate and Cai hesitated to help him, but when he looked at the guy behind the food station, he said "Go on. Help him."

They took seats at a picnic table.

"You okay, man?" Cai asked.

"Second time's no easier."

"I know."

"I gotta get April out of here."

"The more you resist, the more likely they are to kill you."

"I wasn't resisting. I was just looking at my wife."

Cai nodded. He didn't know what to do. Was there anything to do? They were disarmed and isolated, closely guarded. A soldier neared them.

"No talking," he ordered.

Brian flinched. Cai tucked into his food. What else could they do? They were prisoners. He thanked God Marnie hadn't come with him. She would have limited his options and made him weaker when he wasn't all that strong to begin with. On the other hand, he worried about Emmaus. The food being brought into this distribution center came from somewhere ... maybe the Walmart in Emmaus. What would his family do if he didn't come home for 30 days? Would they presume him dead or would Shane come looking for him? Remembering Shane drilling those two National Guardsman in the Kevlar on the night of the bombs, he wasn't sure he wanted Shane's help. Then again, he probably did.

God, why is this happening? Why is it happening to me? Haven't I been good enough?

A sense of dread filled his chest. What if this was a discipling for something ... like being happy after he'd allowed Marie to die for his stupidity? Yeah, Marnie had forgiven him, but maybe God didn't. That left him with this huge hollow cave inside that he dreaded to examine.

Offering Hope

Emmaus, Kansas

With the Internet up intermittently, Rob had endeavored to find out information on Danny Hughes, the kid they were holding for murder. He didn't have a police record, but Rob eventually found him on Facebook. He looked like a normal kid, being raised by his grandmother in a neat frame house in a working class neighborhood of Chicago. Grandma never mentioned a mother or father, but proudly displayed his last report card. The kid was smart and a hard worker.

Joe said the kid believed the pilot had been making a move on him. Maybe so. Jacob could only have seen so much in the doorway and adrenaline might account for the rest. The Burger Barn was up and running again, so Rob took Danny's lunch down to him.

The boy's father had to have been white to account for the lighter skin and eyes. He lay on the floor with his feet on the bunk, staring at the ceiling when Rob glanced through the observation window, but he rolled up off the floor when he heard the keys in the lock. Rob hung them by the door to eliminate any reason for the kid to do something violent.

"Got an actual hamburger for you this time."

"And a milk shake. Thanks!"

The kid sat down on the bunk and began devouring the food.

"When you're done eating, maybe you can tell me what happened in the hanger one more time."

The kid stopped stuffing fries into his mouth, swallowed resolutely, and wiped his mouth.

"Might as well get that out of the way right now. I didn't mean to shoot him. I've tried and tried to think about what happened. I want to believe he made a move on me, but ..." he took a deep breath and let it out slowly. "I didn't mean to shoot him."

"I believe that."

"You do?"

"Yeah. I've been in stressful situations myself. I know how a quick gesture can look like a threat and lead to bad outcomes."

"Do you think a judge will believe me?"

"I don't know. You're only 15, so there's a good chance it's not the rest of your life in jail."

"My grandmother's going to be so angry with me."

Now tears flowed.

The Internet now showed the radioactive zones and Rob doubted Danny still had a grandmother, but there were some refugee camps near Chicago. Rob had managed to get a number to an administrator and asked if Wilma Hughes might be located. Apparently, people were making an effort to connect, so Rob saw no reason to depress the kid further. He shared what he knew.

"Yeah. Thanks." Danny contemplated a fry, but set it down. "You got family you're worried about?"

"My sisters are probably okay. My son Cai left for Wichita Saturday and we haven't heard from him."

"I hope he comes home soon."

"Thank you."

Danny nodded. Rob suspected that under different circumstances, he was probably a good kid, which didn't make the situation any easier. Sooner or later, Danny would have to answer for his crime and Rob had a sneaking suspicion it would be left up to the town to decide what happened to him.

Hello, Tiny Aquanaut

The welder stood back to examine the work and then shut down the rig. Marnie cleared her throat.

"Is it done?" she asked.

The welder pushed back the mask and pulled the hat off.

"Yeah. That should hold it and with a little bit of cosmetics, it shouldn't be obvious we've done this deliberately."

"Um, I know you, right?"

"Nevada Randolph. I brought my daughter in Sunday with a broken arm."

"Right. Sorry. I've been so busy."

"It's fine. You're the only doctor right now, right?"

While Nevada talked, she prepped her next tool.

"So, after I'm done with this, you want those shelves moved in front?"

"Right. We'll put some supplies on them, make it look like it's been there a while and then if they decide to look behind, they'll be unable to open the doors."

"Devious."

Marnie leaned against the wall, fanning her face with her hand.

"How far along are you?" Nevada asked.

"What?"

"You're pregnant, right?"

"How do you ...?"

"You're more emotional than most doctors I know. You've got that glowy, overheated, occasionally wanting to puke look."

"I'm about 11 weeks."

Nevada smiled.

"Tiny little human about the length of your thumb digit. You'll probably feel it start moving in a few weeks."

Marnie brushed a tear away.

"What's wrong?"

"My husband left Saturday for Wichita and he's not back and we haven't heard from him. He doesn't even know and I'm so scared."

"Yeah. I was about 12 weeks when Kim's father decided he didn't want to be a father. It was a scary time, but I wouldn't have missed it for the world. When that baby moved within me, I knew nothing in this world would ever make me turn away."

Marnie dried her tears.

"I have something I have to do upstairs."

"No problem. I'll load those shelves."

"Thank you."

Lila had the ultrasound ready when Marnie got there. The cold gel and Marnie's ticklish white belly complicated matters, but Lila was a good ultrasound technician and she captured a perfect image. Four limbs, a face. Lila had to keep moving to follow the baby.

"Strong little swimmer," she joked. Marnie burst into tears.

"Cai has to see this," she croaked. "What's wrong with me?"

"You're scared," Lila said. "We all are when our first pregnancy is unplanned. It makes sense. You don't feel like you can handle this and everything else that is going on, but you will learn what I already know ... you are stronger than you believe yourself to be. And Cai is out there, trying to get home, so you just hang onto that and don't let go."

The door came open and Abigail stuck her head in.

"I got a farmer out here with a broken foot." She lifted an eyebrow.

"Not a word about this," Lila said.

"No, of course not."

Marnie grabbed some wet wipes to clean off her abdomen. Lila quickly put the ultra sound equipment away. As a final act, Marnie wiped her face to get rid of the tears.

If I'm going to do this, I have to stop being sentimental about it. If Cai doesn't come home, I have got to make the right decision.

Neighbors

Carl Sullivan listened to the radio chatter. He'd been at this for days now. Was this how the Code Talkers had spent their days and nights on those Pacific Islands? He sort of liked the idea that he was performing a vital service to his community from his basement.

Last night he'd been able to hear all the way to Vladivostok, though it really didn't do him any good since he couldn't speak Russian. But he'd talked to a ham operator in Hawaii. Things were going well there. They'd just got a ship hail in rather than going on to California. He'd overheard an American naval vessel in the Pacific talking about some odd ship movements, seeking advice from Cheyenne Mountain.

Far off in the house, he heard the doorbell ring. It made his teeth grind. Why did the world always dig into him like this? He was busy. The doorbell rang again.

He climbed the stairs. Calla Thomas, who lived just two doors down, stood on the side porch.

"What do you want?" he asked.

"Just checking on you." About ninety, Ms. Thomas was always well put together and polite. Her voice reminded him of honey. She was from somewhere south, not Kansas. "How are you doing?"

"I'm listening to the radio broadcasts," he explained. "Rob Delaney asked me to keep an ear out, let him know what's going on out there."

"Good for you. I just wanted to check in since I hadn't seen you much. Let me know if you need anything. Neighbors have to hang together in times like these."

"Yes, ma'am."

She strolled back to her house and he glanced at the calendar on the wall. October 1. That meant he had two more months to live. He wondered how the neighbors would react if he told them what he wanted done when he ran out of meds. No, Miss Calla would try to talk him out of it. Some people were just too nice for their own good.

Food Riot

Great Bend, Kansas

USDA and the Army were taking the corn from Great Bend's elevators and now Mike and his crew were cleaning out the grocery store. When people started gathering in the parking lot, Mike felt a ball of ice form in his gut.

"What do we do, sir?" Kriczek asked.

"Just keep loading the trucks," Mike ordered. "Lawson, Gardino, stand perimeter, but remember, these are Americans, not enemy combatants."

Mike steered a dolly of canned goods over to the back end of one of the trucks. He hated this, one of the worst feelings of his life. He went back inside to get more food. As he levered his dolly backward to go back outside, a shot rang out. He dropped the load and ran out the door, drawing his weapon. Thirty people had guns pointing at 10 Knights, who had drawn their weapons. Lawson's gun looked hot and a civilian lay unmoving on the ground in an expanding pool of blood.

305

Lela Markham

"You're not taking our food," one of the men said.

Mike used his left hand to exert downward pressure on Lawson's rifle, grimacing at the still warm barrel.

"Let's ease up, folks. We're just doing our jobs. There will be food available to you at the central distribution depot."

"You're not taking our food!" someone else hollered.

"Folks, listen, I know this is a bad situation. Nobody wants to be here right now. But we have orders and they come from the highest level. The president says you have to cooperate."

"She isn't my president," one of the women said. "Nobody voted for her."

"Okay, I get it, but let's look at reality here. My men and I are wearing body armor. If it comes to a shootout, we're going to win. Nobody wanted to kill that man, but that's what happens when civilians go up against soldiers. So, we're leaving with this food. The only question here is how many of you are joining your friend on the asphalt."

Mike signaled for his men to get back in the trucks. One by one, they did, but they covered him in the end, so he could get into one of the trucks without taking a bullet in the back.

"You did good there, sir," Jacobson said. "I thought we were going to have to mow down a crowd of civilians, but you kept that from happening."

306

"Yeah." Mike shuddered, thinking of Alicia and Shane having to deal with just this sort of thuggery where they were.

Why are we doing this? There's got to be a better way.

Don't Worry About Me

Emmaus, Kansas

Alex helped Shane rake corn out the back of a dump truck into the hangar while Jacob ran a skid steer to pack the corn into the building. While Alex had his cousins harvesting his fields, he and Shane had tackled Joel Rhys' fields with Alex's old combine. It paid to keep these things in working order. It couldn't harvest as fast as the newer ones could, but they'd cleared one field already and left Poppy to continue while they off-loaded. They'd be done by mid-evening.

With every defunct and mothballed silo pressed into service, Shane had been forced to think innovatively. Jacob had suggested the old hangar, built of concrete. Cleaning the hangar out had been a major chore, but it would hold the portion of Shane's corn he meant to keep. With the last kernel shoveled off the back of the truck, Alex and Shane dropped to the ground to scrape the remainder into the hangar.

"How are you planning to keep it secure?"

"Concrete walls and the lock pins welded to the track. It won't keep truly resourceful thieves out, but it'll slow them down until it pings my phone so I can come shoot them."

Alex stared off at a roofline for a moment before deciding to be brave.

"Keri's worried about you."

"Yeah? She doesn't need to be."

"That haunted look in your eyes ... that from killing people?"

Shane's mouth tightened slightly and he ducked his head so his eyes hid behind the bill of his cap.

"I'm not judging you." Anyone but Shane would have been freaked out by Alex "reading his mind", but Shane had been around Deaf enough to know that the little nuances of body language were like written sentences to folks trained in native signs. "I'm worried about you too."

"You don't need to be." *He's doing it again -- withdrawing behind that glass wall and projecting ... nothing. Or trying to.* "There's a difference between what I did ... did before, and what I'm willing to do now. This is our corn. What we need to survive on. If someone steals it from us, we starve. Shooting someone here is self-defense, not murder."

Alex sighed.

"Yeah, that's what I would say, but I know I'd still regret it."

"After you've had to do it a few times, you won't." Shane glanced at his phone.

"Anything?"

"Nothing so far. The problem is that my handler scrubbed Cai's image, which called the military dogs off, but makes it so much harder for him to find him."

"How so?"

"I don't know. It's not my thing."

"I keep waiting for you to steal the duster and head out looking for him."

The thought has occurred to him.

"Naw. Dad's right. I couldn't find him. If my handler finds him, it'll be like he was in a certain place at a certain time and then maybe I'll go there and search, but for right now … it's needle in a haystack time."

"How's Marnie holding up?"

"I don't know. I try to avoid her as much as possible."

"That's a complicated relationship, I know. Keri's worried about her too. She said she burst into tears yesterday when she just saw Keri."

"Marnie crying? I guess she does love him."

"And you have no feelings left for her?"

Shane rubbed his chin, actually thinking about the question.

"There've been three women since her – two of them fairly long-term. And she's married to my brother. I don't choose to commit adultery with my brother's wife."

"That's good. So, I have to get back to the fields. Hopefully Mark and Pete have got that bunker silo packed by the time I get there."

"Try to talk Mark into joining us for guard training tonight. When the government shows up to confiscate our food, we're going to need to all be on the same page."

"He won't. He's been clear about that. It's a five-year federal sentence for him if he's caught with a gun and he's not risking his family being on their own in this mess."

Shane shrugged.

"I doubt the feds are in any shape to press charges, but that's his choice."

He dropped the door to the hangar and began to gear up for welding. Alex moved to climb into the truck when Jason Breen pulled up in front of him with a panel truck. Alex turned aside to hear what he had to say.

"I went as far as Salinas and got bag silos and lye. They were more than willing to take the corn, but man, their prices were steep. We're not the only ones with this idea."

Jason opened the back of the truck and Shane stared at the contents with a calculating expression.

"What's more valuable to them than corn?"

"I asked that. Corn's top of their list, they just want three times what I had."

"Second?" Alex asked.

"Drugs – pharma drugs."

"Antibiotics will be making the world go round pretty soon." They all stared at Jacob. "None of you remember when we didn't have them. People died of simple cuts, colds that turned into sinus infections that turned into encephalitis. When we first hit the beaches at Normandy, more men died from infection than of the actual bullets, my brother included. Second half of the war, they brought in antibiotics and suddenly you had a chance if you were wounded."

"I doubt my daughter will let any of them go, anyway. She's got them stowed away in the bomb shelter, I hear. So, if you guys want to provide more corn, I'll get more."

"What do you think, Alex?" Shane counted the bags of lye. "That's four bag silos and 12 bags of lye."

"Is four enough to do what you want?" Jacob asked.

"With the two we already had. I think it will satisfy them – or at least give them pause. Is that enough lye, Alex?"

"Probably not. And corn is essentially useless for food without nixilation, so we should fill that truck up."

"I'll go over to Bennett's with two trucks then. Where do you want me to drop this off?"

"The feed store. That Tully girl will let you in."
Jacob always called Jazz that now – that Tully girl.
Alex suspected the old man had a little harmless
crush on her.

"Got it. Thank you, gentlemen, for the good
trading arrangement."

They were paying Jason in corn and lye. Jason
had a lot of mouths to feed.

"I got to get over to the Elevators." Alex swung
up into the truck. "Shane, Keri insists you come to
dinner tonight. Say, six."

"Should I spray myself with baking spray before
I get there?"

"I've made her promise not the grill you too
hard."

"Hey, if you can control my sister, more power
to you. Jason, since you're going to the feed store,
can I catch a ride with you? I left my Jeep there this
morning."

"Sure."

"I just have to weld this door shut and then we
can get going."

"Sounds good. I'm going to go grab a cigarette
away from the oxy acetylene."

There was no reason to hang around other than
that Alex was worried about Shane, so he climbed
up into the truck, then sat for a moment, praying
for his friend without any words.

Welcome Home, Brother

Anders McAuliff entered his office at the Sullivan salt mine, dropping a stack of salt orders into his overflowing inbasket. One of these days, he really ought to move up to the big office next to Joseph Sullivan. On the other hand, he really liked this original battered office. It connected him to the former managing partner, Doug Pomeroy, who had scoffed at Sullivan building the new admin building. The best day of Anders' life had been the day he met Pomeroy. He'd turned wrong on the way to his brother's compound and ended up at the salt mine instead. Pomeroy had been kind. Well, actually, most of the town had been nicer than you would expect them to be toward the brother of the terrorist they'd found in their midst, but Pomeroy had gone above and beyond. He'd invited Anders over for dinner and shown him the town. When Anders said it might be a nice place to live, Pomeroy had asked him if he might want to buy the salt mine. Doug still lived in town, enjoying his retirement and the never-ending quest to hook a huge bass.

Anders poured himself some coffee, looking out the window to where some of his guys were loading bags of rock salt. The last few days had been the busiest period since he took ownership. People were stocking up, imbued with a real sense that the crisis had merely eased for a moment before continuing. Farmers would soon be dropping off harvesters and bag silos to hide in the mine. He turned on his computer to run an inventory, but an alert blinked on the desktop. Someone had been at the silo site.

The Internet was back, but sluggish. It took him a couple of minutes to pull up the CCTV footage. He watched as a van pulled up to the gate. A group of men got out, examined the gate restraints and then got to work bypassing them. What should he do about it? Only one deputy remained on the Emmaus police department, there didn't seem to be a county sheriff's office currently and his mine guards were guarding the interstate entrances. Maybe he could offer Shane Delaney something worth his while. That young man knew his way around force.

And, then it all made sense. Daniel! No, it really was Daniel. Unlike Anders, Daniel had kept his hair, though it seemed lighter. Probably going gray. He looked fairly fit and healthy, though he scanned around him like he expected attack. Which made sense since they had to be recently escaped from prison. Some of the men with him could have been part of Daniel's old crew. They reminded Anders of pictures he'd seen in Daniel's apartment at the site.

How'd you get out, brother? I can't imagine that in the middle of a terrorist attack, they decided to let a bunch of wannabe terrorists out.

Anders' hand wavered toward the phone, but nobody had had any luck with getting through to state or federal governmental agencies. Who would he call? Technically, Daniel still owned the silo site ... Anders was merely trustee. He had considered selling it. Pomeroy had suggested it would make a great kitschy resort and one of his real estate friends had given Anders his card for the future. He'd have put the money in an account for the unlikely event his brother ever saw daylight again. He'd need something to live on. But ....

It's the apocalypse. Nobody will figure this out for a while and, truthfully, I don't care that Daniel is free. I never bought the idea that he was plotting a terrorist attack, at least not against real people.

Anders shut off the CCTV feed and sat back in his chair. *I don't break the law.* A sucking hole began dragging at his guts. *It's the apocalypse he predicted.* He took an uncomfortable breath. *There's no way they got out of prison by walking out the door, right?*

A 3-ton pulled up into the yard, the driver getting out to walk toward the office. Anders rose to meet Jason Breen short of the door.

"You get any?"

"Not much." Breen held out a jar of grayish powder. "They wanted way more in trade than I had. I'm headed back for more stuff for the town, so if you want me to try again -- give me about twice as much salt and I'll come back with the rest of your order."

"You going to charge me more too?"

Jason gave him a sideways look and a grim smile.

"You really don't consider me to be a businessman, do you? Our deal was two bags of salt for every trip and that works for me still."

Anders weighed his options. He didn't much trust Breen not to cut some backdoor deal to enrich himself and then claim a price hike. Of course, there was no way to be sure without going with him.

"All right, I'll have the guys load you up. You hear of any market for iodized table salt?"

"There won't be a lot of seafood flowing this way this winter and iodine protects the thyroid from radiation. The supplier knows that too, which is why he's gouging. You folks going to need anything else? Seems like you don't grow your own food any more than I do."

"I'll line up with everyone else at Huffy's. Thanks for thinking of me. If you can get any meds to add to what the medical center has, I'll pay you for it."

"That's right neighborly of you." Breen liked to affect that country bumpkin accent, but Anders wasn't fooled. He used that to outmaneuver people.

"The community is going to need whatever it can get. I'm just doing my part."

"My daughter appreciates it, I'm sure."

Breen walked with him to the distribution office where Anders detailed the load. Supposedly, this mine had another 100-year supply of salt, so they could essentially buy what they needed with it ... so long as what they needed remained available. Money had been such a convenient concept a week ago, so he'd never really thought about it before. Now, it had just become a data source. He wondered how to pay his employees. Farmers Bank had explained that they couldn't get hold of anyone to straighten out the electronic banking system. They had limited hard funds on hand. Anders had fired off emails to both Joseph and Ren Sullivan this morning, but he hadn't received a reply from either one.

He realized that Breen also had employees.

"How are you planning to pay your guys?"

Breen blinked at him.

"We take a cut of every truck load as our payment and we do a share system. You?"

"Good question."

Breen rubbed the back of his neck.

"You know, according to the salt museum over in Hutchison, the Romans used to pay their soldiers in salt. That's where we get the word 'salary' from."

Anders stared at Breen a moment before laughing.

"Of course. That makes total sense."

"You're welcome," Breen said. "Like I said, I'm a businessman just like you."

"What were you hauling for my brother?"

"Supplies for his community over there. Is that what the stick up your spine is all about?"

"I only know rumors."

"Well, straight talk here. Your brother was building a community of survivalists ... mostly well-off men with families who liked his anarcho-capitalism. As an anarcho-capitalist myself, I liked what they were doing, so I didn't object when my son got involved with them. I didn't know they were under investigation by the FBI."

"And, Shane Delaney found evidence they were plotting terrorism."

"I don't know what Shane found. I think he doesn't know or that they twisted what he found to something it wasn't. That case rested on a couple of sawed-off shotguns and a broken AR15 someone had tried and failed to convert to full auto. The rest of it was pure speculation. You ever read Shane's deposition transcripts?"

"No."

"He heard men talking about revolution, which can mean more than one thing. To a 21-year-old kid whose father was career military before he retired to oh-so-conservative Kansas, that meant shooting at American soldiers, but we don't have to start shooting at the government for a revolution to occur. Your brother was talking about changing minds and hearts, not killing people."

"You think so?"

"Yeah. And, look around. Isn't this the very mess he predicted?"

Breen turned to talk to a mine worker about how many bags to put on the pallet. In 15 minutes, his truck was fully loaded again and Anders had made a decision. He shook Breen's hand before the carter climbed back into the truck, then leaned in and whispered.

"Dan's at the compound."

Maybe He's Not Dead

Beulah, Kansas
County Courthouse

Rob truly did not know what to say to Max Albright as they drove to Beulah. He'd never had to do a death call as mayor. He'd written a few letters to soldiers' wives back in the service, but that whole patriotism rap wasn't going to work here, he knew. He sort of doubted it had worked when he wrote those letters. It wouldn't have worked on Jill.

The county sheriff, Kevin Murdoch met them in the parking lot of the Art Deco courthouse.

"Are you taking us to see Drew?" Max asked.

"You don't want to see those remains," Kevin assured him. "Not sure you could identify them if you did. Car's over this way though."

Beulah County's impound lot was just a block from the court house, which was currently occupied by a rogue National Guard unit. They'd let Kevin keep his office, but taken over most of the building. The mangled and burned-out car Shane had found under the cow catcher of a train had been deposited in one corner of the lot, surrounded by cars confiscated in DUI stops. Max's eyes shined brightly for a moment, but then he frowned. Rob waited.

"I don't think it is Drew's. It's a silver sports car, but Drew's seats were red and what's left there looks like black leather."

There wasn't much left to identify, but they did look like black leather rather than red.

"Was it a Chevy?" Kevin asked.

"No, a Chrysler Sebring."

"Then you're probably right. We found a Chevy emblem."

"Oh, thank God," Max gasped. He smiled and wiped at his tears, then frowned. "But if the poor man who died in this car isn't Drew, where could he be?"

Kevin glanced at Rob and shrugged. Rob didn't know what to say either. Drew's last known location, Chicago, was a nuclear wasteland. He could still be dead, but neither of them wanted to deal with that, so they didn't say anything.

Rob's phone buzzed. He read the message and then cleared his throat.

"I need to get back to Emmaus. Kevin, thanks for helping us out here. Max."

They headed to Rob's truck.

"I can't imagine what the family of that man are going through, wondering where he is."

"Yeah. It's got to be tough for a whole lot of people right now."

"I've been worried sick. I still am. I just don't know what to do with myself."

"Um, the town could use some help. The USDA is headed our way to confiscate food and supplies. The grocery store is hauling its goods to a secure location. You want to help?"

"Certainly. Drew would encourage me to be busy and helpful. Thank you, mayor."

"Rob. I didn't run for election for the title."

"Right. Rob, then. Thank you for taking me and … well, I know it's uncomfortable for you."

"It's just not something I'm used to doing, but you are still a member of my community. Can I drop you at the grocery store? I'm needed elsewhere."

"Of course. I've always like Ms. Huffman."

"Is that what you call her?"

"Yes. Have I got that wrong?"

"Well, her married name is Osimowitz. I don't think she went back to Huffman after he died. But everybody here calls her 'Huffy'."

"That just seems rude."

"Her real name's Mae. She answers to it."

"Thank you." Rob pulled up before the grocery store and Max got out. Yeah, the whole thing was uncomfortable, but life meant discomfort right now. Ordinary circumstances had fled. This just added a different twist to extraordinary that he hadn't ever planned on dealing with. It hardly compared to the USDA coming to confiscate the food.

An Afternoon Caller

Mara Wells, Kansas

Mitchell Rumdale parked his USDA truck in front of Mara Wells' city hall, which consisted of a narrow concrete building with stairs leading to an off-center door.

How do they expect anyone to take them seriously when they are essentially operating out of a storefront? At least Goodland's impressive facade made me feel guilty for teaching them not to argue with their betters.

He really hated wasting time with these hicks while his son waited with his ex-wife in Boise. He straightened his tie and blue jacket with the USDA symbol before he mounted the steps. Upon entering, an L-shaped counter separated the lobby from the office area.

"Can I help you?" The questioner was a tall man wearing jeans and cowboy boots and a mustache that would not have been out of place in a 1970s biker film.

327

Mitchel introduced himself, presenting his credentials.

"I'm Stanley Osimowitz, Mayor of this fair city. What is it you need?"

"For starters, access to the Cosco located here."

"The Cosco? Have you talked to the manager? I can call him for you if you like."

"No, I don't need to talk to the manager and I know the fire department has the means to enter every building in town. We must begin the inventory and securement of the items."

"Excuse me?"

"My team and I are here to protect the resources in that building."

"Building's locked and we've been cooperating with the manager to allow people in as they need supplies. We appreciate the offer, but we don't really need extra guards. Folks around here aren't much into looting."

Apparently, the hick hadn't read the FEMA manual lately.

"I apologize for the confusion, but with the declaration of martial law under President Anna Byers, we've been authorized to confiscate all commercially held food and transport it to a central distribution site for orderly disbursement, per Executive Order 13603."

Mitchel handed Osimowitz the order authorizing his action.

"Now, please unlock the building so we can do our jobs."

"Yeah. Let me find my glasses and read this first." Osimowitz started to move toward the office labeled as his at the back of the lobby, but Mitchell stalled him.

"They're in your left breast pocket, sir." Osimowitz looked startled, patted them, shrugged and laughed and put them on. He took his time reading it.

"Where is this central distribution center and how will Mara residents access it?"

"I can't answer about the location of the distribution center, but there's a number on the order where you can call to discuss the procedures. Now, I'm on a schedule, so we need to move smartly."

Osimowitz stared at him with a hard look. This old man did not yet recognize the new reality. Mitchel had faced a mayor like that yesterday in Goodland ... his town had paid the price for his recalcitrance, though Rumdale thought he'd been more restrained than Obrokowski had been in Sharon Springs.

Osimowitz relaxed his shoulders.

"We have a volunteer fire department hereabouts and I'm not sure where Sherm might be galivanting to right now, so I'll need to let the manager know so he can meet us. My cell's in the office. I'll be back in a jiffy."

The blinds on the small office were closed, so Mitchel couldn't see what the mayor did. Whatever it was took longer than he'd expected ... long enough that he'd been ready to push through the swinging gate in the counter when Osimowitz came out. When he asked what had taken so long, Osimowitz held up the phone.

"I forgot what I'd done with it. Never get used to carrying these new-fangled contraptions and I don't have the Cosco manager's name in my contacts, so I had to look that up."

Secretly chuckling at the hick's ignorance, Mitchel got into his truck. Galena Carboy watched as Osimowitz headed to his truck. She looked smart and official with her strawberry blond hair pulled back in a ponytail, sporting a green jacket and cap with the blue-and-green USDA symbol on both.

"What took so long?"

"These yokels need the rules explained to them, but he was fairly cooperative. He's going to lead us to the Cosco."

Osimowitz didn't waste any time getting there. The manager, dressed in jeans and a flannel shirt, waited in the parking lot.

"I hope you're not expecting much," he said. "We didn't get our shipment last week ... it was due that night. We've had people coming to buy supplies. Of course, I'll need an accounting of whatever you take."

"Of course. We'll do a full inventory."

Mitchel pushed through the side door and paused while the manager hit the lights. They came on in rows, lighting the industrial shelving units. Michael stared about him, stunned because most of the shelves were completely empty.

"My god," Osimowitz averred. "We've been robbed!"

Grant Ellis, the manager, glanced around.

"No, this is about what I expected. We had a week's worth of reserve and it's been a week."

"You have got to be kidding me!" Mitchel wheeled around to stare at Grant. "You're telling me that this is it?"

"There's a little bit in the back warehouse. Come on, I'll show you."

The warehouse had sporting goods, small appliances, rock salt, and a bunch of melted ice cream. Outside, the sun had swung around to the west. A cleared field stood right across the two-lane.

"You pulled your crops early. Where's it stored?" Mitchel demanded of Osimowitz.

"Gone. It was sold to the distributors."

"Why did you clear your fields earlier than other towns?"

"It was an early spring and a hot summer. The corporate fields maybe follow a set schedule, but the folks around here are mostly independents, so they pulled their crops when they were ready."

He's lying! Mitchell's fingers twitched for his gun. He'd never carried one before a week ago, but now he realized that people would have been so much more compliant with it. Cole Packard had reported fields ready to harvest in this area.

Galena, consulting her tablet, cleared her throat. He glanced at her.

"They cleared their fields before the bombs." She handed the laptop to him to show him the satellite photos. Two weeks ago, the fields had been full and the day before the bombs, they had been stripped.

"Why are you plowing?"

"We'll start planting winter wheat and peas this week."

Mitchell turned to Galena.

"Have the crews come in and start searching the houses. Leave a two-week reserve, but everything else goes on the trucks."

Osimowitz's mustache ruffled, perhaps in reaction to an unanticipated move.

"Thank you for your cooperation, mayor. You can go back to your home now in anticipation of an inspection."

Osimowitz looked like he wanted to take Mitchel's head off, but then he breathed deeply and let it out in a slow sigh.

"I really didn't believe it when others said our government would do something like this. I guess I was wrong. I'll be waiting at my house."

He turned toward the exit and didn't look back on his way out. The Cosco manager scuttled past him to wait by the door. Mitchel looked at Galena.

"What do you think we'll find?"

"Homes filled with food they don't need. They didn't anticipate our going door-to-door."

"My thought exactly. You believe that guy? Dumb hick. Why do these rednecks elect people who are that stupid?"

Galena nodded and laughed as they headed to the door.

Stan Osimowitz to Rob Delaney

-They're here. He's about Randi's age, green as grass and overconfident. We'll delay them until sundown. Stan

Match Positive

Jericho Ghoat Town

-Beep. Match positive.

Dylan Rigby looked at the spare computer, seeing a facial recognition match for Cai Delaney. Wichita Kansas, Monday morning. Dylan rolled his chair over and magnified until he could see a disheveled Cai being dragged across a parking lot at the Eisenhower Airport. His hands were cuffed, but he was using his legs, so he had been fairly healthy 30 hours ago.

Dylan ordered the algorithm to trace the truck, then headed upstairs where his parents were chopping vegetables in the kitchen.

"The USDA is in Mara Wells," he reported. "They'll be here tomorrow."

"We've got a plan," Emily Rigby told her eldest child with a laugh. "I feel a proper pirate, I do."

Dylan frowned.

"We're going to use what is known about this place against them," Grant said. "And it was all your mother's idea. It's quite brilliant. Anything else?"

"I found where Cai Delaney was Monday morning."

"Where?"

"Wichita, under arrest by the Army, being tossed into a truck headed I-don't-know-where."

"You put a trace on the truck?"

"I did. I'll let you know what happens. The satellite footage shows this whole area being harvested before the rain. I even scrubbed the satellite images of your boy and others stealing from the train."

"Um, I don't care about that, but you're right, USDA might."

"So, are you going to tell him that you found his brother?"

"Nope! Shane is too valuable to all of us to risk him on a fool's errand. If you find out where Cai's at, hijack Shane's phone and text Sanchez as if you're Shane. Let me read it first because those two are so close, the wording is important. We'll put Sanchez on it and not have to risk Shane at all."

"Wow. Yeah, okay. You know that some people brought a 3-ton truck of I-don't-know-what-all to the hotel a half hour ago."

"I didn't know, but I can't think of a more secure location to hide items. I mean, you've checked it out, right? Could you break into it?"

"Not without knowing the security code or blowing the building up. Exactly what was he planning on doing with that building anyway?"

"Actually, it was renovated by us as a second site when we thought we would have a longer mission following the militia. Then we were ordered in and the hotel was quickly put up for sale. Shane bought it for a song."

"Shane bought it?"

"No, Joel Rhys bought it, but yeah …. Anyway, the security on that building is better than it is on this one, so Shane's right to use it. Where you going?"

"Outside to chop some wood. I didn't mean to spend all day in the basement."

"Hopefully, after tomorrow, we can forego the basement altogether. We can turn the back parlor into our work room. Not yet, though. For now, we've got to keep the business end of this place out of sight because the USDA is probably not on our side."

Dylan's phone vibrated.

"Looks like I got a ping on that truck."

He turned toward the basement door.

"Dylan, go for a walk. I'll check on that. Really, stop being so obsessive."

Dylan sighed.

"Yeah, you're right. A half hour will be fine."

"Clear your head, get the blood flowing. There's a long lonely winter ahead. We all need to learn how to relax. We can't stare at satellite images day in and day out. We'll go mad."

"But isn't that what you were doing before the bombs, honey?" Emily teased.

Dylan liked how his parents were with one another right now. His mother seemed to be enjoying knowing all the secrets. Even his grandparents were opening up to the prospect. *Next thing you know, we'll have the girls analyzing data. Why not? It'll be a long, lonely winter ahead.*

"I'm actually wanting to go for a run. That road that runs along the creek ... that's isolated enough, don't you think?"

"It should be. It's the old road to Emmaus. You start seeing houses after you get past the Delaney fishing cabin, turn back."

"Yes, sir."

A half-mile into his run, Dylan heard voices and saw several men unloading a truck into an old stone foundation. He hung back in the trees while they draped their hiding place with branches and then drove away. He told Grant about it when he got back to the house.

"These people could show us a thing or two about hiding stuff," Grant said admiringly.

"Yeah, or get themselves killed by the cow police."

Grant sighed.

"Still fighting my instinct to tie up and gag Shane and hold him in the basement until this is all over."

"How successful do you think that would be?"

"Not at all, which is why I'm not seriously considering it. Never really could control him."

"That's what you like about him, right? You didn't warn any of the rest of your stable."

"That's true. There's a lot to admire about him, qualities that I'm beginning to realize are passed down from his parents."

Dylan pointed to the screen where Cai Delaney was frozen in the motion of shoveling corn.

"Was he standing behind a tree when ingenuity and risk-taking were handed out?"

"I don't know. The risk of getting to know people through CTV footage is that you really don't know who they are at bottom. I suspect that Cai Delaney is a rule-follower, which is why he became a lawyer. He's got a wife. That changes a man's view of the world. And because he's not been a rebel, he's never had reason to utilize the sorts of skills Shane did. Two men started at the same place, but they took different paths. The interesting question is ... is virtual slavery for a few days going to change who Cai is?"

"What do you think?"

"Don't know. I know ... or think I know ... how it would affect Shane, but his brother ... I just don't know."

"Lunch," Emily called down the stairs.

"Coming," Grant called back. "After dinner, we're going to do another fun family thing and then you wait until tomorrow to come down here again. Got it?"

"Yes, sir. The sun on my face felt good today."

"Good. Outdoors in a place like this means something entirely different than what it meant in San Diego. Hopefully, in time, you'll come to appreciate it."

"Or die of boredom."

They both laughed before heading up the stairs to join the rest of the family.

A Memory of Burning Huts

Mara Wells, Kansas

It reminded him of burning huts in Vietnam only this time, he was one of the villagers. If Stan believed in karma, he'd recognize it biting him in the ass right now. The Belknaps were huddled on the lawn while the USDA were hauling canned goods out of their kitchen. Mr. Belknap had blood streaming down his forehead where he'd been pistol-whipped. Michael Tully sighed beside Stan. His parents had been gone on a trip when the bombs blew up and his sister lived in Emmaus now, so at 19 years old, he was in charge of the family home.

"I always thought my father was crazy when he'd say men like my brothers would come and do this if needed." Michael was tall with long limbs, dark hair and gray eyes. If Stan hadn't known better, he might have mistaken Michael for his own son. He certainly looked more like him than Paul did. "Yeah. That's what they're trained to do. You learn from your dad?"

343

"I hope so. I don't know."

Stan nodded. Everyone who had any place to hide something had hidden it in the last few days. The Wolf's Head mine practically overflowed with food and the farmers had taken their equipment to the Emmaus Salt Mine, hoping that would be enough. But some folks hadn't listened. Some folks hadn't believed. Others didn't trust their fellow citizens. He wondered how much of other people's stuff Michael had crammed into what Bob Tully called "the inner sanctum"?

The good news ... if you could call it that ... was that the sun dropped lower and lower into the west and Stan had detailed a crew to go stop the windmill that supplied power to Mara Wells. After sunset, the power would go down and the USDA wouldn't be able to search as efficiently.

Rumdale's assistant, a very pretty woman, came sashaying up to Stan where he sat on the Tullys' porch.

"This your home?"

"No, it's mine," Michael said.

"How old are you?"

"My parents were out of town when the bombs hit. I'm watching it for them."

"Hmm, I guess that explains the sorry state of your pantry."

"Yeah, they were due back days ago."

"Mayor, where's your house?"

"Two doors down. I left It unlocked for you."

She looked at her clipboard.

"Some interesting dietary choices," she remarked. "Are you a bachelor?"

"Wife and I divorced 15 years ago. I eat what I like."

"Seems like this whole town doesn't have much in the way of food."

"It's the times, miss. We stock up at the Cosco, but when it didn't get the shipment last week ...."

"We keep hearing that from you folks. You do know it's the death penalty if we catch you hoarding?"

"Yeah, I was force rangers in Vietnam. I probably know better than you do."

Rumdale came out of the Tullys' kitchen.

"We got all of it. Sorry, kid. But if you're the only one home, then we can only leave two weeks' for you."

Michael stared straight ahead, avoiding Rumdale's gaze.

"It's okay, kid. There'll be a redistribution center," Stan assured him, hoping he didn't sound too insincere.

The USDA continued down the street as the sun dropped between the trees. Stan could only hope the sun finished its course before the USDA found anything worth finding.

Cost of a Ration Card

Santa Fe, New Mexico

The Southwestern desert nodded in the autumn sun. Alicia Sanchez (or whatever, as she always said in her head upon using her husband's false last name) pulled a wet sheet out of the laundry basket and dropped it over the clothesline, spreading it out, placing pins along the length to keep it in place. Her mother still used the old wooden pins. They felt smooth in her fingers, worn by decades of use.

"Do you want some lemonade, *mijo* ?" Magdela Esquibel had already filled the glass and brought it out to the back yard. It wasn't as if she could turn it down at this point.

"Of course, Mami. Put it on the table. I'll just finish this up and then I'll join you."

Magdela smiled and moved to the table. A moment later, Alicia smelled the familiar stench of her lighting a cigarette.

"Has Miguel called you this morning?"

"No. He can't always get away."

"He needs to work on that." Magdela rolled smoke around in her mouth. Alicia's stomach burbled. She sniffed the pillow case she picked from the basket. The fresh scent of detergent helped. At least Magdela never smoked in the house.

Alicia hadn't realized how much she'd missed Santa Fe until she'd come back here with Mike last week. She loved the architecture and the outdoor living. Two sides of the back yard were formed by the adobe house and the third by the detached adobe garage. The vigas had been extended over a stone patio to make an outdoor living room off the kitchen that Magdela had decorated with a glass table and rattan sofas wrapped in orange outdoor material. A hammered metal chimenea graced one corner of the patio and planters of bright flowers defined the edge. An ash tree shaded a good half of the raked gravel yard beyond the patio and the clothes lines ran from the house to the fence in the other half. A fountain consisting of old wash bins surrounded by some big green plants arranged against the garage wall finished the space that had a decided sit-down-and-relax vibe. Alicia and her brothers had played soccer in a nearby playground and Magdela had often sent them to swim in the arroyo if they complained about not having a swimming pool. Her father, a truck driver, had not been around much. Magdela claimed they were still married, but he bounced back and forth between Mexico and the States and among many women's beds. Alicia knew of at least three half-siblings just north of the border.

Done with the laundry, Alicia sat down on one of the sofas, rubbing the small of her back. At 16 weeks, she felt the changes in her body. She grimaced when Magdela lit a second cigarette from the butt of her first.

"Don't you mock me, *mijo*? It's my life. I'll do what I want."

"Even if it kills you?"

"It hasn't yet."

"Those high blood pressure pills in your medicine chest say different."

Magdela opened her mouth to retort, but down the alleyway, Mrs. Pacheco's dog barked and someone swore roundly. Then a shot rang out across the neighborhood, the crack ringing off the adobe structures and tile roofs.

"Dios mio." . Magdela surged up out of her chair. This wasn't a neighborhood where drivebys happened regularly. Magdela's modest income as a bus driver had assured them a safe neighborhood with neighbors who were too busy working regular jobs to traffic in drugs. Alicia had lived in a neighborhood like that in San Diego. The first drivebys to happen when Mike had been present, he'd asked her to move in together, somewhere else. After her father's laissez faire attitude toward family, she'd been surprised by Mike's domesticity. Being a mercenary aside, he had a soft spot for home and hearth.

"Let's go into the house." Alicia steered her that way. Magdela tossed her cigarette on the ground to stomp on it. Loud voices drifted down the alley. Mrs. Pacheco sounded like she was crying, mixing English and Spanish together liberally. The patio door opened onto the old-fashioned kitchen with its rustic mission style. Beyond the muslin curtains on the front window, they could see a panel truck in the street. "Put Pepe in the bedroom, Mami. I think this is what Mike warned us about."

Swearing in Spanish, Magdela swept up her mini schnauzer from the white-wrapped sofa and carried him into the master bedroom just as the doorbell rang. Alicia took a deep calming breath and answered the door. *My husband is a big bad mercenary. I can do this.*

The white man on the porch smiled. He was tall with vaguely reddish hair and blue eyes.

"Ron Bannon. I'm from FEMA – Federal Emergency Management Administration. I'm sorry to disturb you today, but we've been sent to allocate resources to assure there are no shortages." Alicia wondered if he'd been a used car salesman at some point. He had the same fake sincerity they all had. She'd hate to think that might be bred into some people. "How are you fixed for food?"

"We're getting a little tight." She decided to match his hard sell with a soft sell and see which one worked better. "We have a few more days."

"Do you mind if I come in and take inventory?"

Magdela walked up behind Alicia.

"Que quiere el pendejo?"

"Mami, English please." They had agreed for Magdela to play the simple Mexican woman if it came to that, but Magdela had surprised Alicia by taking to the role.

"Hi, ma'am. Ron Bannon. I'm from FEMA." He held up an official looking badge, apparently unaware that Magdela had called him an idiot. "Just checking to make sure people have adequate food and medicine. I need to come in and inspect."

"We're fine. My sister said you've been giving out ration cards in other neighborhoods. We've got a few more days of food, but then we'll need some help."

"Of course, ma'am. Can I see what you have on hand, please?"

"You want to come into my house?"

"Yes, ma'am."

"Que hacemos?"

"We let him in, Mami."

When he was halfway across the living room, Peppy barked from the bedroom and his hand twitched towards his gun, but he shook his fingers out. Alicia remembered the 45 Mike had insisted on her packing and wished she'd thought to wear it. Of course, if her clothes were any indication, the concealed carry belt wouldn't still fit.

"Thank you for securing the dog. What's in that room?"

"The master bedroom." Alicia wanted very much to keep him from that room because relocating Magedela's bed to hide the entrance to the smuggler room seemed obvious. "The bathroom," she indicated the door to the right. "A guest room." That was the next door to the right. "And there's a bunk room upstairs." A circular staircase graced one corner of the living room. As the only girl, she'd always had that corner bedroom while the boys had shared the bunk room, but Magdela used the bunk room for her art studio now. She made more selling her paintings than she did driving bus these days.

"So where do you keep your food?" Like a lot of houses in New Mexico, the Esquibel house wasn't that large. A lot of living happened on the patio. Some past owner had built a breezeway between the garage and the house and that had been the phenomenally well-stocked pantry until just the other day. Bannon stared around the pantry's mostly barren shelves. They hadn't been able to come up with much to replace all the boxes and bins they'd moved into the smuggling chamber under the house.

"Big room. Lots of shelves."

"When my husband was here, he liked to stock up."

"You don't?"

"No money." That might have been true if Magdela had been sloppy with her money, but she wasn't. So long as the neighbors didn't start talking about their crazy survivalist neighbor ... but

Magdela didn't invite many people into this storeroom. Bannon pointed to the large blank area beside the washing machine.

"What used to be here?"

"Freezer." He raised an eyebrow. "I gave it to my son. Now I buy fresh turkeys."

Bannon smiled, then walked into the kitchen, speaking over his shoulder.

"It's too bad you couldn't stock up." He opened cabinets one by one, then opened the fridge and freezer. "You're right. You only have a few days' food here." He put his clip board on the counter and began filling a form out. "How many people live here?"

"Just the two of us."

"I'm – I'm pregnant."

Bannon stared at her for a moment.

"You married?"

"He was away." She tried to look worried

"Have you heard from him?"

Don't look left.

"No. We lived in San Diego before, so ...." Her voice actually grew hoarse.

"That's too bad." His gaze slid down her body. "Sign this line " He handed Magdela the clipboard and placed three white plastic cards on the counter. "Gotta make sure you're getting milk and stuff." He held a business card out to Alicia. "If you need anything, you can call me." He smiled at her warmly, gaze settling on her chest.

"I'll remember that," she replied, making a show of sliding it under a magnet strip on the fridge. They walked him to the door, all calm and respectful.

"We're so lucky he thought you are pretty," Magdela remarked.

"Yeah, lucky, until he decides he wants payment for the third ration card."

Outside the truck started up and moved through the intersection to the next block. Magdela straightened.

"I'm going to see Mrs. Pacheco and comfort her for the dog. Joe was a good dog."

"He was. Tell her I feel her grief." When Magdela had left, Alicia sat down on the sofa and shivered for a few minutes, thinking how really close they were walking toward death. The television reports said that hoarding carried a death sentence ... but wasn't starvation also a death sentence?

A Friend at Ballard Market

When Wes Marcus saw that the busses were running again, he decided to go to the Ballard Market.

"We need food," he reasoned.

"You will expose us." Geo Tully could be an advertisement for Navy Seals – fit, short hair, clear blue eyes, and single-minded. If he decided to climb Everest tonight with just the gear on hand, he'd do it, plant a flag on top and return in the same night. But he saw everybody outside the door as a potential enemy and Wes had to keep reminding himself that this was Seattle, not Fallujah.

"I'm not as dumb as you think I am and dressed in civilian clothes, they won't know who I am. That's one reason I'm not taking the truck, in case someone is looking for it."

They had stolen a truck to make their escape on Saturday. This morning's news had included the massacre at the shopping center, blaming it on military aggression. There'd been no mention of stolen vehicles, but the owner could well be dead although Knight Industries was claiming only two civilian deaths. Reviewing his memory, Wes thought that could possibly be true. The military had been their targets. The public had just been innocent bystanders. The mayor had felt it necessary to hire Knight Industries to protect the people of Seattle. The military were encamped around Microsoft and Amazon, but the Knights were working to dislodge them. Mayor Sollis told a lurid tale of abuses and illegitimate government leaders issuing unconscionable orders.

"What do you think?" Wes asked.

"I don't know. I saw things ... crowd control. I'm not sure we were on the side of the angels. But my doubts won't keep us alive if we get caught. How are you paying for this?"

"Aunt Joyce had a few hundred squirreled away here."

"If you get caught, don't bring the rain down on me."

"I won't ... get caught or rat on you."

People filled the bus to Ballard Market because Bunnell & Wilson had called a limit on gasoline sales. Wes stood, hanging onto an upright, listening to the people around him talk. Life seemed almost normal except for the discussion of ration cards being issued by Bunnell & Wilson.

"It's almost like they're in control of the country now," one woman whispered to her seatmate.

"I'm not objecting," the man said. "My wife was in the Seattle Center internment camp and they released her yesterday."

"Why was she in the camp?"

"Arguing with a soldier over what shopping center she was supposed to go to. Bunnell & Wilson is at least not locking up civilians."

No, they were just shooting them as they ran away. Or were they? He had been too busy trying to stay alive that he'd not really kept count.

"So, was it easy to get a ration card?" a man asked a woman.

"I had to present ID and they checked my name on the computer, but it wasn't hard."

Wes had brought his driver's license only because he didn't want to risk an association with the military. Maybe they wouldn't delve too deeply. He decided to risk it. Without food, this whole hiding thing wasn't going to last long.

A long line of people waited to get into the Market. Wes kept his head down and developed a newfound practice of prayer. Knights in black Kevlar with side arms but no rifles were in evidence. He hoped his sporting clothes would hide him in plain sight, but then he heard one of the Knights say "Wes?"

He looked up instead of pretending he hadn't heard him and in that instant, he knew he'd been identified. Vic McCann lived three doors down from his parents and they'd been in school together from kindergarten to graduation.

"Hey," Wes said, trying not to show his terror. He saw memory dawn on Vic's face. The last time they'd seen one another, Wes had been wearing his fatigues. Vic glanced over his shoulder and stepped a little closer.

"You need to come with me. There's nothing to be concerned about. Just follow me around the corner." Vic spoke into his shoulder mic. "I'm doing a perimeter check."

Somewhat convinced that Vic didn't mean to haul him away as an enemy combatant, Wes followed him around the building.

"You don't lack for guts," Vic admired in a low voice. "Had you presented ID here, you'd have been hauled away to the detention center."

"So they're not killing us outright?"

"The cooperative ones are being allowed to live, except for the Special Forces. They don't want them getting together and staging a rebellion. Where have you been hiding?"

"I can't tell you that, obviously."

"Right. Sorry." Vic reached into his chest pocket. "Here, take these and get into the other line. Supposedly, they're going to renew monthly. Wilson means well and he's bringing in more food."

"Thanks. Any idea how long this is supposed to last."

"No idea. They got Portland mostly contained. Should be another couple of days. We'll know more then."

"Thank you for this." Wes patted his pocket where three of the four ration cards now nestled.

"I owe you for getting me through algebra, man. Your folks, they looked okay when I went to see mine yesterday, but don't risk coming around. They're watching traffic cams near suspected homes."

"Good to know. I better get my groceries and get out of here before anybody else recognizes me."

Shopping went pretty easily after that. The food cost twice what it had before the bombs, but the ATM machines were working now, so Wes took out a couple hundred before heading back to Ballard.

"You sure you weren't followed," Geo asked when he told him what had happened.

"There are not a lot of people out on the streets and I didn't see anyone behind me. I even doubled back once to make sure."

Geo scanned the street through a crack in the curtains.

"You didn't tell him where you were staying?"

"No! I'm not an idiot. And, you should know, they're executing guys like you. Special Forces – they see it as a control technique."

Geo's blue eyes caught the light for a moment and then he turned away.

"Then I guess you're going to be doing the shopping."

Guys like him ... was fear trained out of them or were they born that way and training just gelled what they had always been?

Death Comes Calling

Mara Wells, Kansas

Stan prepared to text Rob to tell him he'd miscalculated and the USDA would have time to visit Emmaus when angry words sounded down the street and then a shot rang out. By the time he'd run the half block to Gary Carter's place, his friend's body grew cold and the USDA worker who had shot him was in tears. The first kill was always the hardest. Stan still remembered his.

"What the hell?" he bellowed.

"He was going for a weapon," she croaked. "He wouldn't let me in the house and then he was reaching for a gun."

Gary Carter didn't own any guns. A Quaker by birth who had been transplanted to Kansas by love of his wife, he hadn't believed in violence, even in self-defense. They'd never know what he was reaching for. She'd fired through the door and his life had ended. Blood pooled on the wood floor under the half-open door. Gary's hands were both empty. He'd died the same way he'd lived. Stan had to force himself to keep his hands at his side and not grab the gun away from her to shoot her in the head.

"These things happen, Anderson," the USDA commander said as he strode up, seemingly fully informed by the earpiece. "Hand over your weapon to Carboy and withdraw to your vehicle. You're not in trouble, Susan, but we need to follow protocol."

Rumdale scanned the street where people began to gather.

"This is what happens when you resist," he called. "Go back into your houses. Did he have family?" The last sentence was quietly spoken, meant for Stan only.

"His wife is probably at their daughter's house."

"My crew will clean this mess up. You should probably go break the news to her." Stan stared at Rumdale in stunned silence. "Do you have a problem with that?"

"A man is dead. It's not a mess. It's a murder."

"That man was reaching for a gun and, trust me, my superiors will believe me over you."

Stan remembered that attitude from Vietnam. He'd been the one to exhibit it. Karma was a total bitch. Rumdale detailed his people to prepare the body for burial and to clean up the blood -- preferable to burning the house down, but barely. When Stan hadn't moved, Rumdale leaned in.

"What part of this don't you understand? We're in charge now and people like you need to comply or we will force compliance from you. Your job is to inform the widow that her husband violated the law and was given the appropriate punishment."

Stan envisioned Rumdale's neck beneath his fingers, but he knew that any attempt of that kind would result in his death, so he turned away from the carnage and strode to his house where his truck waited. He tried to put the key in the ignition, but a lump the size of Mars formed in his throat and tears spilled down his cheeks. Snot leaked into his moustache. They had been so incredibly stupid and these were the consequences of folly.

Water Break

Hutchinson, Kansas

The sun beat down on Cai's head, reminding him of summers haying Schoenfeld's fields, except that Shoenfeld allowed water breaks. Cai shoved his bucket into the truck of corn and heaved it up into the makeshift silo. His neck and forearms ached from the effort at the same time they crisped from the sun.

Where's your sunscreen? Shane, who never burned, had always made sure Cai and Keri remembered the bottle on the way out the door. Sweat dripped into Cai's eyes. He paused to wipe it away. In front of him, he could see a half-dozen exhausted people working in the midday sun. Even Brian looked sunburned.

"Pick up the pace," the vulture soldier ordered.

God, why is this happening? What is it you want me to learn from this?

Ask and you will receive. You have not because you don't ask.

"I'm getting dizzy." Cai's insides quaked with fear. "I've worked out like this before, but we had regular water breaks."

Nobody stopped working and Cai turned back to his task, but then the soldier told him to go get water. Cai didn't hesitate. The water had grown warm in the sun, but at least it was wet. While he drank his bottle slowly, he heard what he had feared. Larry.

"We all need a break." Larry, the labor union organizer, thought they were still living in 21st century America. "If you don't give us water breaks, you're going to disable your work crew."

Everybody stopped working and wiped sweat. Cai took an instinctive step back. The Vulture examined the crew.

"You." Cai gave him his immediate attention. "Get back to work." Cai climbed back up on the truck. "You, lady, climb down. The rest of you get back to work." After that, he let each of them have a water break separately, making Larry wait until the last.

The fairgrounds sweltered in the heat. Being October, it had to break soon. Occasionally, Cai wondered if perhaps the heat wasn't really the sun. Could it be radiation? Nobody's hair was falling out yet, but he supposed they'd be wondering about the unseen danger for a good long time.

The trucks kept coming in. Today, it was all corn, obviously pillaged from grain elevators. There were more efficient ways of transferring the corn,

Cai knew, but apparently FEMA didn't. During those few minutes they had at meals to talk, Larry had offered a "plan" to change things "for the better." If they all stuck together, they could force the soldiers into being more humane.

"There's not many of them. If we refuse to cooperate, they can't make us."

"They have guns." Brian barely spoke above a whisper, rightfully terrified of the stun gun.

"I'm not saying we make a break for the fences. I'm suggesting we negotiate for breaks and water to start."

Well, that had worked, to Cai's immense relief. Water meant a clearer head and a faster pace and those were the keys to avoiding punishment around here. He could only hope Larry's scheme would reflect only on Larry and not on a bunch of other people, including himself. For April's sake, Brian had every reason to go along to get along and so did he. Thirty days was a long time in these circumstances, but it was better than the alternative.

Dinner at the Lufgrens

Emmaus, Kansas

The sun settled low in the west when Shane
arrived. Poppy had been waiting for him and Kerri
heard her launch herself noisily from the porch
stairs where she'd been shelling peas.

Shane swept her into a swirl and the two began
signing as soon as he set her down.

"Where have you been?" Poppy asked.

"Harvesting corn."

"Today, yeah. Before?"

"Before when?"

"Don't be zero-in-brain. Before-way-back!"

Shane sighed, then finger-spelled. That far
away, Keri couldn't read it. Poppy signed San Diego.
She wasn't buying it, however.

"You soldier."

"I don't want to talk about that." Shane had
been signing since he was a kindergartener, so he

knew how to use his body. There was no doubt of his intensions.

"You hero you. Why not?"

"No hero! Killer!"

Shane strode away from her toward the house then, leaving Poppy to look sad.

Why does he tell her what he won't tell us?

Shane paused on the back porch. She could hear him let the screen door close softly. The pause lengthened to where she was about to step out the kitchen door and demand to know what he was waiting for, but then he stepped into the opening.

"Hey, big brother."

She'd hugged softer statues. He'd showered before he'd come and smelled of soap. He didn't put his arms around her, so she held him a little longer than she would have. She felt him stiffen even further. When she pulled her head back to look at him, he quickly covered his distress with an expression she couldn't read.

"You okay?" she asked.

"Yeah. How are you?"

"Worried about my brother."

"Don't be. You need any help with dinner?"

"You're a guest. Alex is taking a shower. You want some lemonade?"

"Sure. I'll get it. You work on dinner. You want a glass?"

Shane opened the cabinet where the glasses used to be kept, frowned at the plates, then laughed.

"Right. This is someone else's kitchen now."

Giggling, she pointed to the cabinet next to the fridge.

"Just for that, I'm not putting ice in your lemonade."

"You still drink it without ice?" He laughed in answer. "Seriously, how are you doing?"

"Life as we knew it ended last week. How do you think I am? Probably about the same as you."

"Things appear to be returning to normal. We have power again."

"Stan called. FEMA is in Mara Wells, stripping what's left in the Cosco."

Alex came down the stairs just in time to hear Shane's announcement.

"I'm only halfway done with my organic field. That's seed for next year if this is going the way you think."

"We'll get it done. We can work tonight, right?"

"Yeah, but we're out of places to stash it."

"No, we're not." Alex raised a sandy eyebrow. "I'm devious by nature, Alex. Trust me."

"Yeah, I do. So, you think we're good until morning?"

"They'll stop at every farm along the way. We got time."

"Good. Then let's get dinner on the table," Keri decided.

Alex stared at her uncertainly, until Shane straightened up from the counter.

"I'll go get Poppy."

"Pete, Mark and Alice too."

"Where are they?"

"Just ring the dinner bell," Alex suggested. "Remember, they can hear you."

Shane's tan was too deep to show if he blushed, but he looked embarrassed. Shane had already met Mark and Pete, but Alice had been at the grocery store when they'd been working in the fields this morning. Keri noted that he'd adapted to the European way of eating. She wondered where he'd picked up eating with the fork in his left hand.

"So, Alex said you're trying to build some sort of defense force for the town?" Mark said as they ate.

"Trying to wake everybody up. When … if FEMA doesn't find what we've hidden, they won't be happy and they'll push it. It can't just be me standing up to them."

"You getting any takers on that?"

"I am. A handful of veterans and the anarchists are up for town defense. Unfortunately, we're so damned spread out. It's going to be hard to protect one another like this."

"Your grandfather had an inspired idea."

"If it works. If it doesn't, that's most of our grain all in one place, easy to take."

"You didn't say anything," Alex noted.

"I didn't have a better idea. And it was an inspired idea. I didn't come up with it. I was thinking an excavator in a field somewhere."

"Yeah, that wouldn't have worked ... not with the time we've got. The damp would have given us hominy."

"Yummo," Keri sang. All five adults laughed.

"So where are we sticking my organic field?"

"What are we talking about?" Pete asked, turning from his signed conversation with Poppy. He was interpreting.

"You've learned sign pretty fast," Shane remarked. He set his fork down and signed for Poppy's sake. "We're talking about hiding corn and how to defend the town."

"Can we do it?" Poppy asked. Remembering that his parents didn't know sign very well, Pete interpreted.

Shane opened his mouth as if to answer, then closed it and looked at the adults.

"We need you to help defend the farm," Alex signed and spoke to Poppy. "What Pete does is his parents' choice."

"You know my situation?" Mark asked Shane.

"I know you're an ex-felon. I understand why you don't want to risk your freedom for a bunch of people you've only just met. And, I hope that works out well for you."

Alice muttered something in Spanish. Mark blushed and Shane laughed. Alice looked flabbergasted.

"He's pretty fluent," Mark reported.

"I lived in Central and South American for a year and my best friend and partner for most of the last five years is Chicano."

"What were you doing in the south?" Mark asked.

Shane hesitated for a heartbeat.

"Flying airplanes."

He's a liar and he's comfortable with it.

"Airplanes filled with ...?"

"Cargo." Mark stared at him. "I didn't get paid to ask."

"Is that what you were doing in the Middle East?" Alice asked. Shane stared at her. "People talk."

"Of course, they do, especially about me. Sometimes I flew airplanes, sometimes I drove trucks."

"That's not what folks are saying," Alex said.

"They wondering where I got the small-arms skills?"

Poppy's eyes were like Delft saucers.

"Something like that. It might be easier if you just told them the truth."

"I can't. I told you. I signed agreements not to talk about it. So, can we change the subject?"

"We'd better finish up eating and get out to the fields." Alex nodded to where the window started to reflect their images. "We can lead you to a good place, but we can't make you stay."

"No, you can't."

Always the realist, Shane sounded comfortable with his lot in life, but his eyes seemed sad. He pushed back his plate.

"I'm heading out to get started. We're hiding the corn in the hotel. I installed a bag silo in the basement. And it's more secure than the bank, so I think it'll hold it."

Poppy and Pete followed him out the door.

"Is he right?" Mark asked as Alex wiped his mouth.

"Right? About?"

"What's coming?"

"Probably, but there's lots of people available to take up guns. What I need from you is your mechanics skills."

"Good, because my kids and wife need me this side of the bars."

"I told him that."

"What did he mean by he hoped it worked out okay for me?"

"I don't know, but you know, you'll be working with him all night, so maybe you should ask him."

Alex grabbed his cap and kissed Keri on the mouth.

"When you get cleaned up in here, we could use your help."

"I'll be there."

He and Mark went out the back door. Keri stared after them, stomach tightening. Alice began to collect plates. What more could they do? Keri could see Shane frightened Alice and Keri agreed with her. This wasn't her brother. It was just a man with his face who happened to have the best ideas for how to survive this mess.

Trust No One

Hutchinson, Kansas

Jared of FEMA, who really did seem like a nice guy, was using a cell phone and that meant there had to be service now. Cai wet his shirt with water from the hose and flipped up his collar to sooth his sunburn. His hands were burned too, but he couldn't do much about those in the time he had. Jared slid his phone back in his pocket and came to where Cai was trying to cool down.

"Ouch. That looks painful."

"It would have been so much worse If I hadn't already have had a tan. Can I ask a favor?"

"Sunscreen? I haven't seen any come through, but I can ask if we can get some ... not just for you, but for everyone else."

"That's great, but what I was hoping is that you'd let me use your cell phone." Jared's eyebrow quirked. "I just want to let my wife know that I'm okay."

"Can't do it, man. The soldiers have been clear on that subject."

"Then if I gave you the number, could you call her?"

Jared frowned, but then nodded. Cai told him the numbers ... both Marnie's cell phone and his parents' house phone ... and Jared wrote it down on a notebook.

"It'll be tonight."

"Thank you."

"Don't tell anyone. I can't do it for everyone."

"Got it."

"And I won't tell her where you are, just that you're all right. We can't have families showing up here, breaking the shelter-in-place order."

"I understand. Thank you."

Cai headed back to his work assignment, mood buoyed by the suspicion that Shane had the means to track the call's location. Brian looked ready to explode as Cai joined him in unloading boxes from a truck.

"You okay, man?"

"No. I haven't seen April all day and I'm getting worried."

"They probably just took her to work remotely. It'll be okay."

"She's not your wife."

"I know, but what else are you going to do, but wait?"

They worked steadily, Cai's sunburned skin growing hot again, until the guards called meal break. They lined up for the chow line, a bedraggled looking April a few lines away, when two soldiers braced Cai. The jolt of electricity chased away any thought of protest or resistance and then they dragged him away from the line.

"When are you people going to learn?" The Vulture followed behind Cai and the two soldiers who were there to make sure he kept moving. When Cai stumbled and went down on one knee, the stun gun reminded him that he had better not do it again. The air felt cool as they approached a row of connexes in the RV parking lot.

"I don't understand. Why are you doing this?"

They walked him into one of the connexes.

The stun gun in his side sent him to his knees and then a fist smacked down on his right ear and the side of his face. A foot slammed into his left hip. The Vulture leaned in and whispered.

"Stop arguing or we will be forced to kill you."

The second stun gunning left him gasping and innervated on the floor. They slammed the door as Cai struggled to regain his feet. He pushed against it with shaking hands, knowing he couldn't open it. His nose wasn't broken, but blood flowed down his upper lip and into his mouth. Taking a deep breath hurt. Except for some light that leaked through the crack between the two door-halves, he had no light. He felt around the walls and found nothing until his foot encountered a bucket in the far corner.

Solitary confinement? But why? What had he done to deserve this?

And then it occurred to him. He'd trusted Jared.

Dance of the Combines

Emmaus, Kansas

Shane and Mark admired how Alex and Micah coordinated running two harvesters at the same time while their support crew raked up stray stalks and cobs and hauled them away.

While Mark and Shane worked pitchforks, Mark tried to explain his reticence to help defend the town.

"Just staying in a house where there are guns is a federal crime for me. I wouldn't have agreed to it a week ago. If there's no federal government anymore ... or one so disorganized it can't come looking for me ... I'll change my way of doing things, but right now ... my family is my priority."

"I get it," Shane assured him. "But time is coming fast when protecting yourself is going to be needed. That's all I'm saying. I don't think any of us are getting out of this unscathed."

"I hear what you're saying."

Micah's son Nehemiah gave a whoop to let everybody who could hear know that Micah had finished his circuit. A moment later, Alex flashed his lights to let everybody know he'd finished too. Nehemiah ran for the truck to haul the trailer away while Micah climbed down to begin unhitching it. Poppy already had the truck ready for Alex's load.

"They really know what they're doing, don't they?" Mark said, indicating the two teenagers.

"You grow up on a farm, you get good at what you do."

"What would have happened to them if the bombs hadn't gone off?"

"You mean because they're deaf?" Mark nodded. "Same thing that happens to most teenagers. Poppy was applying to Gallaudet. She wanted to be a teacher. I'm not sure about Nehemiah, but he likely would have inherited the farm, leaving his younger siblings to decide what they want to do with their lives. Deaf can do any job that doesn't require hearing. If people accommodate the deafness, that's a huge range of jobs."

"And now?"

"They know what they're doing and we're the grunt laborers."

Mark laughed.

With the two trucks gone, Shane and Mark joined Alex and Micah on Micah's harvester.

"We did," Micah proclaimed proudly, a big grin on his jovial face. Shane leaned back against the cab and stared up at the stars. They'd won this battle, but a larger war loomed. Would they all still be alive tomorrow? A shiver ran down his back. The sound of glass clinking together brought his attention back to earth. Micah had set a cooler on the tire and held out a bottle of Samuel Addams to Shane.

"Nice you here you," Micah signed as Shane took the bottle.

"Glad here me," Shane replied.

"You kid drink?" Micah asked Mark who of course didn't understand. Alex interpreted.

"He's underage."

"Don't care me," Micah said. "Give Poppy, okay?"

"One," Alex signed. Mark's mouth dropped open. "You sure?" Micah asked, this time through Shane.

"You won't get more work out of him tonight."

"Work's done. Beer. Duh."

Mark laughed.

"He can have one."

Shane indicated the cooler.

"I'll take. Want to check."

Shane slid the cooler into the bed of Alex's truck and headed toward the Jericho hotel where he'd left a basement window open so they could fill the bag silo. He could hear Alice and Keri shoveling corn into the ancient conveyor Alex had resurrected from his bone yard. Shane had worked the elevators one summer and knew from the sound that the silo was about quarter full. He walked around the front of the two trucks, carrying the cooler and nearly tripped over Pete and Poppy on the ground, kissing passionately. Pete exhaled in surprise, which alerted Poppy. She hastily buttoned the top of her shirt.

Laughing, Shane put the cooler up on the hood.

"Victory beers," he said for Pete's sake and so Keri and Alice could hear him too. "After you're done. Your folks said you could each have one and one only. The rest are for the ladies." Then, silently, he signed. "Come here."

He gestured for them to follow him around to the front of the trucks. He talked and signed at the same time, no easy task.

"That, I don't care about, but you should know that leads to pregnancy and this is not a good time for that. Go get some condoms before you screw it up and, Poppy, go talk to Marnie about your options. C-o-n-t-r-a-c-e-p-t-i-o-n. And, Pete," now Shane stopped signing. "If you're just wanting to get laid and you don't really care about her, walk away. Because if you leave her knocked up, I will kill you and I am not bluffing on that. Go talk to Jason Breen. He's got some women out at his compound who will make you all warm and fuzzy for not that much money. Got it?"

"Yeah." By the wan light of the quarter moon, it was hard to tell if Pete might be blushing. Poppy still was. "We were just ...."

"I know what you were just." Shane resumed talking and signing at the same time. "And, like I said, I don't care. That's not the answer you would have gotten from Alex." Pete's eyes widened. Poppy looked even more embarrassed.

"You tell him you?" she asked.

"No. But don't be stupid. Okay?"

She nodded. Pete swallowed audibly, probably contemplating what it would feel like for Alex to break every bone in his body.

"You two have known each other a week – two. Maybe this is going a little fast."

"We weren't ...." Poppy signed.

"It's a small step from kissing on the ground with your shirt unbuttoned to making babies."

Pete definitely blushed at Shane's sign for sex.

"Enough said. One each, no more and stay away from each other after because beer makes you forget good sense."

Still laughing, Shane headed back to the truck, leaving the two teenagers staring after him, a clear six inches apart.

Raw Nerves

Hutchinson, Kansas

Mike Sanchez arrived at Hutchinson, Kansas with his last shred of patience tattered. They were two hours behind schedule because they'd stopped in Hayes to pick up another package for Sullivan. He had only eaten some bread from an MRE since breakfast. The water was warm and the smell of cigarettes from the back of the truck started to annoy him. Hell, he'd been annoyed already. Killing civilians had never been part of the deal. He had no problem with killing foreigners who rebelled against American control, but these were Americans and that bothered him. What bothered him more was that some of the men on his crew didn't seem at all concerned about it.

Back when Eric ... er, Shane ... had been his partner, they'd occasionally talked about it. Thinking back, it should have been clear that Ric wasn't just a mercenary, but his thoughts on some subjects might have kept a smarter man guessing. He'd objected to abusing the Miristani. He sympathized with them over the American invasion of their country. He'd also been the one to note that the Knights who had been trained by the US military were much more willing to abuse the citizenry than the freelancers were. Mike had observed it after Ric had pointed it out and now he saw seeing it on parade ... writ large.

This is not what I signed up for. I have standards. I don't kill Americans.

When his phone vibrated, he thought it would be Crispin responding to his request for guidance. Lawson had been acting way too amped up and it had nearly led to another shooting at the next town. Even the other Knights were beginning to suggest they tie the kid up before he killed someone who they couldn't find an excuse to kill.

-I need help & it coincides w your assignment. My bro Cai is in Hutchinson. We think he's detained. Can you claim him for your crew & bring him to our town? That probably merges w your assignment for SullCorp. Ric

Mike considered the text for a moment. Of course, he would help Ric retrieve his brother, but he wasn't sure how he would manage that with this particular crew. Maybe Ric had forgotten that he'd always been the brains of the two of them.

-Curious how you know my assignment. I'll see what I can do for you.

The streets of Hutchinson were dark and quiet as they rolled up to the fairground gates. Except for a cat that ran across their path, everybody seemed to be honoring the curfew. Mike got out to speak to the gatekeeper, who spoke to his higher ups. The gates were rolled open to admit their three trucks. According to Mike's phone, the fairgrounds had become a redistribution center manned by a patrol under Lieutenant Wilkins, who was acting as provost martial. FEMA had a contingent of agents here, but mostly they were utilizing people who had violated martial law provisions. There were perhaps 300 detainees, 50 FEMA workers and two dozen soldiers.

"Lieutenant Wilkins says you can bunk in B Tent," a FEMA worker named Jared said. He seemed really nervous about something. ""We'll get a crew working on unloading the trucks."

"Number 87 actually should be filled with food stuffs. We're on orders from the Governor's Office." Mike showed the order on his phone, which Jared took a copy of. Jared ordered a worker to set a crew on loading the truck. Lawson and Gallante were to assist and then guard.

"It'll be ready for you in the morning. How are things in Wichita?"

"They're starting to experience some shortages."

"That stinks. The rural districts are resistant to handing over their excess, but we're getting it done."

"Good. Um, I was told to look for a detainee here .... Malacai Delaney."

A shadow passed across Jared's face and his eyes averted to the left.

"I don't know the name, but I'll ask around."

"He's related to the Governor, so we want to take him with us when we go."

"Like I said, I don't think he's here, but I'll ask."

As they walked to their tent for the night, Jacobson eased up beside Mike.

"There's something fishy going on here."

"You mean fishier than keeping American citizens on slave gangs?"

"Yeah. You expect some things like that during martial law, but there's something ... the FEMA workers won't meet our eyes. It's like they're scared."

"Don't get caught, but see what you can find out."

Jacobson dropped back and away, dissolving into the night, his black uniform making him one with the shadows. Mike continued to the tent where his men would sleep.

Sing Your Praise to the Lord

Cai leaned in the corner of two steel walls, hands tucked into his underarms, shivering. He'd been more comfortable during his night in the culvert. At least there, he'd had a jacket to keep him warm in his wet clothes. His stomach rumbled with hunger and his tongue clung to the roof of his mouth. The cold had chilled the water in his shirt and made his sunburn sear that much hotter. He could hear sounds out in the fairgrounds ... trucks and voices. Were they bringing in more prisoners? Maybe to replace the other people he could hear shivering in adjacent connexes.

Marnie, I'm sorry.

She hadn't fought hard for him not to go to Wichita, but she'd expressed doubts about the wisdom of it. She thought Rob should send Shane. At that time, Cai had wondered if she meant she thought Shane was more capable of a diplomatic mission than Cai, but now he thought she'd been afraid for Cai. And he hadn't heeded her warning. He'd actually prickled at her suggestion.

If I'd listened, I'd be home safe now, probably getting sunburned helping to harvest corn.

He twisted his wedding ring on his finger, all that really remained of his home. How long had it been since he'd left there? Really only three days? It felt like a lifetime since he'd seen her.

"God, why are You doing this?"

His words echoed emptily in the metal box. God wasn't doing this. People were doing this. And what would those people do tomorrow? Kill someone to make their point? Where was God in this black time? Certainly not protecting Cai from pain and suffering … not protecting anyone. They all stood a good chance of ending up dead before this ended. Ironic that they would survive the bombs, running from the Army and the rain only for him to die trapped in this stupid metal box.

Someone off to his left started humming. The person wept, so it sounded like a keen. Cai listened for a bit, trying to remember the lyrics. He knew the tune. The person stopped before he could remember it, but now his brain sought music, so he began to hum himself. At first, he just hummed to distract himself from the cold and to settle his fear, but then he recognized the song.

Though Satan should buffet, though trials
should come,
Let this blest assurance control,
That Christ has regarded my helpless estate,
And hath shed His own blood for my soul.

The person to his left joined him, her voice quavering in the chill darkness.

"It is well ... it is well ... with my soul."

They sang every verse Cai knew twice before moving on to *Amazing Grace* . When a guard stopped outside the connex, Cai halted for a moment and then he felt a surge of defiance and began belting out *Shall We Gather at the River* . The guard didn't interrupt them, but the lack of water silenced the two prisoners after a while. It had been enough, though. Cai fell asleep with the tune of *My Boat is So Small* spiraling around his brain.

Entangled Spirits

Emmaus, Kansas

"Hold my hand," Cai said. She reached for him, but his hand melted like sugar in the rain.

Marnie sat up in bed, listening to the silence of the house. No light shone at the window yet ... too early even for Shane or Jacob to be awake. Belle the cat yawned at her from the bedside chair.

What awakened her and what song played in her head? An old bluegrass gospel tune. Something about a boat in a wide ocean ... the sort of thing Cai would play with Jacob and Rob. She didn't remember the words.

It had felt like Cai lay in the bed beside her.

God, where is he? She shook her head. *Why am I asking you? It's not like I've been acknowledging you a whole lot in recent weeks.*

She remembered that first sweet feeling of forgiveness the night she'd kneeled in her room at Lawrence, giving into the gospel she'd heard for years and refused to accept. She remembered feeling God's presence even a few weeks ago. She'd been so certain of her future with Cai and living as a Christian. She'd even pushed her past with Shane far back into history. She'd been at peace for the first time in her life. So, what had happened?

What besides bombs and 100s of people dying under my watch? A baby I didn't plan. A husband who is never coming back. A brother-in-law who treats me like I have leprosy. She slipped her hand over to Cai's side of the bed. Cold.

I never promised you a rose garden.

"No, You didn't," she whispered. "I get that, but I didn't expect this."

The disciples all died violent deaths. You thought being a Christian would be easy?

She'd thought it would be ... not like this. She'd anticipated a couple of years living with the Delaneys while she and Cai paid off their school debts and then maybe moving to Denver or a similar city where she could enjoy the fruits of being a doctor married to a lawyer. Denver was glowing glass now and the world as they knew it had gone crazy. Christians were in this world, so what else could she expect but crazy?

"I expected for Cai to be here."

But I'm here, foolish child. I will always be with you ... as I am with Cai right now.

Some through the waters, some through the flood

Some through the fire, but all through the blood

The memory of Cai's hands settled on her shoulders, worked at the kinks in her muscles.

"I love you."

Marnie wiped tears away. Was Cai somewhere thinking of her too? She leaned back against the pillow. Under her hand, her belly gave this odd flutter. She blinked. It was too soon, right? And yet it felt … it felt like a tiny swimmer moving around in there.

"Oh, Cai, you need to come home," she whispered.

It is well … it is well … with my soul.

Marnie slipped back into sleep with that song drifting through her mind and thoughts of Cai somewhere else thinking of her.

Wednesday

Seven Days after the End of Life As They Knew It

Food Scarcity

Casa Blanca Hotel
New York City, Times Square

Katharine couldn't believe they were doing this, lining up at a food distribution truck for the three days of meals. With the hotel running low, no longer able to get food through regular channels, this became necessary for survival. The chef would combine their individual boxes into something delicious, she knew.

"I'll be back," Julian informed her and the Michaels. He left the line and strolled over to where the truck driver enjoyed a smoke. He offered the man a pack of cigarettes.

"I didn't know he smoked," Tamara Michaels said.

"He doesn't. He picked up a couple of cartons yesterday saying they were good for barter."

"Huh?" Phillip said. *This is why I'm paying their bills. These people lack common sense.* Julian and the trucker were standing close, whispering.

Katharine stepped up to the front of the line to accept her box, pointed to Julian and asked if she could have his too. The FEMA worker frowned, but watched Julian for a moment and then agreed. Julian finished his conversation with the trucker and hurried over to take his box.

"What was that all about?"

"Transportation out of here," he told her. "Let's get this inside and then I'll tell you."

Once they'd deposited their boxes on a table in the restaurant, they drew off to a corner.

"Walking out of this town is impossible and getting a private vehicle is also ridiculous. So, I got to thinking that these truck drivers must do more than just the food distribution. I was right. He's got a load of people going with him to Jersey tomorrow night."

"How much is that going to cost?"

"Well, that's the hard news. He wants $1000 each."

She had that, but her childhood training told her to hold that information close to her chest.

"Wow. That's a lot. When does he want it by?"

"He'll be here at 4 pm tomorrow. We need to be ready to go then. He's headed to a warehouse in Jersey and that's as far as the ride goes."

"But we'd be outside the city?"

"Patterson. Supposedly, Uber is up and running there, so we could get a car to somewhere west."

"If Uber's operating that means credit cards are too."

"My thought, yeah."

"Great. I'll get ready. Are we going together to the banks?"

"Yes. I hear ATMs are also working today, still with the $100 limit."

"Great. I'll meet you in half an hour."

"Katharine, pack light. Only bring what you can carry."

Kate Lansing didn't like the sound of that, but Katharine Sullivan knew that lovely clothes could be replaced, assuming that the hotel wasn't willing to hold her things until she could return for them.

She headed up the stairs to get ready for their circuit today, buoyed with the knowledge that she would be that much closer to going home.

As she passed what had been Lillian's room, she saw Mr. Gillam and Marvin the door man in there. Gillam turned when she paused.

"I'm trying to reach her family to see what they want done with her things," he explained. *Of course you are.* "In the meantime, we'll put her bags in the store room."

"I got this, boss," Marvin assured him. "You should get back to the front desk."

Gillam thanked him and moved past Katharine.

"Do you need help, Marvin?"

"No, ma'am. Company, maybe."

Katharine swallowed and walked into the room. It looked mostly like hers, just a bit smaller.

"I got something for you," Marvin's hands were huge, but they didn't quite hide what he offered.

"What am I supposed to do with this?" Lillian had been right. A Saturday Night Special wasn't much of a gun.

"If you're going with Mr. Raines, you should take that along. It's a dangerous world out there."

Katharine nodded and slid the small revolver into her purse.

"Marvin ... thank you for ... everything. You should go home to your family. I think things are going to get worse before they get better. If there's any way to get off Manhattan ... it's gotta be safer in Brooklyn than here."

For just a moment, she heard a hint of her own Queens accent.

Marvin nodded.

"You be safe going west, Mrs. Sullivan."

She held out her hand and they shook before she went back to her room to hide her funds and the very illegal handgun she had in her purse.

Does It Matter Who
the POTUS Is?

Syracuse, New York

"Katharine must be worried sick," Joseph said to Perry as he paid over $100 for 10 gallons of gasoline. "And this having to stop every few miles to refill with gas is starting to get annoying. Sir, is there anyway, for a generous fee, that you would let me fill my entire tank?"

"I'm sorry, sir, but my boss says only 10 gallons at a time."

They had been stuck all day in Columbus and then only made it to Youngstown last night. Now they were in Syracuse, but would have to get gas in Buffalo. With the military having closed down the interstates and so many of them now impacted by radiation, this must be the most convoluted way to cross the United States Perry had ever considered.

"We'll make Scranton tonight. Maybe Patterson. There's no guarantee they'll let us into the city."

"I hear they're keeping a really tight entry policy. Why are you going there?" the clerk asked.

"My wife is there."

"Well, if you can get her to come out, that might be easier. They are letting people out of the city once they've been vetted as not part of the terrorist organization. That's what I hear."

Perry pumped the 10 gallons. Yeah, Scranton. And then maybe they could get another 10 gallons.

"Don't worry, sir. We'll get to her," he told Joseph when he got back into the truck.

"We should have bargained for a newer truck with better gas mileage. Hindsight 20-20."

Perry liked the old Chevy. It just kept going. It needed some antifreeze every 500 miles and a top off on oil and it drank gasoline like a fish drinks water, but it kept running and that was all Perry cared about. That and it didn't look worth stealing, which meant he didn't have to shoot anyone to defend it.

He turned on the radio, hoping to catch some news. Two pundits talked about whether Marshall Ellerby or Anna Byers was President of the United States. Meanwhile, they drove by broken store fronts to get into a long line of cars trying to get where they needed to go on a two-lane. Was this the United States any longer? And if it wasn't, did it matter who the president was?

Who Authorizes This Insurrection?

Hutchinson, Kansas

At 0430, Mike Sanchez brushed his teeth in the bathroom trailer as Jacobson entered. He checked the stalls before sidling up to Mike.

"So, the provost here is Lieutenant Wilkins. You ever run across him before?" He held his phone so Mike could see the photo.

"Doesn't ring a bell."

"You never served in Iraq?"

"Miristan."

"Well, he was D company for a while."

Mike waited for Jacobson to say more, but he didn't.

"And, then?"

"It's why I left the Army. Delta company killed a bunch of Iraqi civies. I requested a transfer, but they left Wilkins in place, so I didn't re-up. One of our unit blew the whistle and the Army rotated

Wilkins and me home on the same flight. I figured he'd be court-martialed, but here he is. He was a major back then. Now he's a lieutenant, so they busted him a little bit, but I kind of wonder what happened to my friend who reported him. I think he's probably dead."

"If you want to frag him, be my guest. Just don't compromise our mission. What else did you learn?"

"They have about 25 people penned up in some connexes the other side of the fairground." He flipped through the photos on his phone and showed him a guy with a bruised face and bloody nose being escorted into one of those connexes by two stun-gun-wielding soldiers backed up by a third who carried a rifle at the ready. "That your guy?"

"Yeah. How'd you get this?"

"They never disabled the crowd control cameras. That was yesterday afternoon about a half-hour before we got here."

"You access any records about what got him in there?"

"It doesn't matter with Wilkins. He could have not eaten his oatmeal correctly. That's what I've been trying ...."

Jacobson cut off what he was saying as they heard voices approaching outside and combat boots on the stairs. Mike scooped water into his mouth to rinse as a cover and Jacobson hotfooted it into a stall and hit the flusher as he closed the door.

A soldier entered the trailer.

"Sanchez, the Lieutenant wants to see you now."

Mike wiped water off his chin. The soldier's name patch read Cowles.

"Okay, sounds good. Where?"

"Dillon Hall. I'm to escort you."

Mike shoved his toothbrush and paste into his kit and followed Cowles out. He heard the stall door swing open as they stepped through the door. Knights had each other's backs ... he hoped.

Dillon Hall had been set up as a sort of officers' mess. Saliva squirted into Mike's mouth as he entered. It smelled divine, wiping away all thoughts of the MRE breakfast he'd eaten just a half-hour ago.

There were few men in the services who were taller or more muscular than Mike Sanchez, so pretty much every one was diminutive in his eyes. Wilkins was short even by ordinary standards. When he stood up, he might as well have been sitting down. Mike held out a hand to shake, but Wilkins saluted him instead.

"I've never been in the military, Lieutenant." Best to get that out of the way right at the start. Shane always had and officers usually appreciated his candor.

"You and your men will now serve under my command, Mr. Sanchez. The Knights ... isn't that what you call yourselves? ... have been nationalized under President Anna Byers."

"Have they been? I haven't heard from my own command on that."

"Who is your commander?"

"Crispin, Richard Crispin. Our HQ is Wichita, Kansas Governor's office."

"Cowles, the man wants to hear from his HQ on this. See to it."

Cowles exuded fear and he moved much too quickly to obey the lieutenant. Other men around the lieutenant didn't seem so nervous. Shane would have said every wolf has his inner pack, the ones who know they won't be the first to fall, but were careful not to piss off the alpha. Mike started to see what Shane had meant.

"I understand you're looking for someone we have in custody here."

Mike rapidly weighed the value of lying, but decided not to.

"Um, yeah. Malacai Delaney. He's related to an advisor of the Governor."

"He's an insurrectionist."

"Excuse me?"

"He's been fomenting insurrection among the other prisoners. Lawyers, you know? They think they know the constitution and they forget that times like these require different rules."

"Yeah." *Jacobson is right. This guy is a madman.* "Any chance you could release him to me so I can make my HQ happy?"

"No. Apparently you don't understand the situation. We have got to get this country under control. Men like Delaney must learn to obey orders or be eliminated. What is your rank among your hierarchy?"

"I'm a sergeant, hence the four bars on my patch."

"You will, of course, retain that rank under the nationalization, at least until we have things under control."

"Sir, I need to call my command. I can't just accept your word for it."

"Cowles will be back momentarily."

Wilkins glanced at one of his aides, who stepped over to the door Cowles had disappeared into. Someone, perhaps Cowles, handed him a sheet of paper, which he gave over to Lieutenant Wilkins. Wilkins handed it to Mike without even reading it.

Mike read the letter written below a Knight Industry logo and signed by someone claiming to be Commander Crispin. It said to fully cooperate with the armed forces.

"Of course, sir. I'll let my men know."

"Oh, and Sergeant, you should know that we cannot spare the supplies that were loaded onto your truck last night. We'll have to off-load those items today."

"Yes, sir. I'll have my men start with that right away."

"They can eat breakfast first and I'll need several of them on prisoner detail. Unfortunately, this insurrection has been very hard to put down."

"Of course, sir." Mike saluted, silently thanking Ric for teaching him what a correct salute looked like. *Best not to piss off the megalomaniac by performing his religious rites incorrectly."*

"You will join me for breakfast tomorrow morning, Sergeant."

"Yes, sir." Mike held the salute, though he desperately wanted to salute in a less respectful way. Wilkins saluted him quickly and Mike released his own salute.

"Dismissed."

Mike stepped back and away, carefully folding the paper and putting it in his breast pocket. Jacobson waited outside the door.

"What now?"

"Gather, Kriczek and Gallante and ask them to join us at the truck. Meeting commences when you arrive."

Mike paused and allowed Jacobson to go ahead. Against the dawn, he could see a figure being hoisted up a power pole, a struggling shadow against the light. He stepped between a building and a bush and pulled out his phone, snapped a pic of the letter and attached it to a text.

-Situation FUBAR. Please advise."

He hit SEND to Crispin and then duplicated the same message to Ric. Despite his change of name, he remained his best friend and a constant companion.

As he stepped out into public view again, Mike saw Lawson talking to some of the Army soldiers. *Good to know. Not that I trusted you before.*

The others had arrived at the truck by the time Mike got there. He handed the letter around their small circle, watching each man's eyes register shock.

"You see my problem, yes?"

"We do, sir," Jacobson said. The other two smiled tightly and nodded.

"Good. Kriczek, Gallante, you're on prisoner duty. Take four guys each. Salute and say "sir" a lot. Jacobson, take the rest of the crew, mingle with the soldiers. We're expected to unload the truck sometime today. You know my orders. Jacobson, what we talked about? 1750. Select your crew. Explain to Blanc and Rojas."

Jacobson's eyebrows shot up, then he grinned and nodded.

"Yes, s-sir," he said. "And then?"

"I'll let you know. Lawson is not in the loop. We need to assume he's dark side. Watch your phones. Protocol 54."

They all nodded. Protocol 54 meant they were to protect civilian life, but could fire on any combatants. Mike's phone vibrated. He read the message he found there and passed the phone around to his men. Each of them nodded before passing it on. Crispin had not heard they'd been nationalized and recommended he seek disengagement as soon as possible. Jacobson saluted, so the others imitated him with varying degrees of success. Mike saluted them back, making a show of the correct form, which they imitated and then they each went their separate ways. Knights had each other's backs ... he hoped.

Newbies

Cai woke at the sound of a generator starting. He couldn't see around him, but the light at the door crack suggested it was dawn. Maybe it would warm up soon. After shivering for half the night with his hands tucked into his armpits, he'd welcome a little heat stroke.

No, not really. He needed water desperately enough to consider drinking his urine from the day before. He didn't think he could survive another day in this connex.

Bracing himself in the corner, he climbed to his feet, every joint aching. He could still feel his fingers and toes. He didn't have frostbite. His collar moved across his sunburn, reminding him that he had only working out in the hot sun as an alternative to this box. Could he take another day and night of this?

"Hey," the woman to his left said. "Thank you for last night."

"Wherever two or three are gathered in His name, He will be there."

"I'm praying for you."

"Me too." Lest he forget, Cai offered prayers that moment for the faceless, nameless woman who had reached into his cell last night and reminded him that he was not alone.

When the door clanged open and two soldiers came in, Cai braced for another stun gunning, but one of them handed him a bottle of water instead. He glanced over his left shoulder, hoping to catch a glimpse of his friend, but the connex stood open and empty. Two men dressed in black Kevlar escorted him pushed him across the fairgrounds toward Dillon Hall. He feared to ask questions. Asking questions had gotten him nowhere as of yet. He tried not to trip or drag his feet along the way. He just drank his water and walked. There were people awaiting sentencing in the provost chamber. The guards pushed him into a folding chair in the front row.

"So, you didn't learn anything from the first sentence, I see," Lieutenant Wilkins remarked. "Talking while working. Interacting with other inmates in express violation of the rules. Trying to contact outside assistance." The provost smiled. "I'm going to give you another 30 days for that infraction." He stared at Cai. "No protests. That's good, because protesting would see you with 10 stripes across your back. We're not playing with you people anymore. Understand that. You're all guilty of crimes and under the Code of Military Justice, I can sentence you to death, so stop acting like this is a game. Get back to work, prisoner. Dismissed. Next."

Cai glanced out at the crowd of newbies as the guards jerked him to his feet. They looked stunned, dumbfounded. They were Americans. This didn't happen in America. Cai vaguely remembered believing that. Had it only been two days?

The guards didn't stun gun him this time. They shoved bread and another bottle of water into his hands, told him to sit on the ground and get ready for work. While he washed down crumbs, he saw a bruised Jared being escorted into the provost court. He moved with that shakiness Cai now associated with stun gunning. Was he being punished for offering to make a phone call?

The black-clothed Knight Industry mercs came forward as he finished the bottle of water.

"Get up. You need to get cleaned up before you go to work." They dragged Cai to his feet and herded him toward the bathrooms. Cai washed the dried blood from his three-day-old scruff and rinsed his mouth with water. He could just imagine how he smelled. He asked for and received permission to use the facilities. Then a soldier walked him out the back door. As they crossed the midway, he glanced up to see a man, bound and gagged, hanging from a power pole. He recognized that shirt. It was Larry.

"Fomenting resistance will not be tolerated," the soldier said.

How am I fomenting resistance? If I knew, I'm pretty sure I'd stop.

The soldier set him to loading bags of rice onto a waiting truck, which seemed odd as they'd spent the last couple of days unloading trucks. His bruised ribs screamed in protest, but he knew that complaints would be construed as resistance and he did not want to be seen resisting in anyway. He wasn't positive that would keep him alive, but it seemed more likely to result in survival than being seen as an instigator. He could only hope.

Becoming Acquainted

Kentucky

Trying to make their way west meant threading transportation needles between radiation zones. They'd spent all day Tuesday traveling 2-lanes to get to Louisville, Kentucky. Predawn Wednesday morning, the desk manager at the Best Western consulted the information website and told them they would need to cross the Mississippi at Memphis, go north to the Mark Twain Bridge or try crossing at Cairo. Javi sighed and asked Ami what she thought.

"I've never seen either, so I don't care. I doubt Graceland is open, but I hear Memphis has some great architecture."

"Memphis it is then."

When they got into the car, Ami sprang it on him.

"I think we should try for Cairo."

"Why?"

"Fewer people. Hopefully less scrutiny."

"Why are we avoiding scrutiny?"

"I don't know why you are, but I just plain don't like military juntas. Egyptian. Go figure."

Javi laughed.

"It makes no difference to me." He checked his phone for distances. "It's a bit shorter distance, but you're right, the crossing shouldn't be as crowded. You take your iodine tablets today?"

"I did. Did you?"

"For sure.

They filled up with drinking water and put their faces toward the west, only to come to a grinding halt west of Paducah. With the 2-lane bumper to bumper, Javi shut the engine off and rolled a window down for air.

"Another checkpoint, I guess. You know any road trip games?"

"Not in English." She rolled down her window too. "You?"

"We'll see how long this lasts. I might invent some. So, you grew up in Egypt. What brought you to the US?"

"My father pissed off the powers that be in Cairo. That's funny."

"Huh? Oh, yeah. That's ironic. I didn't think of it because you pronounced it Karo like they do."

"I didn't realize it was Cairo until I saw the sign. I mean, did you know there was a Cairo, Illinois?"

"I read Huckleberry Finn, so yeah, but I've never been here before. It wasn't until the desk clerk said Karo that I remembered the musical version of Huck Finn, some stupid song based on the name of the town."

"Americans don't really learn history, do they?"

"Our own? Hell, no! We've spent two generations learning to be ashamed of being the evil nation, so why would we want to study our history except the wars." She giggled, so he had hit his mark. "So, was your dad a politician or ...?"

"Or. He was just a businessman, but people listened to him and the government didn't like it." She stared out at the countryside, clearly seeing something else. "One night, a friend shows up at the door and says we should go, the security forces are surveilling us. Baba bought plane tickets for us the next day, but he didn't show up for the plane. We had relatives in Baltimore."

"Did he ...?"

"I don't know. During the various regime changes, I tried to find out, but I didn't have any luck. I was 13, my sister was 4. My mother died two years later of cancer and our aunt took us in. She was ... tough. Insisted I get good grades, scholarships ... her husband was a doctor, so when I excelled in school, he recommended me to medical school."

"So, they raised your sister?"

"Hmm, not really. They were older ... a lot older than my parents. She was my father's oldest sibling. They had grandchildren already and weren't really interested in raising more children. They tried, but really, I raised Christine. Except in matters of faith, they didn't interfere with me much."

"Matters of faith? Wouldn't you both be Copts?"

"No, they are Baptists."

"He was American?"

"Egyptian parents, but yes, he was raised here. They are quite devout and they took Christine to church regularly."

"But not you?"

"I was 16 when I moved in with them, so they allowed me to make my own choices. What about you?"

Javi could have lied, but he didn't want to.

"Parents died when I was little ... car accident. I was raised in foster homes. A couple of them were really good people. The others ... well, paid parenting isn't probably the best parenting."

"Were you a good student?"

"I got good grades. I was pretty rebellious, though."

"So, you became a sheet rocker?"

Javi watched workmen at a Protestant church sorting out groceries into trucks.

"I shouldn't delve that deeply, should I?"

Javi laughed. She joined him.

"You aren't an escaped criminal, so I don't need to worry about an aiding and abetting charge at least."

"My last arrest, I was 17 ... well, the last time I was arrested for something I actually did."

She frowned at him.

"Are you tossing me clues?"

"Something like that. I shouldn't tell you at all, but .... I like this whole real-people feeling."

She snorted lightly.

"Next thing you'll be telling me that you're Jason Bourne."

Javi blinked at her, surprised she'd gotten so close. She giggled and then sobered, reading his expression.

"Seriously? You expect me to believe that you're an assassin?"

"I'm not telling you anything, but you have good instincts. Not an assassin, but you're close."

She stared out at those workmen for a while. Five trucks, 15 men. One by one, they drove away.

"So, why are you headed west?"

"Someone I know is where I'm headed and it should be safe there."

"Safe from what?"

"You don't need to ask. Why are we bouncing all over the map like a ping pong ball? These people wouldn't be there if it weren't safe."

"I see. Well, no, I don't, but .... From the moment you stepped out of those bushes, I've felt like I could trust you, so I'm trying not to ask too many questions."

"Thank you."

The car in front of them rolled forward eight feet and stopped. The car behind them beeped impatiently. Javi started the car, rolled forward and shut down the engine again.

"Looks like we're eating breakfast in the car."

"It takes so long to get anywhere. Can you imagine when this was driving cross-country? How did they do it?"

"They didn't know any better. They were driving Model Ts. There were a lot fewer cars on the roads."

"A week ago, I would have been going crazy."

"Me too. And now, I'm just hungry."

"Seriously? I was going to spend some more of Red Cap's money on you, but we do have some stale cheese danish in the cooler." He grinned at her. She laughed. "Coming right up."

Javi hoped that pointing her in the direction of his secret was the smart thing to do. After years of carefully maintaining a cover identity, he totally wanted to just be honest with another human being. He hoped he wouldn't have to kill her to protect himself, but she didn't seem at all to be that sort of person.

Family

Emmaus, Kansas

Marnie waited for more to come up, but decided she was done for the moment, though she still felt nauseous. She flushed the toilet and brushed her teeth. She heard footsteps outside the bathroom door. She had probably awakened Shane again. He'd never been a heavy sleeper, but now he hardly seemed capable of sleeping. If she'd still cared about him, she might have been concerned. Why had he come back?

The knock on the door nearly startled her out of her socks. Jill waited outside with a glass of juice and a sleeve of crackers.

"Let's go to your room," she suggested. Marnie hesitated. "You don't want the men to hear this."

Jill set the crackers on the dresser and handed Marnie the juice.

"You want to have that ready first thing in the morning. Oddly enough, eating regularly keeps the morning sickness from turning into pukes."

"Lila told you?"

"Lila told me nothing. I've been pregnant four times. I know what it looks like. So, just to satisfy my curiosity, were you and Cai faking the whole celibacy thing?"

"No. We really never … until the wedding night, which is so par for Cai's history, isn't it?"

"You're that far along? How do you know?"

"I had an ultrasound yesterday. Eleven weeks."

"You didn't plan for this?"

"Of course I did, but the diaphragm didn't work, I guess. This is such horrible timing. Cai would have been upset anyway because we're so far in debt, but now …."

Tears spilled down Marnie's cheeks.

"Maggie says I should get an abortion. Lila won't do it. I couldn't get any pills. I feel guilty if Cai is still alive and … Oh, god! I am a horrible person."

Jill laughed. Marnie stared at her. Her mother-in-law had always treated her well. When she'd been Shane's girlfriend and when she'd become Cai's friend first, then girlfriend and now wife. She'd never said if she had misgivings … although she had to, didn't she? The local head of the Women's Missionary Union could not have been happy about what Marnie and Shane were doing in high school and college and then for Cai to become friends with her after …. And, yet, here she was, laughing like Marnie wasn't an evil woman.

"You're not a horrible person. You're scared. This situation is ... wow. We're all trying to avoid the topic. What happens if Cai is a casualty of this mess? But a baby makes it hard to ignore the question. Should that happen, and I don't believe that is what's happened, but if ... when Cai married you, you became a member of this family and Rob and I will take care of you on Cai's behalf. I'm positive that he's coming home, though. A mother knows these things. He's alive out there somewhere. You need to trust me and not stress yourself out. It's not good for the baby and, frankly, it makes the morning sickness worse."

"Does Rob know?"

"No. I won't tell him unless you say I can. He and Jacob will probably figure it out though if you keep puking in the morning. Between them, they've been through 10 pregnancies."

"Ten?"

"Vi lost two, had four living. I lost one, had three living."

"Of course. That's a possibility, isn't it? Especially with elevated radiation levels."

"What did my grandchild look like?"

"A tiny little human, all the requisite fingers and toes."

"Then there's a really good chance you won't miscarry."

Marnie took a tiny bite of saltine, wiping at new tears.

"Thank you. I just realized that I really want my baby. I felt it move last night. I think I was terrified that nobody else did."

"Well, you don't need to worry about that. Delaneys don't back down from challenges and every life is precious here."

"Even with everything that's going on?"

"Especially with everything that is going on. Life is precious. It's hard to know that until you create it."

"Someone else said that to me too. I should stop listening to Maggie. I have never listened to her before. I don't know why I'm letting her confuse me now."

"You would think she'd be terrified of abortion, given what happened to Marie."

Marnie sighed, smiling.

"This family doesn't keep secrets, does it?"

"Shane does, but no, the rest of us .... It just wastes too much energy for so little result."

Marnie up-bottomed the juice and sighed.

"Well, off to deal with a continuing crisis. Thank you for this."

Marnie left Jill sitting on her bed and arrived at the clinic to find a broken leg and a child with what appeared to be appendicitis waiting at the clinic doors.

Hiding the Evidence

Dawn blushed the eastern sky as Jazz worked to undo the clips that held the portable conveyor in place. Jacob had texted her to shut it down. The USDA would arrive sometime this morning. She wasn't sure how she was going to release the conveyor from the second-story window and get it into the building by herself, but she supposed she would cross that bridge when she got the clips loosened. When the green Jeep pulled up out front, she didn't know who it was. Seeing Shane stand up out of the driver's door should not have caused a thrill, but he was an extremely attractive male despite being the second-most dangerous person she knew.

"Looking for Jacob?" she asked.

"He's flying a field. He asked me to swing by and help you hide the evidence."

"We're done for sure then?"

"I just filled the bag silos, so yeah. We've done what we can and it's time to seal up the corridor. I'll be up in a second."

The old aircraft factory Jazz lived in had commercial spaces on the ground floor. The Delaney Feed store occupied one end of the block, Nick's Pizza the other end and several small shops operated on one side of the factory. On the other side was a corridor that had been employee break space back in the day. This corridor had most recently been used as a makeshift bomb shelter, but now it had been transformed into a makeshift corn silo. On the apartment level, a trap door in a mop closet had offered access to the corridor to pump the corn into it. She helped Shane pull the conveyor aside and lower it to the ground with ropes. He dropped a purpose-cut and weathered board atop the entire closet floor and then rolled the mop buckets and other items on top of it. Then they dragged the conveyor into the large storage area in the middle of the building. It looked right at home among the farm implements and extra feed bags.

"Who stacked all those bags of dog food in front of the door?"

"I did."

"Really? Mighty Mouse, huh?"

"I'm stronger than I look. The hard part was the top couple of courses, but I found a portable platform I could climb on. Thanks for the help, though. I couldn't have done the conveyor by myself. So how do we hide the inspection window?"

"We're going to put the board back over it and hope they don't notice."

"We really are winging this, aren't we?"

"It's best not to overthink it. Want to help?"

The inspection window had been a transom over a door that went into that corridor. At some point, Jacob or his father had gotten tired of the draft that blew through the store, so they had sealed it off with insulation and plywood. Shane operated the drill as a screwdriver while Jazz held the board in place. As a last touch, he rubbed soil from a planter into the hatch crosses. It really did make it look like the board had been untouched for several decades.

Shane dropped off the desk that had rested in front of this door for as many years as Rob had been the manager. Jazz started down the ladder. He reached to steady her and then they turned face to face, breath comingling as she stared up into his eyes and he gazed down into hers.

His head bent toward her ... and then his spine went rigid and he stepped away.

"You probably should just stay away from me for your own good."

"That didn't feel like that's what you want."

He cocked his head, green eyes darkening.

"I read the shock in your eyes when I killed those people at the Elevators. Remember who I am and turn your attention somewhere else. I dumped Marnie when her sister was barely cold in the grave and her brother was going away to prison for 20 years. I'm not the guy you want to kiss."

He left her standing there in the feed store. She didn't move until she heard the Jeep drive away. What in the world was wrong with him? Maybe she should just admit that if she was attracted to a guy, he'd have a cruel streak a mile wide and it would be best to run in the other direction.

So why wasn't she doing that right now?

Listen to Me

Nehemiah Lufgren plunged a pitchfork into a broken bale of hay and levered the wad up and over the railing to drop it into the stall below. He moved to do it again, but a shiver ran through the building so he looked around. Micah was just inside the door, signing for him to hide. His phone then vibrated. His sister Rachel texted:

-USDA here now. (Rachel)

-Keep me posted. (Nehemiah)

Nehemiah rushed along the gallery of the hay mow so he could peek through a vent to see what was going on outside, slipping behind a stack of hay bales so he wouldn't be seen. Micah had been clear that he wanted Nehemiah to remain out of sight and at 14 Nehemiah listened to his father.

The man who got out of the Ford Ranger smelled of soap and cologne, one of those ones that smelled like lemons or ... grapefruit. Younger than

Dad, he wore a tie under his windbreaker. When he stepped forward to speak to Dad, he stepped in something and spent the next 30 seconds scraping it off the sole of his foot. He seemed less than amused. Of course, Dad couldn't help grinning, though he suppressed it pretty fast. There were a half dozen people with the man along with two big trucks – one a dump truck, the other a panel truck.

As the other USDA workers moved in myriad directions, Micah met the government agent, turning his phone around for him to read his greeting. The man ignored the phone, talking … typical Hearing. From this distance, Nehemiah couldn't see what anyone was saying, but he knew Micah was saying "Deaf". Like most Deaf, he knew a handful of words he could vocalize when he needed them. The USDA leader pushed the phone away from his face and turned to the barn. Dad was irritated, but he followed.

All the Lufgrens had built storm barns over the years. Some were separate earth-bermed Quonset huts, but Micah's storm barn actually was the old cow gallery under the main barn. After he'd built a separate milking shed, he'd hardened it for tornados. It had made a perfect silo for the corn. They'd cleaned it out after the nuclear rain and it had had enough time to dry before the corn was harvested.

-He not listen. (Rachel)

-They strip root cellar. Take all. (Leah)

That didn't include what they'd hidden, of course, but why would they not leave two weeks' worth?

Nehemiah went back to the far end of the gallery and slid behind the bales there. He turned his phone to interpret. When the man and Micah entered the barn, the USDA leader was speaking loudly enough for the phone to pick it up.

"...wrong with you people? These delay tactics are ridiculous. This is a farm. You have food. We need that food to feed people in cities so they don't starve. Stop waving that phone around. Talk to me."

Micah's lips moved. Nehemiah couldn't hear him, but he knew he was saying "Deaf." The phone even picked it up.

"Show me your grain."

The USDA leader walked across the barn floor and then he paused, tapping his foot on the floor. Micah glanced up toward where Nehemiah was hiding. Nehemiah remembered that the floor had a different feeling than floors that didn't have a large space underneath. Did it sound differently?

-Hit Mom. What I do? Mom say don't. (Rachel)

-Then don't. (Nehemiah)

He looked now to see the USDA leader and another worker as they cleared away the straw and uncovered the trap door.

"Hoarding is punishable by death. Franton, get equipment in here to extract the corn. Parish, prepare for an execution. We cannot tolerate this rebellion now or we'll have more rebellion later."

Nehemiah stood, hand closing around the pitchfork, but as the USDA worker moved to grab Micah, he signed with one hand – "Run." Then his arms were restrained and Nehemiah was left to watch in horror as they dragged his father away.

Nehemiah used the windless to drop to the ground and crept behind a hedge toward the house. Micah was kneeling in the driveway. Mom, Rachel and Leah were being held nearby. Nehemiah wanted to get to the shotgun and shoot every one of these horrible people to save his father, but he knew he couldn't. He slipped into the wood lot and begun running down the trail toward Alex's farm.

Grasping at Straws

Hutchinson, Kansas

Larry was still alive. Cai could see him struggling to move as Cai shoveled corn from a dump truck into a connex on wheels. It had to be sufficiently hot in that bag in the full sun, hoisted up on the pole. It somehow reminded Cai of crucifixion. Cai could only guess at the pain Larry felt. Rumor had it they'd whipped him bloody before trussing him up. Cai was more concerned with figuring out how to avoid the same fate. When Brian asked if he'd seen April, Cai had told him to be quiet instead of sympathizing.

Is this how you become a collaborator?

He needed time to think. Clearly, he couldn't trust anyone. They were all potentially compromised by fear, hunger or the other people they loved. There was no escape from this trap and in 57 days he'd be too beat up and starved to make it home. What should he or could he do? He started playing a game of "What would Shane do?" while he worked, hoping to see some weakness he could exploit. Every security weakness he saw didn't outlive his own weaknesses.

While he worked, he began to hum *It is Well with My Soul.* Somehow that helped. He saw that several Knight Industries mercenaries mingled with the soldiers and FEMA workers. They looked to be loading a truck with supplies. The man who seemed to be in charge of their unit looked familiar, kind of like the guy who had helped them in Wichita. He'd said he was Shane's best friend ... only he didn't call him Shane. Something else. Cai didn't remember.

Cai doubted it was him. A lot of the Knights were Hispanic males with shaved heads. He couldn't be sure this was the same guy and it would be too big of a coincidence. And even if it were him, Cai was rapidly learning to trust no one. Only God had his back and he wasn't sure what God had planned ... if anything.

They allowed Cai and Brian to have water break at the same time.

"Sorry I was snippy earlier. Rough night. I wish I could help with April, but I think I'm going to be lucky not to join Larry by the end of the day."

"I have got to find her."

"You're going to get yourself killed."

"Get back to work," the Vulture ordered. Cai moved smartly to obey. Brian looked reluctant, but he moved. For now, if they just did what they were told, maybe they would live through the day. He had no idea how to make it beyond that.

Commuter

Emmaus, Kansas

Shane held his breath as he steered the tractor between the two hangers. Dennis Hoffman's tongue was visible between his teeth as he steered the jet between the two buildings. The wingtip on the right cleared by about an inch and the wingtip on the left cleared by maybe three inches. Shane kept steady pressure on the tow straps. He'd measured how far he had to drag the plane forward to clear the runway. He crept up on the mark, waiting to hear the screech of metal on metal and the crunch of aluminum on wood, but it never came.

Dennis joined him to help undo the tow straps.

"Wow," he said.

"I know. That's a one in a million there." Shane looked at his phone. "Sentry sees movement to the west. Here come the cow cops." He started texting.

"I'll head to the outpost as soon as we get this done."

"So, question. Why are you here helping us?"

Dennis sighed. "My family was in Los Angeles. My parents and fiancé." His throat grew husky for a moment. "There's a part of me that keeps thinking that maybe if I went there ... there are refugee camps and ... but, uh ... realistically --."

They both heard the sound of running feet. Shane dropped the tow strap he was coiling up and drew his gun, but then pointed it down and away as Nehemiah Lufgren came running into view. With bleeding hands, he signed desperately, explaining that he thought Micah was dead and his mother and sisters might be next.

"What's going on?" Dennis asked.

"The USDA has shot his father and his mother and sisters are there." Nehemiah signed. "The USDA didn't appreciate having to deal with Deaf. I'm going to see if I can rescue Joelle and the girls."

"No!" Dennis snapped. "You can't risk yourself on a side mission. That's a distraction we can't afford. I'll go with him." He pulled his own gun out of his holster, checked the clip. "You stay on task."

"You sure? You can't understand him."

"I took a sign class back in college. I understand enough. Go. Do your part. I'll do mine."

Shane explained hastily in sign and Nehemiah nodded. Dennis and he headed toward the truck the copilot had borrowed and drove away. Shane took a deep breath and turned toward the tractor. Time to resume the role he'd always played in Miristan.

My Daughter's Beau

Nevada Randolph appreciated James Vance's help as they stacked bales of hay in the stable loft to block the entrance to Jacob's apartment. She supposed if the USDA didn't look close, they would assume the entire section of the building was filled with hay. The tall, broad-shouldered young man could certainly lift the bales high enough to wedge the last tier up under the roof. That done, he wiped sweat off his brow, then blotted more with the bottom of his t-shirt, revealing an impressive row of abs. He settled his glasses back on his nose.

"Thank you for coming over to help with this. How did you know I needed it, though?"

"Kim texted me. She's feeling sort of helpless with her arm in a cast."

"Yeah. Kind of lousy timing. Your folks didn't need your help?"

"My parents have three other kids to do this sort of work and they know how I feel about Kim."

Nevada paused and stared at him.

"What do you mean?"

"She hasn't told you?"

"Well, I know you went to the movies a couple of times in the summer, but ...."

"She tried to date someone else for a while, but ... well, that doesn't change my feelings for her, you know?"

Nevada licked dry lips.

"You're young. Both of you." His brown eyes seemed to glow behind his glasses. "Don't get in a rush ... especially during a time like this."

He grinned at her. He was a handsome boy, strong, more mature than his years.

"My ... uh ... intentions are honorable. You don't have to worry about that."

"Worry about what?"

"What you're thinking. I won't ... that's not who I am ... who I was raised to be."

"Yeah?"

"Yes, ma'am. I'm too young for a wife. I'm headed to technical college after I graduate. But, if Kim's willing to wait ... maybe ... after." He nodded more to himself than to her, examining their handiwork one more time. "This looks to be done. If it don't fool them, nothing will. Let's see what we can do about hiding that root cellar now."

Word from Columbus

Anders McAuliff pulled his phone out of his pocket.

-Dad. Hope you get this. Tried calling now that the towers are back up here in Columbus, but the lines are jammed. Are you okay? (Rogan)

Anders sat down, unexpected relief temporarily making him dizzy. He'd been assuring himself for days that his kids were okay, but knowing it was different.

We're fine here except for the USDA wants to confiscate the crops and extra food. We're figuring it out. Have you heard from your sister?

He heard the trailer pulling up behind him and turned to see Jill Delaney in her Tahoe, pulling a horse trailer.

"What do you have?"

"The last of the groceries from the Walmart. You look like you're pleased with yourself."

"My son just contacted me. He's good." Jill smiled, but it didn't quite make it to her eyes. "You haven't heard from Cai yet?"

"No, but Shane's got people looking."

Anders wondered exactly how Jill's younger son had those sorts of connections. Supposedly, he wasn't still working for the FBI and if he was, he'd certainly moved beyond a mere informant. But he knew Jill wouldn't tell him anything, even if she knew, which he rather doubted.

"I'm sure he'll be home soon. Pull over there. Randy'll tag the trailer and haul it into the mine." His phone buzzed again.

-Button it up. They're coming over the horizon. (Rob)

"Rob says the USDA is almost here."

Jill nodded sharply, making her dark red hair bounced. Anders stepped back from the car so she could meet Randy and start the switchover. His phone buzzed again.

-I heard from her and Mom. They're together and both are good. They're going to try to get here to Columbus if they can. What about you? (Rogan)

Anders looked around the mine yard, at the workers rushing to and fro, trying to save their

town. A part of him wanted to be with his kids, but
....

-This is home now. You're welcome to join me here
if you need to. I've got lots of room and Emmaus is a
great town. (Anders)

His thumb hovered over the SEND button. He
could so easily just decide to go there instead. He
took a deep breath, thumb moving to the EDIT icon.
Paused. Dan was at the compound. He shouldn't go
before he talked to him. Right? He stopped goofing
around and hit SEND.

Road Trip

Casa Blanca Hotel
New York City, Times Square

Katharine had picked up a backpack at a sporting goods store earlier in the day and now she finished rolling her last bit of clothes into it. She secured the gun in the bottom most pocket where heavy things belonged. She'd packed her other baggage as well and given it to Gillam along with a generous tip to hold it for her. All she was taking were her sturdiest clothes, a photo of Kim, Joseph and her, and her toiletries. She slipped her envelope into her inside pocket. The Casa Blanca had been a safe place, but it wasn't going to stay that way and the sooner she headed west to her family the better. She swung her backpack over her shoulders. Thank God Joseph was into all of that outdoor nonsense. She knew a quality backpack and how to adjust it for herself. She'd selected a comfortable pair of shoes and bought good socks. She assumed this journey would require some walking. She'd packed gloves and a hat too. She remembered her charger. Her laptop was locked up with her other luggage. No, she was ready. Time to go.

Downstairs, people filled the lobby, trying to make the same deal Julian had made for them. The driver dickered with a few of them over the value of their jewelry. Katharine elbowed her way to the front.

"I have cash," she remarked quietly. His eyes flickered toward her. Julian appeared right next to her. "We both do."

"Cool. Just know that once you give it to me, there's no refunds." He turned to the other people. "Sorry, folks, but I'll be full up with them. I'll catch you tomorrow."

Katharine and Julian followed him out to the street where his truck waited, the cargo container already filled with people who wanted out of the city.

"Don't flash your wads here. Wait until we get inside."

Katharine glanced over her shoulder and saw Tamara weeping beside the restaurant door. She couldn't save the whole world. She needed to think for herself. She'd made arrangements for Gillam to keep covering their room with her credit. There was nothing else she could do.

Her phone vibrated as she stepped up into the truck. Startled, juggling the phone and her backpack, she maneuvered into the middle seat with Julian pushing behind.

-I'm in Patterson. I can't get into the city. Can you get to me? I can probably grease the skids if need be. (Joseph).

"Oh, thank God!"

"What?" Julian asked.

"My husband is in Patterson. He'll be waiting for me."

"That's great," Julian said with a smile. "We're going to Ft. Lee, but ...."

"Where are you taking us?" Katharine asked the driver.

He blinked and frowned.

"We're taking the Lincoln Tunnel to a warehouse in Ft. Lee. I'm not stopping for nothing except official checkpoints and I can't take you any further."

"No, what's the address? My husband is going to meet us."

The driver held out his hand and made the international sign for money. Julian and Katharine handed theirs over.

"It takes time these days to get anywhere. It'll be about 11 pm. We're going to the Walmart Super Center in North Bergen, on 88th. Tell him to meet you at Cliffside Park."

"I'll let him know. We can probably take you at least as far as Kansas, Julian."

"Oh, I hope so!"

(Text) I'm fine. Was actually leaving the city anyway. Things are getting scary here. Meet me at Cliffside Park, Ft. Lee about 11 pm. That's near where our ride out of this hellhole drops us."

The driver started the truck.

"I checked. You're neither of you on any hold lists. When we get stopped at a check point, show your ID. Don't act sketchy. Got it?"

They assured him they did.

He drove around the block to get on West 43rd Street, headed toward the Lincoln Tunnel. With the canyons of New York darkening as the sun slid into the west, it was eerie to see how quiet things were. It wasn't curfew yet and the truck was authorized, but it felt dangerous. The street lights didn't come on. The traffic lights were operating though. They stopped at the corner of 9th Avenue and turned left. People hurried away, headed indoors before the mercenaries took to the streets ... or whoever had been exchanging gun fire last night. Garbage was stacked up in front of dumpsters when they could see into the alleys. Katharine shivered. It felt like a dying world out there. But in no time she'd be with Joseph again and Kansas would be safe enough, she thought. Traffic ground to a halt.

"There's a checkpoint before you enter the tunnel," Yancy, the driver, said. He hadn't told them his name, but it was on his jacket. "At least they're not making us pay the toll."

"Who's in charge?" Julian asked.

"Beats me. There's still transit people at the checkpoint, but there's also those Knights ... the guys in black Kevlar. They're like the mayor's personal security now."

"How long is the Lincoln Tunnel?"

"About a mile and a half, but these days it takes a long time to drive it and even longer to get to it."

Yancy settled back and waited. So did Julian. Katharine wanted to get out of the truck and walk the rest of the way, but she knew that wasn't going to work, so she forced herself to sit back into the seat and wait.

Laying a False Trail

Poppy steered the old combine across one of Shane's field, as Pete monitored the wheat as it spread behind the discs. They finished the last row and then climbed down to check the equipment. Pete didn't know how to prep the machine, but he watched carefully, amazed at how Poppy moved with such confidence. She knew what she was about with this and so many other things. She was very comfortable in her own skin. She knew who she was. Pete ... not so much. He fumbled, fingerspelling when he didn't know a sign.

"Why we doing this now?"

"Winter wheat." She mouthed the words to help him. "Plant now."

"Freeze?"

"No! Grow under snow. Spring harvest." She turned back to the hopper.

A blue truck with federal license plates pulled up in front of the combine. Pete bumped Poppy's arm. She glanced once and signed "Oh-oh!" They were close enough to the County Road to see several vehicles go by headed toward Lufgren's Crossing. A woman got out of the truck. A man hung back while she flashed a badge.

"Galena Carboy, USDA." Pete signed for Poppy. "Where's all the corn?"

Poppy frowned and shrugged.

"Harvested. Before bombs."

"Is she deaf?" Carboy asked.

"Yeah. We harvested the corn weeks ago. We're planting winter wheat now."

"What did you do with the corn?"

Poppy's facial expression was priceless. Pete had learned that Deaf communicated as much with facial expressions as with signs.

"It went to the elevators. We don't keep it."

"Donovan's Elevators?"

Poppy nodded. Carboy texted to someone and then turned back to the teens.

"Who owns this field? Your parents?" She looked at the tablet that her assistant showed her. "Where can I find Joel Rhys."

Poppy shot Pete a warning look, but Pete was the son of a felon, so he'd learned not to give information away to authority figures. They'd been told what to do if they had contact with USDA.

"Her brother might know. Lufgren's Farm, just past the crossroads to the right – yellow farm house."

The assistant showed the tablet again.

"Thank you for your help." Then Carboy got back into her truck and backed out to the main road. As she passed out of sight, Poppy signed something Pete felt certain was a swear word.

Hidden in Plain Sight

Mitchell Rumdale looked up from his tablet as Alcott brought the truck to a stop by a pyramid of straw bales. The yellow farm house seemed to drowse in the midday heat. There were cows in a pasture and chickens in a fenced yard. A goat chewed on a rope by the side of the red barn. A dark-haired man mended a nearby fence. A dark-haired woman came out onto the porch. Across the pasture was the largest pile of compost Rumdale had ever seen. Rumdale got out of the truck, telling Alcott to go check the house.

"Can I help you?" the fence-mender asked, wiping sweat off his forehead.

Rumdale introduced himself, showing his credentials.

"Are you the owner here?"

"No, just a worker. The boss took his wife to work this morning and just hasn't come back yet."

459

"Then you won't mind if we have a look around, will you?"

"No. I'm paid by the hour. Moving down the road when the work runs out. Couldn't care less what happens here."

"They got any grain around here?"

"Grain? You mean corn? It's a corn farm, so yeah."

"Where?"

"I'll show you."

The illegal took Rumdale around to the backside of the barn where a bag silo rested on the edge of the pasture.

"It's their seed corn for next year, I think."

"For next year? Half the country's going to starve to death before next year." Rumdale spoke into his radio. "Bring the flat bed around here. We've got a nice haul."

Finally, we're finding something worth finding.

Alcott came out of the house.

"There's maybe a month's worth of food in the root cellar. Shouldn't take too long to take it out. She says seven people live here."

"Where is everybody?"

"School. Missus Keri's a teacher. The kids are in school."

"Either of you got any ID?"

"Sure." They both produced driver's licenses that looked to be legitimate.

"You're American citizens?"

"We are," the woman assured him.

"Well, here's a receipt for the corn. Alcott will get you another one for the groceries."

Myers came out of the barn.

"There's raw milk in there," he reported.

"What?" Rumdale sighed. *Would these people never learn?* "Write a citation. Sorry, but you'll have to give it to your boss. Raw milk is a violation of federal law."

"Of course. I'm sure it was all a misunderstanding. I know they don't sell it."

Rumdale walked away from the man as he spoke, but then he turned back.

"Do you know where else they might be hiding corn?" he asked.

The man nodded.

"Sure. Not my boss, but other farmers. They thought they were being smart. I'll tell you."

Rumdale smiled.

No Joking Matter

Alex held Joelle while she wept. Her jeans and shirt were drenched in Micah's blood. Nehemiah looked like he would burst into tears at any moment. Right now he mourned his dad, but needed to be stoic for his mom. Alex expected he'd shed some tears when he realized he had the second biggest farm in Emmaus and he had to husband it. Alex remembered that feeling at only a few years older. The sense of responsibility had been overwhelming.

"Kill USDA," Nehemiah signed.

"No," Alex replied. "You stay here. Shane him handle."

"He my father he."

Alex nodded, but he couldn't allow Nehemiah to get himself killed. When he'd wanted to go kill a drunk driver, Rob Delaney had pointed out that he had a little sister who needed him. A job was a good focus for rage.

"Help carry into house."

Micah hadn't been as tall as Alex, but he had still been a solid figure. Even with Dennis Hoffman's help, it was a hard job. Alex could hear the girls weeping noisily somewhere in the house. Keri had drawn them away, hoping to save them from further trauma. They laid Micah out on the kitchen table and Alex drew a bucket of water while Dennis cut off Micah's shirt. Joelle cried as she scrubbed blood from around Micah's wound and couldn't continue when she reached his wedding ring. Nehemiah helped her into the living room while Alex finished. He then covered Micah with a sheet.

"I coffin get, open grave Beulah. We (three) carry him root cellar today. Tomorrow, bury."

Nehemiah wiped away tears and snot.

"Shane kill USDA, yes?"

Alex didn't know exactly what Shane had planned. His side of the plan was simply to hand over a bag silo of corn and about 10% of his root cellar. He could only hope Mark and Alice had done it right in his absence. Shane's plan had a lot of moving pieces, but each cog in the machine was simple enough that its failure wouldn't affect the whole … they could hope.

Red Herring

Shane heard them coming before they came into sight. He pulled off the rebreather mask he wore when filling the duster's tanks and waiting. Mark had texted that they had bit for the bag silo and were now coming his way. Shane watched the dust plume on the road resolve itself into a fleet of trucks.

"I'm Mitchel Rumdale of the USDA. You got any corn or food around here."

"Now why would I tell you that?"

Alex's description of the man who had killed Micah matched Rumdale. Shane calculated the odds of drawing and shooting all four of the men here, but he could sense but not see another worker or two out of sight. He needed to be smart about this.

"Because it's a death sentence to be caught hoarding. Do you want me to quote the Executive Order?"

"No. My father's the mayor. I've already read it. I'm not interested in dying. Some of the farmers stored some corn here. Let me show you."

He led them under the wing of the commuter plane to where a bag silo rested at the end of the alley.

"Seriously?" one of the workers asked. "You figured you could hide it like that?"

"I'm a crop duster, not a farmer. I don't have any corn to hide."

Rumdale looked at a female agent who was holding her phone up to Shane as if taking a photo.

"He's not lying," she said. "Irises are reactive for stress."

Yeah, lady! Who wouldn't be nervous with federal agents threatening them with death?

"That lane, can it be reached from the other side?"

"By a small truck, yeah. Go to the end of that alley there."

Rumdale started detailing his crew. Shane itched to go for the gun he'd hidden in the duster's cockpit, but he knew he'd never make it. Besides, after what Rumdale had done to Micah, Shane wanted to do something more up close and personal than merely shooting him. An ice cold ball of fury boiled unquenchable in that part of his psyche where he normally kept his conscience.

"Sir, I have an alert." Rumdale turned to the agent was had run the lie detector.

Shane tried to casually seem to be moving toward his plane, all the while his heart beat furiously. Rigby might have missed something. Maybe he was about to be arrested for shooting two National Guardsman at the Kanorado line a week ago.

Rumdale looked at the agent's phone. He typed orders into his phone before pinning Shane with a gaze that could freeze hell.

"You're the mayor's son, eh? Just the person to take us to meet him. Delaney, right? Rob Delaney?"

He was too far away to reach the gun, but with luck they wouldn't call his bluff before Rob could back him up.

Fun for Mads

Grant held the earphone against one ear. In the darkness, he could sense but not see Emily and Dylan doing the same thing. They were all listening as Jim greeted the USDA at the door. The agent's name was Galena Carboy. To be certain they wouldn't be detected, they had powered everything down except a few internal listening devices. That meant they could only hear parts of the conversation.

"...bed and breakfast?"

"Yes. We were here when the bombs ...."

"... pantry's pretty bare."

"... stuck here all week."

"Just the two of you?"

"... waiting to hear from our daughter."

"Wait, what are you doing?"

"... two weeks."

"But that's all the food we have."

"... distribution center."

" ... van in the garage?"

"... shuttle."

"Chalk ... basement ...?"

"Grandchildren ... precious ...."

The mics went silent. Rigby strained his ears to hear anything more. And then Madelaine's voice came across the line.

"Jim's closing the gates. They only left us with two weeks' worth of food for two people. Whatever will we do?"

"Stay here," Rigby told Emily. He and Dylan arrived at the top of the stairs just as Jim locked the door behind him.

"That was actually kind of fun, wasn't it, Mads?"

"Oh, loads. I never thought I would enjoy pulling the wool over the government's eyes so much."

"Anything we should be concerned about? We could only hear about half of what you said."

"They seemed interested in the satellite dish, but they seemed to buy that it was cable."

"Good. We five are going to sleep downstairs tonight just in case any of them come back, but it looks like we dodged a discovery. You two .... Thank you."

"Anytime," Jim assured him. "For Emily and the grandkids ... and you're starting to grow on me too."

Rigby grinned and then glanced at his mother-in-law Madeleine, but she gave him that barely suppressed look of disapproval and turned away.

Well, bringing excitement into her life as a secret agent was apparently not enough to win her to his side. Would anything ever do the trick? *And why do I care? After 25 years of her disapproval, why do I still care?*

Chaos

The USDA apparently took the view that they didn't need to talk with the mayor to start their confiscation. Rob had been hearing from farms to the north for hours before Mitchell Rumdale entered his office. To finally meet the enemy energized him.

"Now, why should I welcome this unconstitutional show of force in my town?" Rob asked after reading the Executive Order.

"Because if you don't, we'll be forced to shoot you in the town square." Rumdale looked around at Rob, Joe and Shane. "Do you understand what I am saying? Resistance will not be tolerated."

Rob swallowed tightly, trying not to look at Shane, who kept his eyes firmly fixed on the floor.

"Well, I am not giving you permission to tear up my town, but I can't stop you."

"Sir, they've got a prisoner in the holding cells," an agent said from the door.

"Who?"

"His name's Danny Hughes. Just a dumb kid."

"Why are you holding him?"

"For being stupid." Joe frowned and Shane suppressed a grin.

"So we don't need to take him to the nearest provost?"

"Naw. We're just holding him for a few days to teach him a lesson. His folks will be wanting him for planting winter wheat."

"Okay." Rumdale spoke into his radio. "Standard sweep. This is going to take us all afternoon. Try not to shoot anyone, but remember, resistance carries the death penalty." He looked at Rob. "I'm sure you informed your people of that?" he asked Rob.

"Of course, but this is rural Kansas. They're like herding cats."

"Yeah." Rumdale sighed. "I'm starting to see that dynamic. I've got an agent headed to the Walmart. Do you have the means to get in or do we need to find the manager?"

"Joe, you got keys, right?"

"I do. And I know the alarm code. I'll meet him right there."

"Her name is Agent Carboy."

"Yes, sir. Going right now."

"Mayor, perhaps you can take me over to the grocery store so we can get started."

"You are going to make me help you rob my people?"

"You could be replaced."

"I'll take you," Shane offered. Rob could see his face now that Rumdale's back was turned. If Shane got hold of a weapon, Rumdale would be the first to die. The USDA leader reminded Rob of a lot of bureaucrats he'd seen in military brass during his time in the Army. They knew little or nothing about what they were doing. They expected to be obeyed regardless of the stupidity they commanded. And, they had not one thought about the hate they inspired in those they tried to crush. Rob figured Shane had dealt with men like this before and knew the only answer was to meet their incompetence with a razor's edge.

"If you make the mayor the public face of your shit, he won't be able to govern after you leave. Me … they don't give a crap."

"You won't be able to govern if we replace you either."

"So, your goal is to make me a collaborator?" Rob demanded.

"If they see you cooperating, they will be less likely to fight what we need to do."

Shane had predicted this, even said the USDA would offer an almost logical argument for why Rob should be involved. They escorted the USDA leader to Huffman's, where several trucks were getting ready to go. Huffy met them at the door.

"I don't have anything to give you," she said as Rumdale showed his badge.

"Strip the shelves. Do you live above?"

"Yes. You're going to put me out of business."

"Leave two weeks' of food for the family. How many people live here?"

"Myself and my grandson. How can you do this? I can't stay in business with no stock."

"I have orders, ma'am, and the people in the cities are already going hungry."

The shelves of Huffman's were pretty barren. She'd expertly arranged what little she'd left so that it seemed like a company owner trying to make the shelves look full. She complained and whined and showed her acting chops. Rob remembered when she'd been the lead in Our Town in the community theater the year that he and Jill had moved back to town.

In the end, they found about a truck's worth of food, mostly canned goods.

"Do you have a warehouse?"

Huffy pointed to the back area.

"That's it. I've got no place to hide anything."

Somewhere a couple of blocks away, they heard gunfire. Everyone flinched, but Huffman's walls protected them.

"My God," Rob whispered.

"Resistance will not be tolerated," Rumdale announced. "We want to do this peaceably, but if you don't cooperate, I'll hang the town leaders from the overpass next to your son."

Rob blinked as an agent walked up behind Shane and cuffed him.

"Shane Delaney, you have been found guilty of food hoarding, which carries the death penalty."

Rob stared in horror as they dragged Shane to the door. There were five agents besides Rumdale. The odds weren't in his favor. He'd die if he tried and yet every fiber of his being wanted to. Fortunately, Shane had a cooler head.

"Dad, tell Keri I'll understand."

Then they dragged him up into a truck.

"You expect me to cooperate with the murder of my son?"

"Of course not, but if you try to interfere, we'll kill you and leave your town without leadership."

Rumdale got into his own truck and drove away. Rob whipped out his phone and began texting furiously.

Down the street, in front of the bank, the USDA had dragged three townspeople up against the wall to be shot. A splat of concrete caused the agents to jerk, flinch, cower and cover. The townspeople ran away. One agent moved to shoot them in the back, but another splat of concrete sent him scrambling instead. Brilliant idea Stan had had to silence the muzzles.

Rob sent the text and ran for his truck. He couldn't do much for the town that they weren't already doing for themselves, but he had to save Shane and that became his new mission.

Miss Calla's a Hero

Carl Sullivan answered the door sincerely thinking it was Miss Calla being too friendly. When it turned out to be strangers, the demon voices in his head warned him to beware.

"We're with the USDA. We need to check your house for excess food."

The man in charge of these three agents flashed a badge and pushed past Carl. Or tried to. A big man, Carl decided not to be moved.

"This is my house and I haven't broken the law. You go away now."

"Sir, we have the authority of the President, per Executive Order 13603. Please get out of my way so that I can do my job."

He pushed again. As the USDA agents pushed, Carl's hand slipped from the door knob and he was shoved backward into the living room. His foot slipped on a plastic bag and he went down heavily.

The gooks are here to get you, boy. Get on your feet! Get your rifle. .

479

He'd been 19 and there'd been faceless Vietnamese firing from the jungle. He heard the rat-tat-tat of their rifles even now. He'd reached his knees when the small, white haired woman knelt beside him.

"Stay down, Carl," Miss Calla ordered. "They'll be done soon enough."

He could hear them going in and out of the back door to a truck waiting in the driveway.

"Who are they?"

She was real and he clung to that reality even as the gook women chatter in his head..

"United States Department of Agriculture."

"Who gave them the authority to do this?"

"I'm afraid we did, Carl. We voted for leaders who let things happen this way. We didn't know."

The guy with the badge came back into the room from the kitchen.

"I'm sorry we had to get rough with you, fella, but we can't have arguments at every house. Especially not here. You have months' worth of food in there. There's folks in the cities going hungry."

"That's my food. I paid for it. If the folks in the cities need food, they ought to pay it for themselves."

Badge guy ignored him. Calla held tight to his arm with a knobby hand.

"I'm too old to kneel on the floor like this," she informed him. "You help me get up."

He lumbered to his feet and then helped her up. A mysterious odor issued from the couch when they sat down. Badge man came out again with a receipt for what they'd taken from the pantry. Carl scowled at the paper in his hand.

Outside, angry words and weeping got their attention. They were hauling Miss Calla's son-in-law away in handcuffs.

"What part of ... there can be no hoarding do you not understand?" a USDA agent demanded. "They have a winter's worth of food in the garage attic. Clean it out. Leave them with two weeks."

"What are you doing with him?" Calla demanded.

"He'll be detained at Hutchinson Redistribution Center for whatever term the provost dictates. Let that be a lesson to you."

Carl stood alone on his weed-choked lawn, staring after the truck, trying to remember why he hadn't hidden his food like Jacob Delaney had told him to. But apparently, if you hid your food, the gooks dragged you away to China and who would want that. No, not the gooks. The USDA ... our own government. *Hard to believe I fought a war for these scum bag thieves.*

Head Space

Shane wanted to go to the place in his head where pain didn't matter so that he could dislocate his left thumb and get his hand free of the cuffs, but Rumdale was talking and that sort of distracted him.

"I wish I didn't have to do this, but my orders are clear and if I allow this town to get away with hoarding, they will be problems later. It's good luck that you're the mayor's son. The advertising value of hanging you compared to the others will be so powerful."

"I'm not an advert," Shane said. "I'm a human being and all I did was ignore what somebody else did."

"Then turn those people over and maybe I'll let you live."

"I don't believe that and I don't think you do cithcr. As soon as you put thc cuffs on mc, you had decided my fate."

Rumsdale frowned, perhaps surprised that Shane knew his thoughts. Then he grinned.

"You're right, of course. I can't allow your town to get out of control and you are a perfect object lesson that nobody is going to be given a pass for food hoarding."

"If you think killing me is going to make my father more cooperative, you're wrong."

"No, but I think the townspeople will remember you a bit better than they would remember some guy without a famous name."

The truck slowed to go around a truck where agents were hauling boxes out of a house. There was a body on the lawn. Shane couldn't remember who lived there, but it was another reason for him to drive a spike through Rumdale's head.

Leadership

Hutchinson, Kansas

The Army gathered for dinner in Dillion Hall. Jacobson had distributed devices to two others while Mike and the others checked weapons to assure they wouldn't have any miscalculations during this process. There were still lots of workers out on the fairgrounds, but the Army seemed uncommonly excited to be able to turn some duties over to the Knights, so they were all gathering for dinner, to "celebrate a job well done" Wilkins had explained to Mike. It worked for his plan, so he had nothing to complain about.

The guy hanging from the power pole had stopped moving a couple of hours ago, but Dershowitz, one of Wilkins' most trusted soldiers, seemed determined to replace him with Cai Delaney or the blue-eyed brother who kept asking to see his wife. Dershowitz seemed insulted that the wife was white ... or maybe insulted that the husband clearly was biracial.

It had to be because these were Americans. It had never bothered Mike in Miristan that they treated the locals like slaves. That had been Ric's beef. Even after Mike had more or less come to agree with him, the actual treatment hadn't really bothered him. He could find excuses for why they needed to be treated that way. But not this time. Now he wanted to teach Dershowitz and Wilkins a lesson.

And, then he also wanted to fulfill his mission. Deliver food to Sullivan's home town. Take Cai Delaney home to his family. Ric had always been good at focusing on what they were supposed to do. Mike had always thought himself incapable of that sort of attention, but now, as the sun swept toward the west, he saw his plan coming to fruition and he wished Ric were here to see it.

I'm not just a grunt anymore. I'm stepping into this leadership role and it's working.

He watched as Dershowitz entered the Dillion Hall. That was the last of them, he thought, except Wilkins who was still in his trailer. He'd given Jacobson permission to frag Wilkins, but they were only using flash-bangs in Dillon Hall. Mike sent a text to his team, minus Lawson who was guarding the truck with Kriczek, who had orders to subdue him if necessary.

-We're a go. Hit it!

Passing to Paradise

Emmaus, Kansas

Dick and Trisha Vance heard the USDA truck before it reached them. You could see the dust plume above the driveway.

"That was quicker than I thought it would be. You should probably go into the house. We should look like we weren't expecting them."

Trish nodded and turned toward the farm house. Dick turned back to the hopper he was filling with winter wheat seed. David came out of the barn dragging a hose for water. Johnathan straightened from stacking firewood as the truck rounded the corner into the farm yard.

The USDA introduced themselves. Frank Isenberg, the lead agent, cited an Executive Order and then his crew fanned out to inspect what Dick hadn't hidden. He could only hope then didn't find his two bunker silos. He'd done his best to hide them and the rest of his corn was in bag silos in the salt mine and the secondary site Shane had come up with.

It seemed to be going well when a shriek came from the chicken shed and an agent came out dragging Kitty by the arm.

"I found her hiding eggs."

"I wasn't hiding eggs. I missed a couple this morning, is all."

"Prodish, that sounds like normal farm activity …."

It all happened so fast. Kitty kicked the agent in the ankle and he punched her. Dick leapt forward to grab his arm before he could land the second blow as Kitty cowered on the ground. David stepped forward with the spanner wrench raised. Shots rang out. An agent grabbed the wrench from David and clubbed him with it while another intersected Jonathan from interfering.

Sound returned as pain washed over Dick. He slumped to the ground, crying out feebly. He could hear Trisha screaming up on the porch.

"Take her into custody. Ma'am, nobody is to blame for this but your family. You people must stop resisting."

Trisha. Kitty

"There's not much here," an agent said.

"Good. We'll take her. Is he okay?"

"When he wakes up, he'll remember that you shouldn't argue with the people in charge."

Dick tried to get up, but something was wrong with his legs. The ground under his hands had grown sticky with blood. He heard the truck start and then Trish came flying to him. She wept as she ripped off her shirt to try to staunch the blood. Dick couldn't breathe. He coughed feebly. The sound of another truck coming made his heart flutter, but he recognized it as one of theirs.

"David?"

"Unconscious, but breathing," Jonathan answered Trish. One side of his face was red and swollen where he'd been slapped. At 14, he wasn't big enough yet to put up much of a fight. "I'm calling 911. Damn. I couldn't stop them."

They won't come. The USDA won't let them.

"What happened?" James demanded, kneeling on the other side of him, the stark blue sky behind him. Dick felt a warm hand upon his shoulder as his body melted into the ground.

"James …. Remember … remember what I taught you."

His soul stepped free of his meat suit and into the welcoming arms of his Savior.

"I've still got work to do."

"No, My child. Your work is finished. You've done well. Come along."

Ahead was paradise and behind … he'd loved and been loved and he couldn't quite remember what it was that was so urgent back there now.

A Past Not Forgotten

Mark and Alice sat on the porch steps, basking in the warm sun and congratulating themselves on a well-wrought deception.

"I was scared that we'd give something away."

"But we didn't, so .... How Lisa?" Their little girl was not yet two. She played hard and slept just as hard.

"Still sleeping, I'm sure. I'll check on her in a minute."

Before Alice could move a truck started up the driveway at speed.

"Oh-oh. Go check on her. Stay out of sight."

Alice ran to the camper, leaving Mark to stand alone before the farm house. Lisa slept on her bed, her dark curls damp with sweat. Alice listened at the screened window.

"Marco Pedro Ramirez?" She didn't recognize this agent. He'd not been one of those who had been here before. He had his badge out like he thought he was a cop.

"Yes."

Guns came out immediately and the agents ordered Mark to lie face down on the ground. He didn't argue. He assumed the position. As they zip-stripped his hands behind his back, they explained that all felons were being rounded up for the protection of the public.

"I'm not wanted for anything. I'm not even on parole. I have a wife and kids who need me."

"It doesn't matter. We can't have people like you just wandering around in times like these. You're a threat to public order."

Alice watched helplessly as her husband was put in the truck and driven away. As the truck turned left toward town, Keri's car turned in from the west. Alice met her as she pulled to a stop.

"They took Mark for being a felon."

"What? Oh, god, these people are out of control. Micah's dead. The USDA shot him."

"What do I do?"

Keri stared around her in shock for only a moment.

"I'm supposed to be somewhere that might help. You said you know how to shoot a rifle? What are you willing to do for your husband?"

"Anything. I can't do this without him."

"You can, but that's beside the point. Is Lisa okay on her own for a few minutes?" Alice nodded. "Text Pete to come. I'll be right back."

"I can't tell him. He'll want to be involved."

"Then just say we need to go and for them to watch her."

Within minutes, they were climbing the Emmaus water tower with rifles across their backs and replacement magazines in their pockets. From the maintenance deck of the town's tertiary water source, they could see the trucks out on the Interstate. Jos Osimowitz had already climbed all the way to the top of the water tank. He leaned out enough for Alice to see him. The height made her slightly sick.

"Now what?"

"We watch and wait and shoot when we're ready." Keri pointed to the overpass and the trucks that were clearly visible there. "They're following the same pattern they did yesterday, holding their vehicles on the overpass. My brother missed his calling. He should have joined the military. So, check it out through the scope. Unless we absolutely have to, we're not killing anyone, but punching holes in their tires and scaring them half to death should make them think twice about taking our people, if not our food. The rest is up to Shane, but I believe he can do it."

Insurrection

Hutchinson, Kansas

Kris Lawson had begun to think Sergeant Sanchez had something against him. He'd spent all day guarding a truck they'd been ordered to unload. Every time he'd asked Jacobson why they weren't unloading it, he'd been told to mind his own business and just do what he was told. That just made Kris paranoid. He knew these guys considered him to be an interloper and some of them had had real issues with him shooting that townie back at the grocery store. They didn't have what it takes. That's why they were mercs rather than real soldiers. Bunch of pansies, his dad would say. Weak. Poorly trained .....

Bang! Pop! Bang!

Kris ducked and then moved to draw his weapon. Kriczek pressed the barrel of his gun against the nape of Kris' neck.

"Sorry, man. Maybe you'd be on our side. Maybe you wouldn't. Let me just take this for now." He pulled Kris' service weapon free of the holster.

Something blew up in Dillon Hall. Something else blew up over at the Lieutenant's trailer. People screamed. Soldiers fell. FEMA workers hit the deck. The prisoners cowered.

"What the hell is going on?"

"Wilkins is off the rails. We're taking command."

"My god, that's illegal."

"Who says what's legal anymore, man? I doubt it's legal to keep all these people prisoner or to shoot guys in parking lots."

"He had a gun. It was him or me."

"Yeah, maybe, but Sergeant Sanchez doesn't trust you and we're doing what we have to do."

"You're going to end up court-martialed for this."

"I'm not a soldier, Lawson. I'm a contractor. Remember?"

A chill ran down Lawson's back as black-clothed mercs swept the midway, working as a unit toward the RV parking lot. How stupid of Wilkins to trust these bastards!

A Flash of Light

Missouri

They had miscalculated the sunset and were still far from the next town when the sky blushed in colors.

"I've got a tarp," Javi announced. "And an extra sleeping bag. I picked it up in Columbus."

"Great. Too bad we don't have any marshmallows."

They pulled off Route 60 into a conservation area with a lakeside campground. Javi picked the lock on the gate and drove around to the back side of the campground where terrain and a stand of oak trees would shield them from the road. With Ami's help, he built a fire in a pit and as the last light faded from the sky overhead, they sat down to parcel out an MRI dinner.

"The apple sauce isn't bad," she remarked. "This will be my first camp out."

"Really? I had a few when I was in the Army."

Her amber eyes glowed in dying sunset as she stared at him.

"I'm not going to ask," she said, then flopped back on the tarp to stare up at the sky as the first stars were just spreading across the deep purple canvas.

"If I may, if I might, have the wish I wish tonight." She closed her eyes to make her wish. Javi looked up into the sky. He didn't have the heart to tell her that the "star" she was wishing on was a satellite. Light burst across his vision and then everything went dark. He blinked. He turned toward Ami, who had the fire behind her, but everything was dark, including her and the fire.

"What the hell?" he whispered.

Who Do You Trust?

New York City

"How long does it take to get there?" Julian asked the driver, who said his name was Lou. Yancy was his last name, he explained. They had just cleared the checkpoint going into the Lincoln Tunnel, the high walls on either side embracing the truck as they dropped into the two lane 1.5-mile long coffin.

"It'll take a while. There's a checkpoint at the other end. Maybe an hour."

Katharine texted that to Joseph, who said they were headed that way now. She had always hated tunnels. Even as a kid, going into one had always felt like being buried alive. The headlights of the other cars reflected off the tiled walls and roof. The only other light was small maintenance lights along the top of the wall, which caused shadows like prison bars to be cast against the right-hand wall. It made her shiver. She especially hated that this was bumper to bumper, slow-crawl traffic. She had time to wonder about the maintenance doors off the left-hand pedestrian deck. Probably for lighting. She wondered if any of them were for air.

Katharine glanced at her phone. It was a message from Allison, dated two days ago. She hastily texted back, amazed that she had service in the tunnel.

-Dad and I are fine. We're about to meet just outside the city. Hang in there. Tell Ren we'll be there in a few days. (Katharine)

She looked up, smiling happily that the traffic was all moving, if slowly. And then everything went dark.

Execution

Emmaus, Kansas

Rob pulled up behind Rumdale's truck on the onramp and got out to walk the rest of the way. He could hear men talking up on the overpass. When he got there, he saw a collection of about dozen men under the guard of three USDA agents, but only one of them was armed. Alex' farm hand Mark, several other men and two woman knelt with hands zip-stripped behind their backs. Rob recognized Frank Damaron who had been a couple of years ahead of Cai in high school and Andrew Bennett, who had obviously been hard to subdue. His oldest boy was part of the group too. There were a couple of people from over near Mara Wells. Sharon Laughlin and Kitty Vance were the two women. Sharon looked ready to eat Rumdale's liver while Kitty just looked stunned. Shane knelt in the same line. He and three others had nooses strung looscly around their necks, the other end tied to the overpass railing.

"I don't want to kill anyone," Rumdale insisted, as if these people would care about whether their deaths would bother him or not. "I truly don't, but people have got to learn to cooperate. You've all been found guilty of crimes that carry the death penalty."

"I told you to go jump a tree when you wanted to come into my house," Sharon snapped. "Are you familiar with the 1st Amendment?"

The young USDA agent backhanded her. Blood flowed from her nose. She spat blood at him.

"Are you familiar with the provisions of martial law? Those two first."

Two guards grabbed Kitty Vance and dragged her to her feet. Her stunned silence became wailing protests as they approached the railing. Two other guards dragged Shane to his feet and tried to lift him over the railing.

"What the hell are you doing?" Rob demanded, stepped out from the shadow of the trucks.

"Now!" Frank hollered and launched himself at the guard with the rifle. Several of the male prisoners and Sharon surged to their feet and head butted the unarmed guards. Rumdale drew his sidearm and pointed it right at Rob's face as chaos erupted behind him. Rob pulled his own gun.

"You stop this now!" he ordered. Shane put up an incredible fight at the railing. One agent had blood flowing down his face. Rumdale shook his head and then a shot rang out. Blood blossomed from Rumdale's right shoulder. He dropped the gun, his fingers innervated. Frank had somehow gotten his hands in front of him. With his doubled fists around the barrel of the USDA agent's rifle, he clubbed the man into bloody unconsciousness as behind Rumdale, first Kitty and then Shane rolled over the railing and dropped out of sight.

The End

A Taste of *Thanatosis*

"I've been shot," Mitchel Rumdale complained. "I need a doctor."

"The doctor is busy with a critical patient right now," Jill Delaney snapped, grasping his upper arm with one hand just about the elbow while plying her scissors on the hastily applied bandana around his arm and then his suit and shirt. "It's a crease, barely worth the first aid."

She almost didn't want to do first aid on him. What she really wanted was to shoot Rumdale dead right where he sat, right this moment. How many people were dead or dying because Rumdale had been following orders? She'd known people like him in the Army. She had hated them then as she hated Rumdale and his squad now, but her feelings today were much more personal ... deeply, intensely personal. If she'd had a gun right then, he might not have survived five minutes.

In the end, she did bandage his arm, but decided not to bother with an antibiotic shot or pain relief. Why waste the resources? She had just cuffed Rumdale's injured arm to the table when Rob entered the examination room. Their gazes met. He shook his head almost imperceptibly. Tears sprang to Jill's eyes, but then she got out of Rob's way as he advanced across the room with his sidearm drawn. His hand didn't shake one bit as he put the barrel against Rumdale's forehead.

"Do you know what happens to a body when an inadequate noose snaps tight on the neck and the weight of that body stretches the spinal cord?

Rumdale looked terrified as Rob thumbed off the safety and stood there, clearly considering pulling the trigger.

The Story Continues

Other Lela Markham Titles

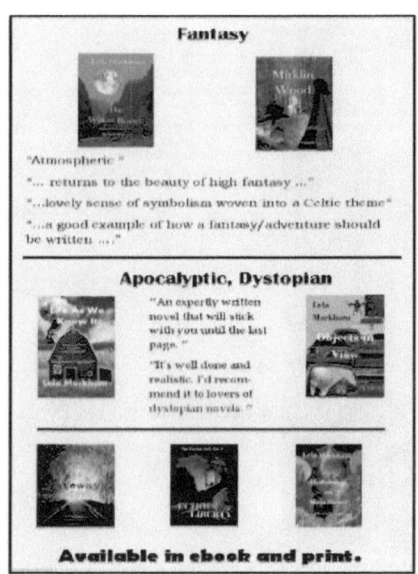

Other Great
Breakwater Harbor Books

Moscow, 2138. With the world only beginning to recover from the complete societal collapse of the late 21st Century, Zoya scrapes by prepping corpses for funerals and dreams of saving enough money to have a child. When her brother forces her to bring him a mysterious package, she witnesses his murder and finds herself on the run from ruthless mobsters. Frantically trying to stay alive and save her loved ones, Zoya opens the package and discovers two unusual data cards, one that allows her to fight back against the mafia and another which may hold the key to everlasting life.

www.breakwaterharborbooks.com

Meet Lela Markham

Hi. I was raised in a house made of books in Alaska and told tales from the time I could talk. A teacher eventually made me write one of them down. I hated the exercise, but it was the spark that ignited a fire that has never gone out.

My daring husband, two fearless offspring and I live the adventure of a lifetime here on the Last Frontier where the midnight sun encourages wandering the wilderness and the long dark winters favor reading, writing and staring at the northern lights ... hence the moniker Aurorawatcher.

It's all about the aurora watching!